# Colours of Prejudice

# Colours of Prejudice

*Robert Bishop*

# Colours of Prejudice

All Rights Reserved. Copyright © 2011 Robert Bishop

No part of this book may be reproduced or transmitted in any form or by any means, graphic, electronic, or mechanical, including photocopying, recording, taping or by any information storage or retrieval system, without the permission in writing from the copyright holder.

The right of Robert Bishop to be identified as the author of this work has been asserted in accordance with the Copyright, Designs and Patents Act 1988 sections 77 and 78.

Spiderwize
3rd Floor
207 Regent Street
London
W1B 3HH
UK

www.spiderwize.com

This is a work of fiction. Names, characters and incidents are products of the author's imagination. Any resemblance to persons living or dead is entirely coincidental.

The views expressed in this work are solely those of the author and do not necessarily reflect the views of the publisher, and the publisher hereby disclaims any responsibility for them.

ISBN: 978-1-908128-26-3

To Suzanne who saw the good in everyone.

# CONTENTS

ACKNOWLEDGEMENTS..........................................................ix

PREFACE     COLOURS OF PREJUDICE ........................ xi

CHAPTER 1    FRIEND OR FOE? – BELFAST 1974 .......... 1

CHAPTER 2    BLOOD BROTHERS – COOKSTOWN 1949............................................................... 5

CHAPTER 3    CAREFULLY TAUGHT – BELFAST 1957................................................................. 15

CHAPTER 4    DIFFERENT WAYS – ALDERSHOT 1962................................................................. 22

CHAPTER 5    DIVIDE AND RULE – DUBLIN 1966 ....... 40

CHAPTER 6    HOME TRUTHS – BELFAST 1966 .......... 55

CHAPTER 7    THE SPECIALIST – FORT BRAGG, USA 1966...................................................... 71

CHAPTER 8    THE DROP – SALISBURY 1967 ............... 81

CHAPTER 9    THE MARCH – DERRY 1968-69............... 91

CHAPTER 10   THE CRISIS – DERRY 1969 .................... 111

CHAPTER 11   THE INVITATION – BELFAST 1971...... 123

| CHAPTER 12 | DEMETRIUS – BALLYMURPHY 1971.. 131 |
| --- | --- |
| CHAPTER 13 | ANOTHER FINE MESS – LISBURN 1971 ............................................................ 136 |
| CHAPTER 14 | OLD FRIENDS – HOLYWOOD 1971 ...... 144 |
| CHAPTER 15 | BLOODY SUNDAY - DERRY 1972 ........ 165 |
| CHAPTER 16 | DANNY BOY – LONDON 1972 .............. 178 |
| CHAPTER 17 | MEN OF HONOUR – CYPRUS 1976 ..... 191 |
| CHAPTER 18 | THE MISSION – DONEGAL 1976 .......... 200 |
| CHAPTER 19 | THE INTERROGATION – HEREFORD 1976 ............................................................ 215 |
| CHAPTER 20 | THE RECKONING – BELFAST 1976 ..... 229 |
| CHAPTER 21 | THE PARADE – LONDON 1976 ............. 237 |

# ACKNOWLEDGEMENTS

It has been a long journey and because of that I have lived to see the light at the end of the tunnel gaining ground.

As Bill Bryson says, "Growing up was easy. It required no thought or effort on my part."

The Year 1969 was a very rude awakening.

This book started off as a personal therapy and hopefully may be of help to all those who believe in a future.

Strange to say, the book wrote itself. However, it was only through the help of friends that it survived. Those friends have my thanks already but it is good to declare it here in the open. My thanks are especially due to David Avery and Simon Palmer, my original mentors, Richard Roberts and our son Simon for their final push to finish at long last.

They say behind every man there is a woman. Believe me, it is not always behind. This book fulfils a promise made a long time ago to my wife Rhena for her belief and understanding.

Hope springs eternal. May that hope work for all those who have suffered and continue to suffer unmentionable pain, both physically and mentally.

# PREFACE

## Colours of Prejudice

**TWO BOYS**, Colin Monro, a Protestant, and Tom O'Neill, a Catholic, both born at the beginning of the Second World War, become blood brothers in the innocence of childhood friendship.

Both boys grow into men along with the expectations of their communities, Colin becoming an Officer in the Parachute Regiment and Special Air Service, Tom a solicitor and a leader of the Provisional IRA.

Through their eyes and those of their family and friends we experience the influence of a closed environment on the social history of a Province, which can lead to man's inhumanity, even to the people they love.

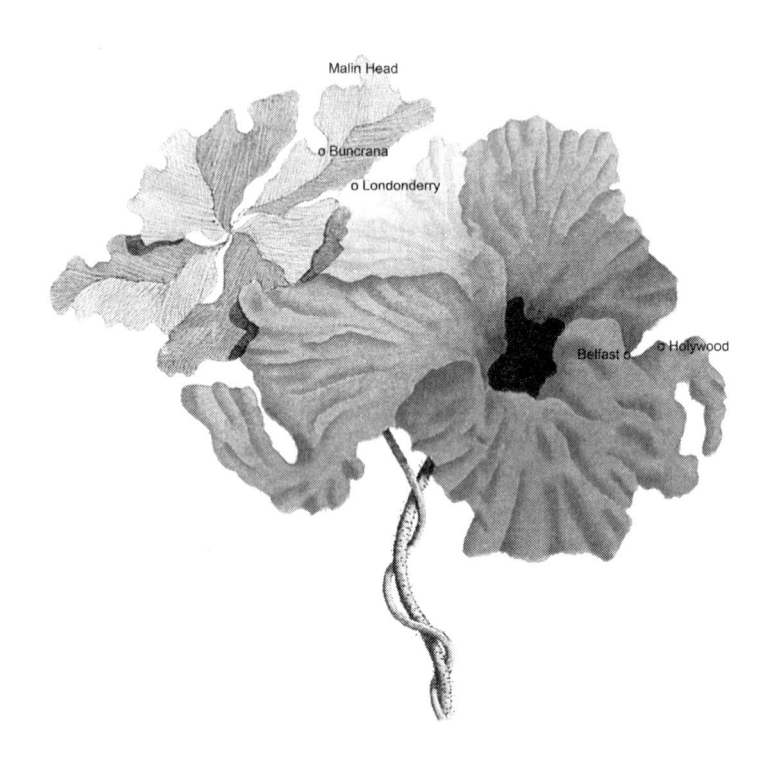

Malin Head
o Buncrana
o Londonderry
Belfast o   o Holywood

# CHAPTER ONE

## FRIEND OR FOE? – BELFAST 1974

**T**HE TIPS OF THE HUGE BLADES dipped and flexed, lifting the helicopter clear of the pines, sliding to the right, passing low over the main Holywood road heading out towards Belfast Lough.

It was dark and drizzling in Ireland, where time never meant too much—history being the exception, of course. Standing in the open door of the Wessex, the man hugged himself, knowing there was no protection from the elements. He cursed softly in a local accent. A native of Belfast, he wore no rank or insignia.

"We're ready down here." He held the throat mike close to his Adam's apple.

"All checks completed," the crewman added, trying to move the figure away from the open door.

"OK, two minutes," the pilot replied.

The man tightened his grip on the door strut, bracing his body, moving his feet to balance, shaking his head against the Irish drizzle. He shuddered somebody had just walked over his grave. Jesus, where did that come from?

"Did you see that?" the Cortina driver asked, spittle flying.

"Wouldn't a blind man?" came the excited chorus from the back.

Their eyes followed the flashing strobes out onto the reflected water.

"For fuck sake," the driver swore, "road block!"

"Shit," they chorused, running sweaty fingers through untidy hair, licking dry lips, their Bangor pints and the helicopter forgotten.

The pilot adjusted his line on the dark promontory on the far shore, known to locals as Napoleon's Nose; he checked the lights of Carrickfergus off to the right, adjusted the controls and eased the large transport helicopter in their direction.

"Flying with the side door open."

"Affirmative," the crewman replied.

"Colin," the man at the door turned inwards, responding to the familiar voice on his headset, "this one's awake." His accent was closer to the border, Portadown, maybe Banbridge.

"About bloody time," Colin acknowledged as he hooked his right boot under the body, turning it face up.

Tom felt the boot force his body onto his back, releasing the putrid smell of stale vomit. He could feel the bile rise in his throat, spreading upwards into his nose, filling the sinuses until there was no escape. He gagged, spewing his relief, tasting his fear.

Colin felt the dampness seep into his leg. "Bastard!" He brushed at the remains sticking to his thigh. "Paddy, help me move him closer to the door. That's good. Now, prop that bastard Rourke next to the other one at the door... No, not there, in the middle. I want Rourke to have a grandstand view." The request came as an order. He didn't know any other way. Both men worked methodically, each man shifting and organizing the inert limbs until, finally, the bodies of the three prisoners were in their allocated places.

Tom could feel his captors rearrange their body positions but couldn't hear a bloody thing. Even his fillings hurt. The rotors forced the air pressure down to meet the forward slipstream, the mix funnelling in through the open door, probing for loose clothing, forcing tear ducts to cry. He accepted the pain of the pinched flesh as strong fingers grasped wet clothing. His teeth began to chatter—fear or cold? Both...it didn't matter. He was beyond struggling. "Bastards...

Fucking English Bastards!" he shouted, knowing no one would hear him.

He felt better… no, he didn't.

"Jesus…" he prayed softly. He felt his head jerk sideways, then back again, like one of those stupid dogs in rear car windows. It didn't belong to his body but the fucking pain did. His eyes ached and his ears were full of his brains. Everything had shifted. The smell… the noise… Christ, Jesus Christ! He gagged again. His mind sought refuge. Escape into memories. Childhood memories….

But the smell followed. There was no escape.

Pictures flooded his brain.

Black and white pictures.

Bodies twisted in eternal agony.

Open graves.

The wrong memories.

The wrong file from his memory bank.

It had selected fear.

The Judgment Day.

Sin and retribution.

The Man on the cross.

He felt the draught of the cold chapel. Fingers over eyes. Our Lady, her head bowed, always weeping, never smiling.

Tangled bodies, feet and legs everywhere. Open coffins. Soundless screams.

No comfort there.

More feet, then legs.

Real legs.

Para boots.

He lifted his eyes to a jigsaw face of shadows and hidden cheeks. Nightmare eyes, amber bright. Turnip eyes, in a Halloween mask.

Colin's eyes.

He was back with them, back to pain.

There was no escape.

The raw wind mocked his howl of fear, lashing his cheeks with cold reality. He looked out beyond the bodies next to him, out and down into that black hole of Hades. He knew the rest of the living nightmare and he knew the ending.

He felt his body begin to rock.

Backwards and forwards, backwards and forwards.

Childhood escapism.

They'd promised. Those bastards at Westminster had promised. Never again would they allow them a free hand. Colin didn't have the authority.

This was England.

Wrong... Ireland.

What the fuck did it matter. The bastard wouldn't do it. He couldn't. Not after Bloody Sunday.

Why had he returned?

What offers had the faceless ones made this time?

How long had they been friends?

Enemies?

Cookstown... a different world.

— o —

# CHAPTER TWO

## BLOOD BROTHERS – COOKSTOWN 1949

**TOM HELD THE SMALL PHOTOGRAPH** closer to the bedroom window. His fingers wiped at the creases of neglect highlighted by the sun's rays criss-crossing the black and white picture showing two small boys holding up their jam-jar trophies displaying their catch.

— o —

"What's you doing?"

Tom heard Colin's words as if it were yesterday. He remembered how the cornered stickleback had seized its chance and darted for open water over the top of the net. Gone.

"Nothing now," he'd answered, shaking the empty net at the end of the bamboo rod.

"Can I try?" Colin asked, his voice excited, keeping his gaze fixed on the goggle-eyed sticklebacks circling in the large jam-jar. It was one of those really big jars. The jam could last a whole week if his mother had her way.

"Where's your things?" Tom asked, looking around the immediate vicinity. Nothing. "Haven't you anything?" he asked incredulously. "A net, a jar, nothing at all?" he questioned, shaking his head in disbelief. "And you're wearing socks and shoes," he chastised.

Colin looked down at his companion's feet, so white and bent in the clear cold water. "I'll take my shoes and socks off," he volunteered, tugging eagerly at his lace balancing on one foot. The knot was impossible. He pulled desperately at the toe, then the heel. "Bloody," he exclaimed, determined to impress.

"Hey, watch what you're doing," Tom cautioned, looking in disgust at Colin's shoe which had landed dangerously close to the startled spricks. His hand quickly covered the churned water of splashed excitement spilling over the brim of the jar, threatening a mass escape. Colin hung onto the heel of his sock, too scared to move as Tom checked the jar.

"Here," Tom offered in a puzzled voice, holding out the offending shoe. "You might as well take the other one off now. No, not here, you idiot, over there," he stated. Exasperated, he pointed.

"Sorry," Colin apologised, scrabbling with the other foot. "I've never fished before," he explained, plucking at another knot.

"Never?" Tom asked incredulously.

"Never!" Colin confirmed.

Tom felt guilty. He'd heard his mother talk of deprived children. Everyone caught spricks. Even girls tried. This boy was really funny and he spoke funny as well. He noticed the blazer for the first time. It had a badge on the breast pocket and silver buttons. He dried his hands on the front of his crumpled pullover. "Where do you come from?" he questioned, curiosity turning to suspicion.

"Up the road," Colin answered.

"What road?"

"That road."

"You're not from here," Tom challenged.

"No, but my uncle is," Colin defended. "I'm from Belfast," he admitted.

"Belfast?" Tom sat down on the grass. He'd never met anyone from Belfast before. "That's where the war was," he stated. Everyone knew that and he knew that this boy wasn't a German. No, he'd seen films and those Germans talked even funnier than this one. "What's your name?" he tested, just in case.

"Colin."

"I'm Tom," he replied, relieved. "You want a go now?" he asked, offering his net.

"Yes please." Colin gave one last pull and the sock came off in his hand.

"You'll have to take your coat off and roll up your sleeves," Tom added quickly.

"Thanks."

Tom watched the boy struggle free from the blazer determined not to release his hold on the net. He noticed that the inside-out sleeves had white stuff right up to the shoulders.

"Is that Okay?" Colin called from the middle of the stream. "What do I do now?" he asked. The forgotten jacket lay between the socks and shoes watched over by the forgotten spricks.

"You did all right," Tom praised his new friend's efforts. "Want another one?" he asked, offering his bundle of jam sandwiches.

"Yes please," Colin replied anxiously as he fingered the dark crust of the thick white slices into the corner of his mouth. "Makes you hungry, doesn't it?" he observed, capturing a dribble of enjoyment at the other corner of his mouth. "What do you call that again?" he asked, biting into the rich yellow filling.

"Butter," Tom answered, puzzled. "My mother makes it." He felt stupid, explaining simple things. Didn't everyone's mother make butter?

"What from?" Colin persisted.

Tom kicked at the ground. He watched the stone bounce once before splashing into the stream. "We'd better go now. You can carry the fish if you want." He made himself busy, not knowing what to think.

They walked in silence as Colin concentrated on not spilling the water.

"What's it like in Belfast?" Tom asked, fed up with the silence.

"Okay."

"Did you see any German bombers?" Tom asked. He stopped, waiting for the answer. This was important.

"Yes... Well... my Dad did."

"How many?"

"Lots. My Dad said they had been after the shipyard. He makes things for the shipyard."

"What?"

"I'm not allowed to say. What does your Dad do then?" Colin pressed his advantage.

"He makes things too," Tom answered.

"What like?"

"Things," Tom defended.

"What for?" Colin pressed.

"For people... watch, you're spilling the water," Tom scolded.

"What sort of people?" Colin wouldn't let go.

"Dead people," Tom whispered.

"Coffins?" Colin whispered back.

"No silly," Tom laughed, relieved. "Wills. They call them wills."

"Wills?" Colin queried. "Wills—what are they for?"

"For dead people's things. You know... what they give away when they die." This boy knew nothing.

"How can they give away things when they're dead?" Colin smirked.

"They don't, silly. My Dad does it for them. He's a solicitor," Tom smiled back.

Colin walked on holding his hand over the top of the jar. "What does he wear to work?" he asked suddenly.

"A suit," Tom replied instantly.

"So does mine," Colin responded.

The boys continued down the long straight road leading into Cookstown. Their world was everything they could see. Colin squinted his eyes against a sun set in the clear blue sky. A bumblebee hovered. He just knew that even the Germans couldn't find this place. Nobody would ever bomb here, he reckoned. A few nosy cows rested their jowls on the stone wall, their doleful eyes reflecting the boys' progress. Tom pointed to the swaying udders.

"They're making their own butter," he quipped, laughing at his own joke.

Colin laughed with him but he couldn't share in the joke. "I live over there," Tom pointed.

"Can I see you tomorrow then?" Colin asked.

"Sure, keep the spricks," Tom called over his shoulder. It was nice to have a new friend.

"Thanks." Colin waved back. "I'm here for the summer," he called after the retreating back.

— o —

"It's too tight."

"No it's not."

"We have to mix our blood," Colin explained, pulling the string tighter, watching their flesh rise like a butcher's Sunday joint.

"You're supposed to use a knife, stupid," Tom grimaced.

"We haven't got a knife, have we?"

"We could get one."

"How?"

"I don't know."

"So, who's stupid then?"

The two boys watched their blood mingle, feeling no pain happy for each other. Blood brothers. They didn't know about fate, society and the eleven plus, the examination that pigeon-holed you for life. They had agreed to work on a farm, make real butter and fish for the big ones. Trout, and maybe even salmon. But they didn't know how to fail or how to lie.

Then suddenly it was all over, their glorious summers gone, and with them the end of childhood innocence. Colin, to the big school in Belfast and Tom to Omagh. Both to be carefully taught.

They had sent postcards their first two summers apart. He from Portnoo in Donegal and Colin from Bangor in County Down. He still had it somewhere. A picture of a great big swimming pool, Pickie Pool, all green and cold looking.

There was no swimming pool in Portnoo, that's for sure. Rock pools galore full of crabs and things, but no friend, no blood brother to share with and big boys didn't write to each other.

— o —

It had been Tom's family's fourth summer at Portnoo after the last postcard from Bangor. The teacups rattled in their saucers, spreading the latest gossip. It was true then, a new family wanting to buy, and them Protestants. Not rent, but to buy a summer place.

"A Protestant family right enough," his mother confirmed over lunch, "but a professor of history no less and couldn't we be doing with an educated family around here no matter where they come from?" she challenged. And she was off visiting.

"Lovely women," she informed them over supper, "no airs and graces—they're not like some I could mention. None whatsoever," she emphasised. "No boys," she looked directly at her son, "a daughter and a dog, fifteen, the girl that is, not the dog, a young lady no doubt, not like the dog." She pulled at her cardigan. Always a bad sign. "Do you know what they call that poor animal?" she asked knowingly. "Bugger," she whispered.

"The dog?" his father queried, suddenly interested.

"The dog for sure—who else would you call Bugger in an educated house?"

"It could have been worse I suppose," his father teased.

"How?"

"Billy," he suggested, bringing instant laughter to the room.

— o —

Old Willie John had spied her first. "I see they're here then," he told the bar, wiping the Guinness ring from his stubble.

"Who?" the barman asked needlessly.

"You know who... those ones from Belfast" Willie added equally needlessly. "Have you seen the daughter?" he queried.

"What's she like then?" The bar waited.

Willie took another mouthful with closed eyes. "Like," he beamed as if his horse had come in, "like a young filly, legs like a racehorse and breasts like a wet greyhound's nose." He whistled softly. "Makes you glad there are things you've best forgotten," he grimaced. "I'll have another pint when you're ready," he ordered, lowering the remainder in one. "Aye, best forgotten," he sighed, regretfully.

— o —

"Bugger, here boy, here." The voice carried on the wind. The dog was stuck in the hedge.

"Bloody townie," Tom cursed softly to himself. "Hold still, you stupid animal."

"He is not," the voice right above him now changed, angry. The dog shook free, wagging its bottom like a jelly on a plate, licking her hand. Tom stood dumbstruck; in love, helpless.

"Don't be a silly Bugger," she chastised. Her laughter was uninhibited, clear and honest. "Not you," she corrected, "Him," she pointed. "He's the Bugger, that's his name."

Tom knew that he had a silly grin on his face and he had spent the last week avoiding his mother's invitation to visit.

"Tom," he heard his voice explain.

"Oh, so you're Tom?"

"Yes," he said. He couldn't figure out if the 'Oh' was good or bad.

He'd noticed his first pimple the next morning. He was in love. He showed her his secret caves. The whirlpool with its stranded crabs the size of shovels, well, small shovels. They ran. They touched. He wrote unseen poetry. She was better than any boy.

Tom sat hugging his knees looking out to sea. He felt the breeze stiffen, becoming a wind on his cliff-top vantage point, clearing the remainder of the morning mist. This was his favourite time—time for private thoughts as he looked down on his witch's cauldron of hidden secrets and future promises. He understood Macbeth's temptation; to be offered all that lay before him and to control the elements of life. Dorothy would be his forever; he would make a pact with the Devil if necessary. He shivered as the last cloud crossed the sun chasing after its companions, then out came the sun again painting the sea in sparkling blues and greens highlighting the black rocks below. She was late this morning but it didn't matter, they had all day together alone except for Bugger and he didn't really count.

The voices were excited, mingled together. He stood indignant, surprised at the intrusion, trying to identify the cause. He lifted his hand to shield his eyes from the morning sun. She waved back immediately, taking her companion's hand, rushing her upwards to their meeting point. Bugger circled them both equally excited.

"Tom," she gasped, "meet my bestest friend, Sheila. Sheila, this is Tom."

"Hello," was all he could say in reply. Their faces shone with friendship. Suddenly he was alone again.

"Isn't this a real surprise?" she continued. "Her dad decided to call on impulse—they've been doing the lakes on a boat from Ballyshannon. A cabin cruiser. Would you believe it? They're staying the night."

— o —

Sheila bloody Hart without an 'E'. Tom fiddled with his napkin, bloody napkin, no bloody use anyway. He shook the crumbs onto Bugger's back. He glared across the table at Sheila Hart but it was useless, she didn't even know he was there. And neither did Dorothy. Why had he agreed to come?

"Have you been to France?"

Tom realised the conversation had died and Mister bloody Hart was asking him a question.

"No," he replied rudely. And I just want to go home, he thought.

"Pity, you'd love it. Wouldn't he, Dorothy?" he smiled down the table at Dorothy's joyous face, taking another slurp of his red bloody French wine. "We're going for the rest of the hols, the Dordogne is beautiful in August, hot but beautiful." They all agreed. Well, they would, wouldn't they? "Goodness me, I nearly forgot," his smile filled his face.

Tom felt his heart stop. He felt sick. He knew the question.

"Why don't you come with us, Dorothy?"

"Can I mummy?" He never heard the rest, just Bugger's howl as he trod on his tail and his childish request for a postcard.

— o —

He hid in his secret places all the next morning watching her search for him watching them leave. His Dorothy and her best friend Sheila bloody Hart without a heart.

— o —

He burnt the letter unopened but kept the postcard.
Bloody Eiffel Tower.

— o —

He replaced the creased photograph beside the postcards.

# CHAPTER THREE

## CAREFULLY TAUGHT – BELFAST 1957

TOM PACKED THE PHOTOGRAPH and postcards carefully within the folds of his spare trousers and shirts. He smiled as he fantasised, "This is Your Life…so far." What had the Man with The Red Book in store for him? He closed the suitcase, his second, his mother having packed the first.

He hadn't intended to follow his father into the practice, it had just happened. School had been good to him. Although no intellectual, he had no problem with exams, allowing him the luxury to play both games, hurling and football. Not your everyday soccer, not his football, Gaelic football. And now it had become the fly in the ointment. He had a choice, Queen's University Belfast, QUB, or University College Dublin, UCD. As usual, his father had solved the problem: Queen's for his degree followed by a post graduate at UCD.

"Feeling nervous?"

"Yes," Tom replied, startled.

"The door was open," his father observed. "Would you like to talk?" he asked, crossing the floor to the window. "Man to man like." He sat down on the chair by the window looking out at the rolling countryside. "Some things never change," he said, pointing with his pipe to the hills and Slieve Gallion beyond the lower meadow. "Your Grandfather bought those fields in 1921, when he was forced to leave Belfast. They say that he was a stubborn man proud of his heritage and determined to remain in the North. It had always been our home, you see. It was Cookstown that offered him refuge away from the greed of men who should have known better. Land was cheap here and the Protestants weren't interested in anything beyond Portadown. They clung to the edges of Belfast where the money was; developing its port, building factories, spreading out into its hinterland along the Lagan Valley, Lisburn, Lurgan and Portadown. The Orange strongholds. We were left alone, left to get on with life, no obvious threat." He opened his tobacco pouch feeling for a fill, fingering the leaf into the pipe bowl. "We developed the land to meet our personal needs. You only have to look at the breadth of the main street to see it was plentiful. Plenty of room for a horse and cart or a motor car if you had real money. You should see some of the old photographs! Talk about the Wild West, my goodness, it is difficult to tell them apart. Mind you, there was still poverty, but nobody starved. That's what neighbours are for and still are."

He fingered the tobacco, testing the consistency; satisfied, the Meerschaum was set aside. He never smoked in the house. The greenhouse was insect free and more importantly his sole domain. There was a bell-pull for emergencies, real emergencies, business, not domestic. "We built the chapel on the high ground and clustered within its protective shadow, secure and safe. Everyone knew their place in the community and accepted its rules. People got on with living and dying as the good Lord intended." He picked up the pipe and sucked at the clearance, tasting the flavour. "The countryside hasn't changed and that's true enough, but time stands still for no man, they say, and that's equally true, especially in war." He put down his pipe once again with a heartfelt sigh. "Men are never the same after a war. They experience things and places which were never meant to be seen... makes them dissatisfied with their lot. And now we have this picture thing, television they call it. Pictures in your home, live pictures, they say. They'll be bringing war into your very parlour next. God protect us," he said with a never-to-happen smile. The smile had gone and the brows had narrowed. "It was the war right enough," he continued. "Socialism, Communism, call it what you want. Utopia, there's no such thing, never. You see, men aren't meant to be equal—we have to work for what we get. At least the Calvinists got that right. The trouble with them is that they moved God backwards; they replaced the crown of thorns with their own crown, making the state and Crown inseparable. Question the status quo and you question Ulster's existence. And that is seen as treason." He leant forward, touching his son's shoulder gently but firmly. "What I'm really trying to say is that your world in the photograph is fast fading away, possibly leaving a vacuum which every Tom, Dick and Harry will fill with their own ideas and prejudices. It's happening already. We all need to move closer together, accept history for what it is... a lesson in life. Learn from our mistakes; teach a common doctrine with a common syllabus within an integrated educational system. Children have enough to cope with just growing up without this ridiculous educational segregation dictated by religious belief. Why should young friends, with open minds, be separated by the out-dated thinking and prejudice of their church elders? When will we ever learn?"

His father picked up his pipe, ready to escape to the greenhouse. He'd said more than enough.

"Thanks Dad, thanks for caring." Tom stepped forward to embrace his father. He could feel the body tense and slowly relax.

"Some talk," his father said, recovering. "More like a sermon," he half joked. "Your Grandmother wanted me for the priesthood. Aren't you lucky your Grandfather won?" He smiled knowingly.

— o —

Tom loved dances but hated dancing. Two left feet. He'd matured, a young man, his mother said, ready to make his way in the big world. He sipped at his Guinness, his eyes searching the smoke-filled hall. Colin had to be here, he'd seen his name on the fresher's list for Queen's University. Would they recognize each other? Had it been seven years? Had he changed? Would he have a partner? He was alone himself, conscious of his doubts and his place.

"Tom, Tom; over here." He knew the voice instantly. Everyone had turned in his direction.

Why didn't they look at her? He could feel his cheeks redden, unable to escape, his feet rooted to the spot. He watched the crowd part following her progress. She was by his side, her arms around his neck kissing his cheek. Everyone was smiling at them. His hands patted her bare back.

"Tom, how marvellous to see you, you never replied to my letter," she scolded. "You remember Sheila my....."

Bloody Sheila Hart without an 'E'. Dorothy never finished her introduction. Tom heard only one voice.

"What's you doing?"

"Nothing now," Tom replied.

The two old friends embraced their destiny.

The square was complete, the players assembled.

"You and Sheila an item?" Tom couldn't keep the surprise out of his voice.

"Always have been ever since I went to Paris with her brother."

"Nineteen forty nine!"

"How the hell did you…"

"Never mind, it's just great to see you again."

"Still, can't believe it and a bloody lawyer I see. History myself, good on dates. Talking of dates, here come ours. You have to wonder what they do in the powder room. By the by, Dorothy is being chased but is still side-stepping, so you had better move fast."

"What…"

"Isn't this unbelievable, meeting again, after all those years and you going to be a lawyer and all," Sheila smiled at Dorothy. "She always said you would be," she continued, ignoring Dorothy's blushes. "I bet you she still has that stupid photograph; you know, the one she asked Colin for, holding those silly spricks in a jam-jar."

"Dance?" Colin took Sheila's hand.

"You don't."

"Yes I do," he insisted. He held her close, trying not to look at Dorothy and Tom. "They don't need your help," he whispered into his partner's ear.

"Who says?" she whispered back. "We shall see," she smiled sweetly.

— o —

"Why didn't you go home with Tom?" Colin asked.

"Because he didn't ask?" Dorothy replied.

Sheila nudged Colin's side and smiled knowingly.

— o —

The weeks had turned into months before they stopped to think. Sheila had insisted that he call Tom and arrange a foursome. "That Alistair Hall is making his move on Dorothy's parents," she explained.

"Can't allow that," he agreed.

— o —

"Run that past me again, Tom," Colin quizzed. They were alone for the first time that evening. Sheila and Dorothy had gone in search of the ladies' room. Good for fifteen minutes and an extra pint. "You don't or can't play rugby," he questioned

"Both," Tom sighed, knowing he was in for a hard time. "Look, its dead simple. If I play rugby I'm barred from playing hurling and Gaelic football."

"Who says?"

"The GAA."

"Who are they?"

"The Gaelic Athletic Association, the governing body for Irish sports."

"Fair enough," agreed Colin. "So how come the Irish rugby team is selected from the whole of Ireland?"

"Ah, now there's a thing. Have you ever noticed that not one Catholic from the north has ever played rugby for Ireland?"

"Don't talk daft," Colin took a swallow of his beer.

"Think about it. Check it out."

"Not one?"

"You really didn't notice? You didn't know that any Catholic who played rugby in the north would be banned for life from playing Gaelic football and hurling in Ireland?"

"Jesus man, that's strange... what about soccer?"

"That's different."

"How come?"

"It's our law," said Tom.

"Stupid bloody law if you ask me."

"It's still the law."

"Change the law—you're a lawyer, or will be."

"Goodness me, don't we look serious about something!" Sheila observed. "Most likely the empty glasses. Have you had nothing else since we left?" she asked incredulously.

"Just some poison," Colin replied cryptically.

"Grab him, Dorothy," she ordered as Tom tried to escape with the empty glasses. "Let's dance," she guided them to the floor.

— o —

Tom had become one of the family. Colin's parents had even offered him a room in his final year but he had become used to his independence. Sheila had given up on her matchmaking but was still convinced she knew best despite Dorothy's engagement to the hot favourite, Mr Hall.

— o —

They had guested at weekends for opposite sports, switching places, thumbing their noses at the establishment. Everyone knew of course, all the players and some of the spectators, only the referees didn't and they knew bugger all anyway according to both the players and the spectators. Both had played against the army side at Holywood Barracks; stuffed they were, by the Duke of something. Two England internationals and three rugby league, national bloody service players. Taught us a lesson, they did; it takes all sorts to make a team. "Half of them Catholics," Tom had remarked ruefully. The British didn't give a toss who played for them, so long as they won. They got us drunk and signed us up to visit some bloody place with an unpronounceable Welsh name, in the middle of nowhere. After that, Tom was going to be a judge advocate or such-like and Colin agreed to settle for being a hero.

— o —

# CHAPTER FOUR

## DIFFERENT WAYS – ALDERSHOT 1962

COLIN WRAPPED HIS OVERCOAT tightly to his body. He blinked his eyes at the steady drizzle and leaned further out from the deck rail. Stretching on tiptoe, he watched the disturbed droplets leave the rail and fall into the oily water below, swallowed forever between hull and jetty.

There they were, his farewell party, each face a stage in his life leading to this miserable moment. There they stood, staring accusingly up at him, their faces stretched and wet, ghostly skulls framed in scarves and hats. He recalled his Uncle Tommy's story, the one who went to America, the one who sent food parcels during the war; bubble-gum and Dick Tracy comics. "Did you know that when immigrants got on the boat at Cork for America, those left behind held a wake for the departed dead? That's what they were, right enough, or might as well have been for they would never see them again." He swore that it was true. He'd sent an ashtray with the ship's picture engraved on the bottom, in colour, and nobody was allowed to use it.

And now he was doing the same. Well, not quite the same but it still bloody hurt. He was a shit, a bastard to cause all this needless pain. Hadn't he been offered a good job, a secure career for life, rugby, golf, family friends—and Sheila: what about Sheila? He could see Tom, good old dependable, home-loving Tom. There he stood; a comforting arm around his mother and Sheila, Dorothy close by; strange bloody relationship that, Tom and Dorothy. She called him her brother but he knew that Tom wasn't happy with the arrangement. But sure it was none of his business. And wasn't Tom off to Omagh, to do his articles in a friend of his father's practice. Articles, what the hell were articles? Something you lost in the washing machine. Like socks! Why was he so bloody content looking for socks? Hadn't they gone to Wales together? Followed the Yellow Brick Road? Agreed to take the Queen's shilling, well a bit more than that, to get pissed in Wales and hadn't they both liked the mess life, its cheap booze and servants, stewards, whatever? It was a really good pub. Then he'd taken cold feet, so it was half his fault anyway.

Jesus and Joseph! His heart was in his mouth. Bloody foghorn, on a night like this, wasn't it only drizzle?

Must be an English captain.

The steamer drifted sideways away from the jetty, casting its magic lantern show upon the dark rainbow waters. Row upon row of twinkling lights reflected her silent passage.

He felt the tingle of her turbines through his feet, their pulse quickening towards the open water. The woman beside him wiped the wet hankie up and down each cheek. His stomach churned with each throb of the screw, digging a pit of emptiness. He was hollow, a chocolate soldier drained of emotion, empty. He knew as never before, it was Sheila he loved… Her words rang in his ears… "Why, why if you love us all so much, why do you choose to leave us? What have you got in common with those strangers across the water?" He felt his tears mingle with the soft drizzle, trickling down his cheeks. He wiped them away, not caring who saw. Tom was still visible, his umbrella sheltering his women from the rain. His father stood alone; umbrellas were for women, golf courses and Englishmen. It suddenly dawned on him that he had never asked her to marry him. He didn't need to, did he? He'd gone to school with her brother; hadn't the families been friends for years. Wasn't it expected? They were made for each other, people said.

The figures slipped away into the night and he was alone with his doubts. Slowly he became aware of his new surroundings, passing through a valley of gantries and cranes, resting in silence, awaiting the bustle and hubbub of a new day's build. Men worked on those slippery trestles, in all weathers, giving birth to ships of all shapes and sizes. It was known by a name in the outside world but here it was known simply as 'The Yard'. They'd built the Titanic, God rest her souls, and borne her cross of guilt down the generations like a well-worn coat.

The steamer gave a final warning blast as she nosed out of the lough into open sea and Liverpool.

He needed a drink. Only a small sign on a picket gate and years of conditioning separated the haves and the have-nots. A chorus of Danny Boy drifted up to the first class. No, he'd forgo the drink—he had a long way to go.

— o —

The cabin door hit the back stop with a twang. He'd just got to sleep in the airless sauna. The overhead light revealed a crumpled night.

"Good morning Sir, six o'clock and all is well. My, we didn't have a good night, did we Sir? Up and down were we? Where would you like your tray Sir, on your lap?"

He had six pairs of hands and a cheerful grin. Colin made a grab for the sheet... Too late.

"Here let me help. There we go Sir. Everything ship shape." He twirled to the washstand. "Now don't you fuss yourself, I'll just help myself from the change." And he did, every last penny.

The fresh salty air helped to blow away the cobwebs as black-headed gulls swooped and soared, shrieking their right of monopoly to their mobile canteen. A jigsaw of images lurked on the horizon, mingling with the drifting clouds. Then, as if by magic, Liverpool appeared in its grey frame, Belfast without the hills.

Colin followed the bleary-eyed stream of zombies down the slippery gangway of hope. Head down, they trudged to their second class space, past the exclusive emptiness of the first class compartments with its buffet car attached. He joined the trail of hope. First class ship, second class train, so much for an Officer and Gentleman.

— o —

The young officer looked in the mirror for the umpteenth time. Why couldn't they accept progress like everyone else? What was wrong with a clip-on anyway? Tradition, that's what, stupid bloody tradition. Tradition was all right in its proper place but not when you had thumbs for fingers. And then some smart alec would pull it undone, just for a laugh. Bastard! He closed his eyes, how did it go? Left over right, right under, round the bloody tree, back up and pull tight...Voilà! Another fine mess, Stanley.

He had passed, he had survived the self-doubt, the humiliation and loneliness; a new experience. He had beaten the bastards and this bow tie wasn't going to win. They had taught him to command and obey, your obedient servant, within a defined chain of command and social etiquette. To be worthy to hold the Queen's Commission.

He opened his eyes. The reflection showed a perfect bow tie nestling below a winged collar. How in hell's name had he done that? He smiled at the familiar face in the mirror, it winked back. Never admit defeat, it mouthed.

The Mess Corporal held open the massive oak door; he returned the salute still self-conscious of his recent elevation. A steward advanced with a tray of sherry glasses. Not enough to fill a tooth, his father would say. They were here for the parade, his parents and Sheila.

"Sweet or dry, Sir?"

"Dry…thank you."

He took a sip and inhaled deeply, remembering his first visit to this great hall. He had pushed the door open and walked into the past.

— o —

His footsteps echoed his presence from marbled floor to vaulted dome, surrounded by draped folds of decaying embroidery of a once great empire. He felt small and an uninvited intruder. He turned quickly, but he was still alone. Alone with the ghosts who haunted those colourful shrouds of widowhood. Christ, it was like a church on weekdays.

He realised that he was tiptoeing to closed doors, listening like a thief. His third door, nothing. He knocked louder, convinced he could leave. He could feel his heart thumping. He stepped back.

"Enter."

He dropped his cap.

"Enter," a voice boomed.

He turned the knob and pushed. The silken hinges swished him into the room.

"Don't worry," it was the same voice, plummy and authoritative. "Bloody door catches everyone first time. Right Horatio?"

Colin recognized the insignia of a captain in the Brigade of Guards. Horatio wagged his polished tail in agreement and closed his eyes.

"Sorry Sir, nice dog."

"Thank you." He had lost his tongue. Silence screamed its embarrassment.

"You have a name and a reason for being here?" the voice was friendly like the face, not unlike Horatio's.

"Yes Sir, Monro Sir."

"Do I take that as Sir Monro or Monro Sir?"

"Sir?"

"Never mind. Now Mister Monro, as the door you're still holding is not for sale, do you have any other business in this establishment?"

"Sorry Sir, yes Sir." God he was beginning to sound like a nursery rhyme. "A message for Major Phillips from Staff Smith."

"Ah, well done," he congratulated, turning away. "Neville, for you, a colonial messenger from Staff Smith." Horatio took one last sniff before following his master to the open fire. Colin shut the door.

The room stretched forever into a draped bay revealing manicured lawns beyond, croquet hoops in evidence. Silverware of all sizes and shapes mirrored their presence on satin surface mahogany. Stern portraits, fully aware of their own importance, stared down crusty noses. All gathered in an aroma of leather, polish and tobacco smoke, declaring this the den of a male species.

The leather chair sighed as the tall distinguished figure uncurled from its comfortable mould, immaculate even in a loose sweater, the light blue of the specialist parachute wings on the upper arm of the sweater the only colour in a sea of brown. The long legs crossed the room in fluid movement, pausing briefly to empty the remains of his glass over two frantic whippets struggling to retain the breed. "Scrawny breed, makes the whole thing look positively indecent," he confided to an open-mouthed Colin on arrival.

That was his introduction to his mentor from whom he was to learn much during the next sixteen weeks. "Know your weaknesses, respect and control them but never ignore them, otherwise you will grow to fear them and soldiers can smell fear."

— o —


The Regimental Colours crackled in the breeze announcing the next guest. Colin raised his eyes to the domed ceiling, reading the names listed. Alone with his thoughts, he promised that he would never let his men die for foolish causes. There would be no widows and fatherless children on his conscience.

"Strange what men will die for." Colin knew the Major's voice immediately. "Especially the masses. You should study your own countrymen and the Somme. All those men willing to make the ultimate sacrifice, a chain of belief of which you are now part and really beyond logic to the outsider." The voice changed, dispelling the past. "Come, enough gloom, tonight we celebrate your future. I hear you are off to Abingdon, subject to Pre-Para," he smiled knowingly. "Remind me to give you some introductions before leaving," he offered, ushering his pupil into the dining room.

And the band played on.


— o —


Colin peered into the cold damp curtain of sea mist as the steamer edged its way into the last few miles of the lough and into the heart of Belfast. The early morning light fought to disperse the grey gloom, allowing him a glimpse of the shore line at the foot of the Holywood Hills before entering the Grand Canyon of 'The Yard'. Here was the high altar of the Protestant work ethic. Here, where men touched their caps to royal portraits but where no man had the opportunity to cross himself. Catholics were not welcome. Some had tried, foolish but brave men, his grandfather had admitted. Lucky they could swim, tossed like flotsam on the incoming tide, never to return. He had enjoyed his grandfather's stories as stories, war stories, historic stories, the folklore of his people. The past was past, people had moved on. The past couldn't hurt. That closed shop of religious prejudice described by his grandfather had no place in today's world. "Fall out the Roman Catholics and Jews." He was learning to respect other people's views.

— o —

"A penny for your thoughts Sir," Sheila asked. He hadn't heard her approach.

"Hi, they're not even worth that," he confessed. He felt her hand grip his sleeve.

"Your Dad wants a hand with the luggage. He says never again, once is once too many. He's not doing that again even if they make you a general," she laughed.

"He enjoyed himself, didn't he?" said Colin, seeking reassurance.

"Of course he did, and your Mother. They are both very proud but maybe a wee bit scared at the same time, like myself," she confessed. Her face spoke volumes, volumes he didn't want to read.

"I know Sheila, so am I." He hugged her tightly, "So am I."

— o —

The brown bags stood in the middle of the kitchen table. Beer for the lads, Martini for the girls and Bacardi for the brave.

"Whose place is it anyway?" Colin asked between mouthfuls of bottled Guinness.

"A friend's," Tom winked. "Don't I have my own place in Omagh," he smiled knowingly.

"You're a lucky sod right enough, I knew that I shouldn't have left." Colin winked back.

"Why don't you try pulling the other one?" Tom's voice had changed, even a slight slurring he had missed before. It had become harsh and penetrating.

Colin hesitated, suddenly alone. People had stopped talking. He needed to break the silence. "I know that you won't believe it, but I've never pressed so many creases, nor polished so many boots."

"And licked so many English arses," an unknown voice from the corner raised a chorus of agreement.

"Nobody made you go," Tom again.

The room was silent.

"You can't say I didn't warn you." Tom opened another bottle, taking a long swig. "You saw it for yourself in Wales, those con merchants with their superior Oxbridge accents. Who do they think they are? Who do they think we are? Do they think we're impressed, like the blacks and the wogs? What do they call us? Paddywacks, Micks or Taigs? No, they wouldn't know Taigs."

Heads nodded in agreement. Tom drained his bottle.

Colin was dumbstruck. Nobody moved.

"Come on Tom, get a grip man," he tried to sound flippant, "they don't all go to bloody Oxford or speak with a plum in their mouths." He pushed a fresh bottle across the table.

Tom pushed the bottle back, leaned on the table to get closer. "But their clergy do, those who become bishops do, their theologians do, those self-righteous bastards who pulled off the greatest con trick of all."

Colin was lost, the others excited in a strange way. Tom slapped the table. Anxious hands steadied the bottles. "The bloody House of Orange," he said standing. "That was their greatest con, they were the ones who invited the Dutchman, a wee Protestant poofter with a handy wife in tow, who needed to keep the Anglican throne and save their arses from another Oxford fire."

Chairs scraped the floor, showing people's unease. Things were getting out of hand; it had gone on too long.

"Colin, we need a drink here," Sheila's voice.

The crowd broke up, the baiting over. Tom sheepishly extended his hand. "Sorry," he mumbled.
"Forget it, what are friends for?" Colin asked.
What indeed, Tom thought?

— o —

The remainder of his leave had flown past, one duty visit after another. "Just a wee cup of tea in your hand and a wee slice of cake." The slice would have choked a donkey. "Wouldn't dream of keeping you, I know you're dying to see other people. Now have you seen?" and a list of names was ticked off, including some he couldn't remember. He'd seen everybody and then some, and he'd only been away three bloody months. Tom hadn't mentioned his outburst again, and although he'd telephoned to wish him bon voyage, as they say in Armagh, he joked; the end pause was long and painful to both of them, followed by hurried promises, promises. The seeds of doubt festered in his mind, threatening the brotherhood of youth with the reality of manhood. Somehow he had crossed a line, he'd become piggy in the middle, an anglophile. In three months? Don't talk daft. What if Sheila felt like Tom? Had she hidden doubts? Would she accept change? Would she Change? God, he was becoming paranoid. Para was the word.

— o —

Para pre-selection had come and gone in a series of exercises in mental and physical torture. The log race, the milling, both designed to test men to their personal limitations. Those bastards were sadists; these were the good guys, subtle and devious.

RAF Abingdon, home of the Parachute Training School. The Brits, the only country in the world to use RAF instructors to train their parachute forces. There was a rumour that New Zealand was thinking of copying the Brits, but nobody really cared. The first two descents from a static balloon, followed by six from aircraft; two carrying an equipment container, and a final night descent.

A winged-horse my ass, more like Dumbo, who flew in fairy tales but this was no fairy tale.

"Go…go….," he woke at night hearing that command ringing in his ears. At least the accent was friendly, soft and round, moulded in the peaceful beauty of County Kerry. The Sergeant instructor, known as Paddy to his friends and Yes Sergeant Leary or No Sergeant Leary to his pupils, was built like the proverbial shit house, broad as he was long with the waist and strut of a silver-back gorilla.

"Goooooo…" The order could flow from his arse or his head depending on whether he was walking on his hands or his feet. The whole course stood in awe of this human machine who could devour a plate of sausage rolls without leaving one spilled crumb of evidence. Somewhere in the past his maker had decided that this man should teach others not through books but by example.

The man stood before them, knuckles on hips.

"Now then, gentlemen, this is a balloon." He rolled his eyes with his words. The group shuffled their feet with embarrassment. It was the first time they had ever had reason to doubt his word. And pigs can fly! "You all know the drill." He scratched the skin of his knuckles, moving the large freckles like draught pieces. "I'll be taking aboard five at a time. Last man in, first man out. One…two…three… four… and five. Mister Monro draws the lucky one. Lead on number five." He pointed to the canvas-topped wooden cage swinging this way and that below Dumbo's folds. "Any questions?" he asked the condemned. Who ever heard of questions without spittle?

The five victims moved forward in single file, each man carrying his static line and D-ring attachment like a personal hangman's noose. Feet splayed and shoulders hunched, they waddled and bumped with penguin logic following their leader. Canvas flapped, woodwork creaked and men groaned inwardly. One by one the beast swallowed its load. Feet shuffled to the dark corners assigned to them, avoiding the covered but very obvious aperture in the floor through which they would drop if they survived the first descent from the door. Door? There was no bloody door, just a gap where a door should be and a skinny piece of metal bar to prevent you from falling out… before your allotted time! Tom was right, they were only cannon fodder.

"Number five, static line. Lean forward son," the voice and touch were gentle. "That's it, don't worry, you won't fall out… yet," he joked. Joked! He helped each jumper in turn, freeing the umbilical cord of the parachute, checking the buckle D-ring, securing them to the overhead bar and inserting the safety pin to prevent any slipping out.

"Number one OK!" he asked, pulling on the static line, testing the security of the D-ring.

"Number one OK!" The reply schoolboy clear.

All checks completed, he placed the metal bar across the gap. "OK lads, hold tight now," a truly needless suggestion. "Here we go then. Up eight hundred feet, five men jumping!" he yelled through the gap to the elephant trainer on the winch.

"Up eight hundred feet, five men jumping," confirmed the elephant trainer.

The five men made no comment. They heard the winch-man release his brake and the noise of the drum spilling out the hawser wire, allowing the cage to shift and drift. Knuckles already stretched bloodless, tightened their sweaty grip. The beast shook itself, took a deep breath, bowed its head and with a grateful ripple of freedom lurched skywards. The cage swung violently, plunging its occupants into deeper despair. The floor levelled out at two hundred feet allowing fingers to relax a little and blood to flow to extremities. Toes uncurled within sweaty socks. The wind had become more pronounced, plucking at their protective canvas roof screen, identifying gaps, letting in shafts of light, revealing unseeing eyes.

"Right lads, the drill's the same; no need to think. So what should we do to pass the time? How's about a song? Ten green bottles? No? Sure, doesn't everyone know that one? No again. Now let me think... jokes... no, maybe not a good idea. Ah! What about the view? Don't people pay a lot of money to see that view from one of those hot air contraptions?"

They felt him move to one side taking the floor with him. Fingers clutched for handholds once again. "There now..." They heard the rustle of canvas side screen being parted. "Would you look at that..." he invited.

The cage swung violently once more as they flapped to a halt, announcing their arrival at jump height.

"Here we are, we've arrived as they say. So listen carefully." He'd lowered his voice, making them concentrate, gathering them mentally. "Now you remember that I explained how we can only jump when the man on the ground waves a green flag at us? Good lads," he counted their nodding head agreement. "Well, would one of you be a darling and look over your side to see what colour of flag the nice man is waving at us?"

Nobody moved a muscle...

"OK, everybody relax... can't I see him myself..." He unclipped the bar and stowed it neatly away. "Mister Monro... come forward... nice and slow lad... there's no hurry... I have you," he confirmed, gripping the jumper's shoulder, holding his static line clear, checking. "Stand in the door..." the order was clear, matter of fact... "Steady..."

Colin struggled with the logic of survival. He was oblivious to the other jumpers' presence, he was an island of numbness, unafraid; fear didn't exist, he was beyond that point. The healing hand held him steady, knowledge and confidence flowing from its touch. He knew the voice, he trusted it...

"OK Sir, I still have you... look straight ahead... Gooooooo..."

The order of command triggered the response implanted in training. His legs drove his body out the door into the unknown. He felt his legs snap together, watched his arms fold independently across his chest resting on top of his reserve chute, felt his fingers confirm the existence of the red rip cord handle as instinct forced his head backwards searching for the nylon streamer that would blossom into his life saver. He was falling... falling... his stomach still in the doorway..."Please God make it work... name your price!"

The canopy billowed, blanking out the balloon. His helmet forced his head forward as the leg straps cut into his crotch and buckles bit at his shoulders. His stomach caught up with him confirming he would live.

The view was marvellous, life was wonderful, the world incredible.

"Number one... look up... check your canopy... free your leg straps... feet back... pull down on your back lift-webs... Number one... wake up..."

Feet, then arse and finally head, he had landed back in the real world.

— o —

Had it been only four weeks, four weeks? He had survived again, had been accepted into an elite club. The Wings Parade over, he marched back to the mess, very conscious of the new wings on his shoulder. A hot bath, a cold pint and a Chinese with the gang. And Sheila's weekly letter.

— o —

The letter lay in his lap. How could she? The sound of water cascading onto the bathroom floor brought him back to reality. He pulled the plug, ignoring the sodden sleeve. He returned to the armchair. He couldn't think straight. He read the Dear John once more:

*Dearest Colin,*

*I waited until you had finished your course before writing to you. I hope I got the dates right what with the weather and everything. I am truly sorry that we cannot talk face to face, but then that is really the heart of the problem. We have grown apart through no fault on either side. Absence does not make the heart grow fonder; it eats away at security and opens up a Pandora's Box of doubt.*

*I agree with Tom…*

He felt his hand squeeze the life out of the offending page, cursing the Judas friend, swearing into the darkness. His fingers eased their pressure; frozen in position, he flexed his fingers, smoothed the damp pages.

*…that you have changed, perhaps it was meant to be? Your career has become your life and I see no place for me in England. Please try not to be angry, I know that you will meet some nice English girl, who will make a home for you and help you in your career. Maybe another officer's daughter?*

*I know that it will hurt for a while but time heals all wounds, they say. You'll see. Try to understand Colin that this is my home, my people, my place in life and I cannot surrender all it offers. I cannot leave and I wouldn't ask you to return.*

*There is no one else, I swear. Please let us remain friends. I do hope so. I still love you.*

*Always,*

*Sheila.*

What would his parents say? His friends? He had no friends, no old friends, only new friends. Screw her and her Judas Tom. There were other fish in the sea, English fish who knew how to make men happy.

— o —

Colin pushed open the door to the all ranks club. He was late on parade. Smoke hung in circular clouds above each table, dancing to the vibrations of raised voices competing with the juke-box... "She loves you... Yeah... Yeah... Yeah... Yeah."

"Over here Sir." A few heads turned to view and quickly dismissed him as unimportant.

"Late on parade, Sir," our kid gloated, also known as Acne Ted, each pimple a Belisha beacon. "That's a pound for the kitty and a two-pound fine," he challenged, pausing, waiting for the inevitable slap on the head. He held out a sweaty hand.

"Move your arse, give him a seat," a voice ordered. "Get that down you Sir, you're way behind man." Trust Geordie to get right to the point.

"Good luck," Jimmy toasted, downing his in one. "Again?" he challenged.

— o —

The tree was moving, gently mind you, nothing serious. The contents of his stomach, numbers 4, 7 and 13, unlucky 13, lay at his feet. He hugged the tree. It wasn't fair, it just wasn't fair, life wasn't fair.

"Hello again, are you feeling better?"

"Sheila?" he squinted into the darkness trying to concentrate. She was outlined against mess lights. He knew the voice. Who? He tried to straighten himself, pushing away from the tree.

"You need a cup of tea," she said.

"I'm not very good company," he mumbled. He could smell her perfume, Ginger, the Mess waitress, Ginger the legs!

"Take my arm."

"Thanks," he felt like a small boy.

"What number?"

"Sorry?"

"Your room," she stated matter-of-factly.

"Forty-four."

She turned the key pushing the door and entered his room, switching on the light in passing. He followed.

"I'm a wee bit drunk," he apologized.

— o —

Rays of sunlight warmed his aching eyelids. Another day. He sat upright, headache forgotten, kicked back the sheets. Naked… Jesus! The room was tidy, no sign of last night's disaster. His clothes put away. Jesus! Perfume… Sheila… Barbara! Jesus! He pulled back the curtains. The letters lay side by side, one still wet, drying in the morning rays.

*Colin,*

*A few lines about last night. The Mess manager asked me to organize a clean-up of your room. Having found your letter I kept it safe until the work was finished. Naturally I read it. Sorry. I hope you can forgive me. The rest you know. My telephone number is 274898.*

*Barbara.*

Know… Know… He knew bugger all. Jesus… Sheila… He would fly home, talk to her, and be rejected… Sod her, she had done this to him. Well he was a big boy now… His head ached… He had aspirin somewhere? He pulled out the drawer—there they were beside the telephone book.

He felt better already.

— o —

# CHAPTER FIVE

## DIVIDE AND RULE – DUBLIN 1966

TOM SAT IN FARRELL'S BACK BAR slowly savouring his pint. The world was a great place right enough; circles of cream around the inner glass betrayed his thirsty mouthfuls. He had done it, a two-one from Queen's and completed his articles in Omagh. Dublin was the icing on the cake. Somebody up there had his interests at heart, a mature student in Dublin and on full pay. A whole year to write a thesis, "Irish Law—North and South—Compatible?" Thank you Lord...

Politics had entered his life for the first time but he had put it down to the old dream and pub talk, a few pints of sympathy, a smile of agreement and life went on as ever. Wasn't politics a national hobby, something you sorted every week knowing it would never happen? Like winning the pools. Mind you, he had to admit that his offhand manner wasn't really appreciated but the locals still forced a laugh for the ignorant Northerner when he declared:

"A United Ireland, what the hell for? Sure wasn't the Guinness and craic the same on both sides of the border and only the customs men knew where that was and then only when it suited them." He was given a fool's pardon, refusing to take politics seriously. Jesus, you only had to take a look at those who did to wonder. He had a good life—leave politics to the politicians, he said. Why rock the boat? He took a mouthful of Guinness. The face glared in at the window, its nose distorted, clouding the glass. Now there's a born politician right enough. The figure rubbed at its own reflection. Liam had spotted Tom through the wiped clearing.

The door opened disturbing the comfortable fug of the sporting bar. The voice was instantly recognizable even amongst that cantata of brogues. Soft, cultured even, compared with the harsh vowels of his own Ulster accent.

"What the hell are you doing man?" Liam's words drifted over the general blur of conversation. He sounded serious.

"Weren't you supposed to meet me at the Post Office? You haven't forgotten the meeting, have you?" he challenged.

The thick black eyebrows rose on invisible strings to meet the mass of black curls resting on the questioning forehead. Tom swallowed. They had a thing about post offices. Like Chapel in many ways.

"I'm sorry Liam, I thought it was tomorrow night," he lied openly. "Have a pint and then we've both missed it," he tried bribery. "Couldn't have been important anyway," he said casually, half rising from his chair. He paused to look the standing circle at the bar in the eye, letting them know it was still his seat. That lot enjoyed anyone's conversation. He dug his hand deeper into his jeans. Bloody stupid pockets. His hand stuck halfway down. Liam looked really serious.

"Come on man, you can forget that—take your hand out of your pocket, we've no more time," Liam said turning away. Jesus, this was serious right enough.

Tom swallowed the remainder of his drink in one. The crowd at the bar were alert.

"We haven't time to argue," Liam went on. "You promised and I'm holding you to it," he declared. "We've twenty minutes to make it," he said, already halfway to the door.

Tom followed sheepishly. The leaning bar crowd smiled their enjoyment.

Sometimes Tom wished he had never set eyes on this big curly haired git. The trouble was that he had the makings of an intellectual and like all budding intellectuals he saw the world as an eternal challenge for change. Immediate change and immediate answers. Revolution, not evolution. Liam was way ahead. Tom slowed his pace, fed up with trying to match the long angry strides of his far-away companion. The Guinness swirled gently in his empty belly. He was getting annoyed with himself for being so easily led.

"For God's sake slow down, Liam. Where's the fire?" he called.

"A fire it is, Tom, but not the sort you mean." He had slowed his pace just enough to chastise. "Don't you remember me saying that we had a guest speaker from the North?" he stressed. "Well, if you don't, you should!" he shouted, and he was off again giving Tom no chance to reply.

"Would you hold your horses a minute?" Tom panted. He stopped to fiddle with his shoe lace. "From the North, you say? Not another saviour?" he called. That'll stop the bugger in his tracks. "Who is saving who and from what this time?" he baited.

"You're a lucky man, we're nearly there," Liam threatened over his shoulder. "Look, why don't you listen for once in your life and you might learn something useful? Some real history, first hand, not what you read in those corrupt books from the Black North."

Tom felt himself trip on the still undone lace, only saving himself on Liam's jacket. He hadn't noticed him stop in the middle of the pavement.

"Here we are then," Liam nodded sideways. "In you go," he ordered, breaking Tom's grip.

Tom took in the impressive pillars of the Four Courts Hotel, a favoured meeting place to air national grievances. Liam nosed his way to the back bar.

"Two pints please," he ordered, without consulting. "I suppose you're off for a pee?" he said without malice, not bothering to listen for a reply. His eyes swept the crowded room. He knew a face or two.

The barman was quick. Liam, pushed his sole fiver across the wet bar as if his father printed them.

"And one for yourself," he announced, after deliberation.

The tap on the shoulder made him jump. Everyone was quick tonight.

"Man you're feeling flush. A pint for the barman. Who is he then? The Pope's brother," Tom joked.

Liam looked round in disgust. Tom shrank before the silent rebuke. He panicked. Maybe he was the Pope's brother?

"You'd joke about anything, you Northern heathen, anything at all," Liam ridiculed through creamy lips.

"Not a brother then, just a barman. Never mind, it's a job with influence and control of the tap," Tom said hopefully. Not even a hint of a smile cracked his companion's face.

"You really are a peasant. Don't you know anybody?" Isn't he only the President of the Club, you idiot," Liam corrected.

"Club. What club? Fifteen or eleven players?" Tom asked brightly.

Liam looked embarrassed. He'd lowered his voice. "Why in God's name do you have to reduce everything to the context of kicking a ball?" he hissed. "Try and be serious for just a minute and even you might learn something. That's the President of the United Brotherhood of Ireland. All Ireland," he whispered over his glass.

Tom followed Liam's eyes as he checked that no one had overheard. He knew he shouldn't but it was out before he could stop it.

"You're kidding," he tried to restrain his smile. "Not All Ireland," he stressed. "Both footers can join then. Catholic and Protestant? Just like Lansdowne Road," he rushed.

He was saved only by the President's return.

"Two more pints is it, Liam? Good luck lads," the President toasted. He waved his glass grandly. Tom smiled his thanks; a bloody know all, for sure. The ring of the empty bottle on marble wasn't Waterford but it was effective. Conversation became audible as talkers became obvious. The audience paid attention.

The President swallowed, cleared his throat and called for order. "Gentlemen, it's my privilege to introduce our honoured guest from the North... but don't you all know him anyway?"

he said confidently. Willing hands pushed a table forward. It wasn't every day the wee fella from the North crossed the border. The chair rocked precariously on the uneven floor as himself was patted and praised to his position on the table platform.

Tom's eyes followed the line of raised glasses. A small man stood head bowed, dressed in a jacket of Donegal tweed which had seen better days. Only one tattered button remained, suspended on a much twisted lifeline of unmatched thread. The grey flannel trousers, an inch too long, rested their chewed turn-ups on unpolished shoes. Tiny beads of sweat glistened under the shadowy peak of his greasy flat cap. The man waited for his audience to settle. This was his natural habitat. He was at home, surrounded by a sea of bobbing glasses.

He understood his audience, man and boy.

"Boys..." he spoke the cry, soft and emotional. Danny waited again. Pause... he'd learnt to take his time. He removed his cap, wiping the droplets of sweat on its folds. He knew the effect that single word could have, recognized as a battle cry and a covenant of patriotism. Men sloughed off middle years of inactivity, sucking in the tell-tale flab of employment. "Boys..." the cry echoed. "I'm here to learn, at the coalface you might say, divided by others but united in our future." The applause was deafening. Men spilled precious drink unnoticed. He touched his forehead on the cuff of his jacket as he raised his hands for quiet. "To see for myself your continued support to the cause." He smiled down on them knowing the warm up was now over. The extra ripple died away. "We have with us tonight, friends, old friends and old soldiers who have stood alone against the injustice of the British Empire. And it is to them I turn to for support."

He swallowed slowly, knowing the risk so early on. He was asking their help to overthrow and revise the generations of entrenched philosophy that we can conquer by the gun alone.

He sucked on his bottom plate counting the teeth with his tongue. Not bad for National Health. He knew that they wouldn't like it. Brain engaged tongue and he was off and running.

"To support the Old Cause in a new way, to continue the fight but in a modern world, to insist we have what is rightly ours since 1920....

"One man, one vote....

"A United Ireland....

"Under one flag....

"A United Ireland through the ballot box supported by the working man's vote from the North and South....

"An Irish vote

"A Nationalist vote."

"And the open end of a gun, you wee dummy," a voice shouted.

"Now you're talking," a chorus agreed. Men exchanged knowing glances and settled in for a good evening's entertainment.

They'd always give his like a chance if nothing else. And he looked like he knew his place.

Danny listened to the shuffling of disturbed feet. He looked up fixing his eyes directly on the old guard.

"You're right," Danny declared. "We will always need the gun and more important, the brave boys willing to carry it," he agreed. If that's what they wanted to hear, he was ready to hit them where they wanted it. "And to use it if needed."

They stared up at him, looking for a leader; the cause was in their genes. The hard men were his for the taking.

"But only if needed," he stressed. He had them on board, bloody children, toy soldiers really. "The working man," he opened again, lowering his voice, introducing a confidential pitch. "The working man," he repeated, "has stood back long enough. Misused and abused by landlords and bosses alike on both sides of the border." Danny listened to the feet shuffle to a different tune. "We need to meet them on their own ground. Meet them in Parliament. Any Parliament. Use the vote. Our vote... the Union vote." He smiled teasingly. Playing them... "The Trade Union vote," he continued to their relief. "Your vote. Your rights... Equal rights... and Equal pay. Equal opportunities... and religious freedom. But most of all we demand freedom. Freedom from the Protestant sash and the English yoke."

The room erupted.

Tom found himself on his feet applauding the cry for freedom with the rest. Men clapped each other on the back. Others punched their neighbours' shoulders.

Danny was pleased with himself. He had played them as he would his fiddle. They had allowed him to introduce legal confrontation with Westminster provided he trampled on the Protestant sash.

He tucked his audience under his chin and stroked their emotions.

"We have tried for years," his voice rang, "without success, to break the stronghold of the Orange Order. We have always had the support of the working class. Our own working class. What we need now, today, is the working class men under one banner. An international brotherhood. Catholic and Protestant united against the oppressor. Against the Establishment." His voice high. He'd guessed right. They would go along with him provided they could poke the English lion in the eye.

"A movement led by new young leaders," he continued. "Leaders who can argue the Establishment down. A new intelligentsia." He knew the word would frighten them but he was ready. "Young men. Working men. Like our friend behind the bar." Danny pointed their heads towards a blushing President. He drained his glass. Now for the final push.

"Let's use the new generation. Your sons... Ireland's sons," Danny shouted the battle cry over their heads. "Let's fight the bastards on the streets if need be, but first let's unite and show them what democracy really means. Liberty, Equality and Fraternity."

The applause went on and on. Men stood with their backs straightened, shoulders back calling for more.

The President appeared from nowhere holding a fresh pint aloft for the speaker. Danny raised the glass to his audience. He felt the black liquid slide down his parched throat. They had accepted his proposals. His eyes didn't leave the crowd. He was unaware of the rivulets of sweat coursing down his back. He was back where he belonged. He opened his arms and gathered them in. "Thank you. Thank you lads. I can hear your answer loud and clear.

"Now here's what we do."

With practised ease, he told them the proposals they had already agreed to. Danny watched their heads nod in agreement.

Tom nudged Liam in the ribs and nodded towards the bar. "Quick man, whilst there's still space at the bar," he prompted, pointing. Too late, Liam had answered the call of the bugle.

Carried away with the crowd. Tom elbowed his way against the tide to the bar, trying to ignore his friend's desertion of common sense.

The President, God bless him, had lined up an army of black soldiers, their creamy heads awaiting the invasion of the volunteer lips. There they stood to attention ready for the final, life-giving injection of black gold.

Tom eyed the ranks of temptation. Nobody was looking. Why not? He placed one of the glasses under the nearest tap. His lips touched the rim. Taste buds danced in anticipation.

He recognised the voice of judgement instantly. "It's true then, God helps those that help themselves." The wee man stood smiling at Tom's obvious guilt and confusion.

"I won't be a minute," he promised as he fumbled the buttons of anticipation on his passage to the gents.

"Why don't you join us?" Danny called out over his shoulder. "That table in the corner." He nodded the direction with his head.

Liam pulled a chair out in welcome as Tom approached. The President looked different without his apron. All eyes were on the Gents. Nobody spoke, content to wait, saving their thoughts for the wee bugger in there shaking his dick.

"Good to meet you lad." The handshake was strong and testing but still wet.

"Tom O'Neill, isn't it? I've heard a lot about you," Danny revealed.

Tom gave Liam a knowing look.

"No lad, you're away off mark altogether," Danny defended Liam. "No, you'd need to get much closer to home than that over there," he said with a broad grin. "Sure I'll put you out of your misery. The young lady in question has known you for years. Her Da, the Professor, had a holiday cottage close to your own family's. Now let me see," Danny paused.

"Portnoo," Tom heard his own voice, far away, "Dorothy," he confirmed.

"That's the very girl," Danny nodded his head. "A heart of gold and always willing to give a hand when needed," he told those interested. "She chairs our Action Committee in Belfast," he nodded again.

Tom needed time to think. Dorothy... he hadn't thought of her in years. Chair... Action Committee. What Committee?

Danny recognised his dilemma. "Nothing important. Well not yet anyway. Just a few people of like minds." Danny reached for his glass. "She herself suggested you might be willing to help," Danny pressed. "Act as a link. A sort of go-between. Someone who knows the North and South," he paused, letting his words sink in. "Thanks Liam," Danny said, accepting a fresh glass. "And one for Tom," he winked. He studied Tom's reaction through slow deliberate sips. This one would need careful handling. He was nobody's mug.

— o —

Tom sat silent. Stunned.... Dorothy, Liam, and this strange wee man and himself. What had brought them together? Yes, he had agreed with the evening's issues and could subscribe to their success. But to act as a go-between. A messenger boy. It was just too silly... ridiculous even. The priest's voice droned on and on. Tom couldn't understand a word. That's two careers gone then, priest and doctor! Why couldn't they speak in English? Irish even. Anything but bloody Latin. He moistened his dry lips. God forgive me Father but I could go a mouthful of that wine. The guilt was instant but the Devil won the round. Come on Father, quicken the beat—you of all people know the doors open in ten minutes.

"God forgive me," Tom's lips followed the priest's hand.

— o —

The vision was clear. Tom saw the hands cupped around a pint glass but it wasn't the priest's hands, it was the bloody President's and he was sitting in Farrell's already.

"I needed that right enough," the President announced. "I take it you've been to see the insurance man?" The man's grin was twisted just like himself. "I believe the policy hasn't changed," he smirked. He'd heard some wit crack that one and besides he wasn't feeling wonderful and he never took to Northerners. Not on first meeting. Not ever. "Danny asked me to give you this," he said to Tom. The ungodly hands pushed the envelope across the table.

Tom stared in embarrassed silence at the evidence from the night before. Jesus, he couldn't remember a thing. What the hell was this? A bribe? If so, it was worthwhile by the size of it. God, wouldn't he just love to wipe the smile of that smug bastard's gob.

"He said to tell you it was all simple stuff. You'd have no trouble with the meaning when you could read again." Tom's mind raced in circles tripping over guilt. Falling into embarrassment. The envelope wouldn't go away. They had two more pints each. Funny how sometimes even the cleverest of men couldn't detect a strong spirit in a pint of stout.

They were content to leave when the President was sick in the toilet for the second time. Something he hadn't eaten.

Tom sat alone in the rumpled flat. Liam had gone off in search of Sunday intellectuals.

"Always good for a glass or two of cheap wine and a bit of brie," he'd said. The envelope lay gutted beside the sheaf of typed notes on the table. The proposals were simple; clear, direct and obviously long overdue in a modern society; their reasoning and logic self-evident.

The justice of the demands beyond reproof. He sifted through the pages finding Danny's potted history. He read it again hearing Danny's emotive voice in every single word...

> *We must always remember 1916 and never forget the sacrifice made by those brave but foolish men that Easter morning. A ragbag army of volunteers. Leaderless and on a hiding to nothing. Casement already arrested and their promised weapons scuttled at sea. An army in name only. Enthusiastic patriots. Nothing more than a handful of idealists who dared to challenge the might of the British Empire that Easter Monday in 1916. Men isolated in their beliefs from the Irish populace. That's true enough, a populace sympathetic but already confused by the inhumanity of Flanders.*
>
> *Nobody had cared that a few hot heads had taken over the General Post Office in O'Connell Street. Nor that they called themselves soldiers. Rebel soldiers. Members of the Irish Republican Brotherhood. Only a band of idiots would take on the British Empire and it already at war as well. They were on a hiding to nothing. Born losers one and all. Five day wonders. Rebels on Monday and Traitors on Friday.*
>
> *Captured and shackled like animals, they were mocked by their own. Mocked by a local populace with better things to do. It was then they'd realised that they had lost even the chance of martyrdom. Forgotten men.*

*Born on a Monday and dead on Friday. It was all over. There was no popular support for their cause.*

*Then it happened, a bloody miracle..... The stupid, arrogant English bastards couldn't resist the heaven-sent opportunity to teach the natives a lesson they would never forget. The faceless mandarins of Whitehall poked at the ashes of Irish despair. They awakened a smouldering nation. Phoenix-like, a dormant nation awoke to the vindictive judgements of their absentee masters. Enough was enough. No man should be treated like a mad dog. Strangled, aye strangled, at the end of an English rope.... denied even a soldier's bullet.*

*Sinn Fein was born. Born out of a national hatred. A hatred of British injustice.*

*Memories of the famine, nurtured for generations, were suddenly released. Men, women and children vowed never again would they let foreigners sit in judgement over Irish tragedy. The people demanded a new weapon. The right to vote. To vote for their own destiny. In their own land.*

Tom rubbed at the sleeves of his pullover. He was cold. He crossed to the sink and filled the kettle. The hot tea coursed comforting warmth. He closed his eyes visualising the political wanderings of that stupid line drawn in 1921, called the border, carving out the Calvinist laager called Ulster. The Protestants had looked out upon a South already fighting a bloody civil war. A war forced on them by the invincible pinstriped warriors of Whitehall. Those same faceless mandarins forever envious of Rome's infallibility and scarlet couture. Men who had made themselves the protectors of the Protestant throne. Desperate men who had introduced the opportunists of Orange and Hanover. Obedient servants, capable of initiating a campaign of atrocities and capable of employing a rag bag of psychopathic mercenaries in black and tan uniforms. Capable of sacrificing Michael Collins.

Tom opened his eyes. His new awareness only heightened his previous ignorance of the continued social injustice. He separated Danny's notes, picking up the last few pages.

He read on with a determined interest.

> *The vote wasn't enough. You see we had inherited Collins' legacy. The agreement that he was forced to sign knowing it was his own death warrant. You could say that he was Ulster's first victim. Ironic isn't it? Collins was forced to agree to the establishment of The Orange Boers in his own country. The faceless ones had made him an offer he couldn't refuse; Ulster or war? And Michael Collins had paid for it with his life. The big fellow was executed by his own people in a roadside ambush. The silly bastards couldn't see that it would leave Carson and his Ulster Volunteer Force a clear field to threaten the South. The bastards were armed and prepared for a religious crusade. You can imagine it, can't you; a Calvinist army of tight-mouthed know-alls who fancied their chances against a tired and confused Republican Army self-destructing on mixed principles. The Protestant bully boys won the day... Ulster was a fact of life.*

> *The people had seen enough of death what with every family on the mainland nursing an open wound of personal grief from the war to end all wars. They could take no more. The result was a fudged compromise. Home Rule for the majority. Twenty-six counties in all; established as the new Irish Free State. You see Ulster had surrendered three of her counties. Simply as an expediency. Those smart arses had judged them to be militarily indefensible.*

*The remaining six turned inwards, creating a Protestant stronghold ruled by Protestants for Protestants. Established Catholic families were driven from their homes and herded south to the new Free State. Their Free State, they were told. Those who hesitated got no second chance. Over a hundred innocents died on the streets of Belfast in the riots of 1922. Democracy was the majority and where the majority was in the minority, gerrymandering was standard practice. Any protest was deemed treasonable. Londonderry was split into three wards. The Catholics who made up two-thirds of the total vote were confined to one ward. Returning eight seats. The two smaller Protestant wards returned twelve seats. It was simple arithmetic; twelve to eight ensured a Protestant corporation for all time. 'No Surrender' ruled. Any slippage was covered by the property vote in local elections, where every freehold carried a vote and as the wealth lay in Protestant hands so did the power...*

*'No Surrender'*

*That power, that vote, that mentality is still in existence. It's called Stormont, and provided nobody makes waves Westminster will continue to ignore the minority. Well it's about time we made a few waves. We need people like yourself, reasonable people, educated people who are willing to take Stormont on at its own game. Break down the barriers of prejudice. Banish the philosophy of 'No Surrender'.*

*One vote.*

*One nation.*

It was signed, *'Danny Boy.'*

Tom sat upright in his chair. Why had nobody told him? His father, his teachers, his Church, his friends? My God, this is the sixties. We're talking about a European Community with no barriers. Social, economic or religious. How could such a thing continue to exist within the judiciary of the Mother of Parliaments? How could they permit an electoral system that South Africa would be proud to call its own? Within a province of the United Kingdom there existed a coloured vote. A vote creating a tribal creed of bigotry.

A coloured vote.

Orange or Green?

Colours of Prejudice!

— o —

# CHAPTER SIX

## HOME TRUTHS – BELFAST 1966

COLIN SMILED TO HIMSELF, content with recent memories. It had been four, no, nearer five years now since his last visit home. He had learnt his profession well. Cyprus had knocked off the rough edges and he had survived the self-doubt and mental stresses of the Middle East. Home. Sometimes, like now he had feelings of guilt. The screech of protest as rubber overheated on tarmac broke his reverie announcing the aircraft's arrival. There was no escape. He was home.

He waited for his fellow passengers to collect their hand luggage, peering out of the window at the distant figures huddled against the wind and rain. His stomach rumbled, nerves or hunger? God knows! People smiled their apologies for the aggressive actions of their handbags and briefcases. Modern battering rams of impatience. Triumphant, they emerged one space ahead of their unknown adversary.

He was suddenly alone in the empty cigar tube. Collecting his raincoat he quickly followed the lopsided line of bodies; coat collars raised, secured by thumb and forefinger, they scurried across the open tarmac. The pace quickened as faces became recognisable through the rain-speckled glass of the arrivals lounge. He shrugged his shoulders deeper into his overcoat. Bloody October weather. The glass door slammed closed. He stood in his own puddle. Heads turned to look. The wind ceased. People shook themselves, embraced, the parochial welcome. He stepped aside, suddenly an outsider. How he envied them. If only he could once again accept that touch of confirmation. It was too late. He had severed the umbilical cord of innocence, grown away from them. An anglophile, a person suspected of superior thoughts. Always a welcome guest, but suspect.

"Over here soldier." The voice hadn't changed. Colin wanted to hug him, to be embraced.

"Dad, it's good to see you," he said, offering his hand, recognising the immediate hurt in his father's eyes. What a greeting. The proffered handshake. The English stand-off. Where was the embrace of brotherhood? The telepathy of family? Had he really lost the seed of trust? Awkwardly, they grasped each other's shoulders with their free hands. Then his father's hand moved on. Colin welcomed the full embrace, hugging the old friendship, choked by his feelings of loneliness.

The luggage console hummed to life. He turned away and brushed the corners of his eyes. People turned, jostling their neighbours for position. Normal life resumed.

Colin reached for the service issue holdall but his father had it first, swinging it off in an easy movement. "You don't see many of these here," he said, testing the weight. "You look good son. Mind you, who wouldn't with that tan," he said. "You wouldn't get that in Pickie Pool. Not in a month of Sundays." They laughed aloud. Friends again. People smiled for them. They hadn't changed. The paper walls fell away exposing the core values of family and friendship. He was home.

The car meandered through the unspoilt beauty of his childhood. Nothing had changed. Except possibly the colour of a new crop sown into the eiderdown of patchwork fields.

Colin stretched his arm along the back of his father's seat. "How's Mum? He asked. "Still laying down the law?"

"She looks well," he answered, pausing to consider his conclusion. Colin was grateful the road was empty of traffic. The vehicle returned to its own side, then swerved gently into open space again. The wipers had come to rest at last as the car coasted downhill. The sun had come out again. His father still drove as if petrol was rationed. Neutral gear and freewheel downhill. And still that tuneless whistle. The real talk could wait for the pub.

Belfast lay nestled between the Antrim and Holywood Hills curled around the top of the Lough. His eyes followed the lights of the shipyard stretched out along the far shore. Then a gap, a circle of mushroomed oil tanks before the pine trees of Palace Barracks scattered along the escarpment, dipping gently into Holywood itself. What a posting that must be. What did the poor sods do all day? Paint the kerbstones every year? They should get out and about. Meet some nice girls. Admire the scenery. Watch the locals paint their own kerbstones every July? He'd forgotten that. The tall grass rippled reflected light rolling down the hill towards the lough. Space and more space clear to the far shore. The car slowed and turned off the main road. They drew up outside McGlade's, his father's favourite watering hole.

He placed his glass beside his father's on a corner table. Colin winked one final thank you to a persistent well-wisher. The bar settled into the usual evening banter respecting the family privacy.

— o —

Two days, two fries, two steaks, and two visits. This was the third. His mother had arranged the invitation. "The Malone road," she'd explained as if it were a command performance. They'd just passed the University, branching right at the Botanic Gardens. His mother was talking faster and faster, trying to be informative. "It's Dorothy's house we're going to," she said as they passed the Woodlands. "She's married you know. To Alistair Hall," she informed, quickly. "Position and money, her position and his money," she smiled, disarmingly.

— o —

The large drawing room was decorated in the accepted taste of the successful middle class. Polished mahogany reflected a wealth of silver, lighted by what seemed a multitude of expensively paired lamps. Their brocade shades cast embroidered shadows unto corniced alcoves. Exhaled smoke, filtered of nicotine, hung above the social battlefield. Camembert and cheddar lay slashed and crumbled beneath tired lettuce leaves. Overflowing ashtrays nudged mislaid glasses of warm wine, their lipstick-smeared rims and smudged thumb prints fading evidence of previous owners. Alistair had spotted them immediately. Always the perfect host, always looking to his future. Colin watched him glide across the room without a hint of body movement.

"Delighted you could make it." He sounded as if he meant it. "I hope you're not hungry," he apologised in a concerned voice. They shook hands. "Red or white?" he enquired.

Taking Colin's elbow he guided him to the chosen quarry. They passed the Professor holding forth to an entrapped audience of lesser mortals. Mesmerised they stood, unable to escape, slowly melting before the turf fire, its aroma a reminder of white cottages and a patchwork inheritance still too close to some for social comfort. Momentarily distracted, Colin collided with a glass of red. She glared down her nose, not amused, a very obvious teacher of drama. His apology ignored.

A small wiry figure moved into his line of sight. The face smiled that hello of I know you. Colin knew he was the target. The handshake was severe, its message positive. The voice was unmistakably from Belfast but not the Malone Road.

"I've heard a lot about you," Danny said, scratching his nose with his glass. Colin noticed the lady nearest to them move away.

"They say that you're a man after my own heart. You don't suffer fools gladly," he explained. Sniffing loudly he raised his glass to the now distant lady peeking over her husband's shoulder.

Danny glanced around the room. His voice lowered to a confidential whisper. "Let's get shot of this lot. I've done my duty for tonight. Stick close now," he warned as he carved an escape route to the kitchen. Groups parted unasked. A few smiled knowingly.

"This is more like it." Danny's voice filled the kitchen. "Now then, I don't know about yourself but I could do with a real drink," he said, tipping his wine into the empty sink. He poured the bottles slowly. A picture of concentration. "There you go, my boy, get that down you," he smacked his lips loudly. "Man, that's good enough to put hair on your chest."

"Cheers," Colin replied.

"Cheers," Danny returned, nodding his head, the eyes steady. "Sit down son." He offered a chair turning another around, resting his arm and chin on the back rail. "Tell me about yourself then. Friends tell me you have had some interesting..." he hesitated. "What was the word?"

Colin wasn't prepared to help... Not yet.

"That's it!" Danny exclaimed. "Escapades. Good word that," he winked.

Colin felt uneasy. There had to be a hidden agenda to this wee man's friendliness. What was he doing here at Dorothy's soirée? Mind you, her father always had a need for the common man. And Alistair had political ambitions they said. Well, so his mother said. He needed to know a bit more about this smart alec.

"It's not often the likes of me gets the chance to chat to an officer in the Red Berets. Good film that. Did you see it yourself?" he asked. "Alan Ladd it was, great wee actor. Hard as nails. Pity about the voice," he winked. "Can you stay on?" he invited. "The craic's usually good once the kitchen cabinet gets going. No need to worry about a lift, sure there's plenty of those about," he offered, blocking Colin's refusal.

— o —

Colin's cold feet touched the lukewarm remains of the hot water bottle. He couldn't sleep, his mind refusing to submit to shut down. He remembered telling Danny stories he would have hesitated to tell even to close friends, never mind a total stranger. The craic had been good as promised. Maybe the odd dig but he gave as good as he got. He pulled the blanket up under his chin. What he wouldn't give for a bit of the mess central heating. He watched his breath rise to the high ceiling. He had never acknowledged that politics existed. His youth had been above such mundane things and now he was a servant of the Crown, beyond politics. A professional soldier. Nobody, but nobody had ever mentioned anything about second-class citizens. The Catholics had always played their own sports, gone to chapels, not churches. Were ministered by priests instead of ministers, who were helped by nuns, penguins in long flowing gowns. Both of them married to the church but forbidden to marry each other. And the priest himself endowed with the power to forgive married sins. So his mother said. He'd often wondered what married sins were, but never ever about second-class citizens. He had never needed to think about religion. He knew his. He had been carefully taught. Taught the loyalty of allegiance to God in his Kingdom and to the Queen on the Protestant throne. That was the way things were and everyone accepted it as such. There wasn't a problem. The Catholics played their hurling. The Protestants played rugby. And there was always football for the masses. So everyone was happy. The status quo.

— o —

Colin turned onto his other side trying to escape the thoughts of the night. He tried counting sheep. Catholic sheep followed by Protestant sheep. Protestant sheep followed each other in procession.

— o —

It was the twelfth of July. The month of King Billy and the Battle of the Boyne. The whole of the province took to the streets on that day. OK. Only the Protestants, on Protestant streets. Every village, hamlet and rural crossroads, no matter how small had decorated their territory in red, white and blue. The British colours of power and an open declaration of the people's continued loyalty and allegiance to the larger tribe. Rows and rows of bunting gaily fluttering support, surrounding vivid portraits, painted on cloth banners of gold and silver. Life-sized images of the Man himself. King Billy. The Saviour of the nation and the faith looked down on the grateful from his white horse. Why did every successful bastard have to have a white horse? The Lone Ranger, Roy Roger's Trigger, well sort of blonde white, even the French got in on the act with Napoleon.

Happy children played one-legged hop-scotch on painted kerbstones. Parents, watched by parents, joined in the street games teaching the traditional preparations for the Eleventh Night. The community toiled for long hours in the summer sun as the bonfires grew and grew until they reached gable high. At last, tired but excited, the children ate their thick slices of bread trowelled with jam and waited for dark. Grubby hands rubbed away the threat of sleep as the blackness rolled down from the hills spreading its anonymous cloak. Street doors opened wide releasing shafts of friendly light. Dogs barked and music blared from grey-cupped speakers. A torch was lit. A rowdy circle formed and without ceremony the bonfire sent its message of flame into the black night. Men and women danced in the firelight. Sometimes with each other. The air was filled with voices, cackling and crackling to the Protestant flames as giant sparks flew higher and higher. The crowd ebbed and flowed; arms entwined, they circled in a frenzy of celebration.

Then it was time.

A shout from the deep darkness heralded a chorus of hate. The men dragged a figure from the crowd. Children poked at him with half lit sticks. Women spat their saliva curses, joining their men in a roar of tribal approval. The chant grew louder. Men flexed their muscles. The sacrifice was tossed high onto the bier as scream after scream rent the night asunder. Flying sparks billowed as hungry flames engulfed the arms and legs, eating their way into the body releasing the inners and consuming the hate. Children chanted their parents' curses:

"NO POPE HERE...

"FUCK THE POPE...

"NO POPE HERE!"

The effigy met the flames of hell.

The people were as one. Every door was opened spilling shafts of identifying light onto the pavement. Large ladies with stomachs overtaking their bosoms passed out food and drink to passing revellers. The guardians of the Protestant rights joined their children in the dance. Children lost in a land of giants. Friendly giants, family giants, tribal giants. The hot fire lay dead beneath its mountain of ash. Charcoaled logs smouldered their weak heat as the final door slammed on exhausted emotions and the last revellers escaped from the naked dawn.

The big day had broken.

Indoors, lights still burned. There was no rest for the wicked, they say. Last night's guardian took up the morning chores. Lower lips puffed at matted curls stuck to running foreheads. Strong forearms stamped the hot iron down hard on the damp linen tea towel, hissing and pressing at her man's Sunday best. Satisfied, she climbed the narrow staircase to the empty bedroom. She reached up her eyes avoiding her body filled image on the mirrored wardrobe door and lifted down the round hat box. Her eyes turned to the white shirt and black tie kept for funerals and lodge already unfolded on the bed. Slowly, gentle pressure was applied in a circular process until, reluctantly, the lid lay on the bed. Her coarse fingers opened and smoothed layer after layer of protective tissue paper. The glittering tassels, rough to touch, nestled on thick brocade of Orange. The sash lay exposed. It had been Sammy's father's, father's. A work of art and fit for a king. She smiled despite herself. She cocked her head to the stairs, listening to the snores of the king, her man, still asleep on the downstairs sofa. She smiled to herself; at least she'd had some sleep a night away from those bloody tonsils.

The sash was placed below the bowler hat, worn and acceptable on this day only; the rest of the year it was decried as a symbol of the English middle class. With one last glance she descended the treacherous stairs. The kettle lid bobbed its warning readiness. With measured practise she divided the scalding water between teapot and shaving mug, wiping the condensation from his mirror. Ready at last, she crossed the parlour floor to shake her man.

Her King for the day.

The bandsmen were the first to appear, wrinkling their noses at the acrid smell wafting from the still-smouldering remains of the night's revelry. Assembling their instruments and adjusting their mouth pieces. Praying for spit. Furred tongues flicked nervously over dry lips as pale fingers attempted a run at the bottom scale. The magic notes of the flute floated the length of the street. Children appeared in open doorways, their faces hastily polished, tiny hands hidden behind mugs of steaming sweet tea. Music was the order of the day.

Throats scalded but refreshed, the pipes and drums sounded the call to arms. The king stepped onto the pavement, his knife edge creases hiding wobbly legs. Determined fingers picked the last hint of dandruff from his passing shoulder. Polished and pressed from head to toe and in full regalia, he stood, eased his neck muscles in a nervous twitch and stepped forward in all his glory. Panic stricken, he stopped at the kerb edge, shaky fingers fumbling for the packet of fags; if she'd forgotten! Cursing quietly at her incompetence he pushed the overlooked mothball back into the corner of the lined pocket. The nicotine-

## 64  Colours of Prejudice

stained fingers trembled their need as he found the packet of twenty. In the inside pocket, for fuck sake! He struck the first match of the day, inhaling the sulphur and nicotine deep into delicate lungs. Nerves steadied, he exhaled through his nostrils. Humphrey Bogart? Who he?

The wide-eyed children stood in awe, ever careful not to get underfoot. Swords and pikes, symbols of office, shimmered in the morning sun. Unblemished metal caressed by white gloved hands. The Lodge Master checked his watch. Satisfied, he gave the signal. A whistle blew. The lead players took up station around the banner. Reverently, the rich tapestry was unfurled from its protective sheath. Young boys ran the guide tassels out. Testing the breeze. Everything was ready. Hands raised, head bowed, the blessing was intoned. The whistle blew again. Pole bearers tested the wind. White-gloved hands adjusted their leather pouches into the groin. The big drummer sounded his warning note. Bandsmen pursed their lips, flicking nervous tongues against wet mouthpieces. The bandleader held his baton aloft. The banner flapped its impatience. Lungs expanded. Music sounded. The men moved off in a line stretching back in time to the Battle of the Boyne.

The Twelfth had begun.

— o —

Colin hugged himself, shivering beneath the eiderdown. Well, it wasn't July today. Droplets of rain clung to grey window panes. When would his parents get central heating? He struggled into his dressing gown. He could only find one slipper. He kept to the right of the stairs, avoiding the loose boards.

He poked the fire and adjusted the damper. Tongues of flame announced the beginning of his new day. The tea was hot and sweet. He stretched his bare foot into the hearth and settled down to read Danny's paper. Danny's commandments, he'd called them last night. So simple, so obvious and so true to fair-minded men. But were they workable? Any reasonable man had to see the historic injustices laid out in such logical form. How could this harmless tradition of marching, enjoyed by so many, be in reality an instrument of suppression to his fellow countrymen? Surely the threat was over. A thing of the past. Like Guy Fawkes.

He read on. A shopping list of grievance... How many elected members of Stormont were Catholic? What about councillors? Civil servants? Police, lawyers, doctors and teachers? What about the allocated few. The token Catholics? Token positions of social standing? Never allowed to hold any office of power from which the status quo could be threatened. His tea had gone cold but his foot was warm. The paper slipped from his fingers as he nodded into a troubled sleep.

Colin awoke with a start, knowing the touch immediately. The same huge hand which long ago rocked him to sleep rested on his shoulder "Come on son," it shook him awake. "How long have you been there? You'll burn the foot off yourself," his father warned.

"Sorry Dad, I couldn't sleep," he yawned. His slipper was really hot. "I came down to make a cup of tea. What time is it?" he asked, checking his watch. "Would you like a cup?" he offered.

"Now there's a good idea. A fresh one I take it," his father suggested, glancing at the tea cosy.

Colin carried the evidence of the cold tea to the kitchen and filled the kettle. He looked out at that broad back upon which they had all depended for so many years.

"So what's up with you?" his father called. "Can't sleep?"

"It's nothing really," Colin replied. "I was just thinking about last night. I stayed on as you know. Met all sorts and ended up putting the world to rights."

"Nothing wrong with that," his father advised. The big hand adjusted the tea-cosy to the new pot. "Provided you don't take your conclusions too seriously in the light of day."

Colin looked across the table knowing that he was entering unknown territory. "You've always employed Catholics. Basil, Sean and others. Good workers, you've always said." He tried to sound innocent, matter of fact like. He watched his father straighten immediately.

"That's a damn fool question. If it is one? When you already know the answer already. Two good men. The best," he said defensively.

"Yes, I know Dad, and that's what makes it worse. Well, puzzling. Good men, you've been saying that as long as I can remember, but they have never been promoted in all these years," he rushed on. "Take me, for example, I'm a captain already."

"They're both a bit long in the tooth to be shot at even for promotion," his father joked. The reply was jocular, offering his son a way out. Colin knew he should stop. What was he doing?

"Come on Dad," he heard his own voice, challenging. Oh my God. "It's really nothing to joke about," he blundered on. Holy Jesus man, that had put the cat among the pigeons. He was a dead duck.

The big man hadn't moved. The chair was quiet just like his voice. "I don't know what's brought this on but if you must know, they've never asked and I've never offered. They know I've always gone out of my way to look after them," he growled. The chair creaked its warning. "They earn more than the managers," he explained. "What with bonus and wee jobs here and there, cash jobs, I've always rewarded loyalty and honesty. I couldn't ask for two better men," he stated. The table moved. "You're full of daft questions right enough. I suppose it's your educated friends who have been filling your head with nonsense. Well, you can tell them from me it's as much their fault as mine. Neither Basil nor Sean for that matter has the education needed to make managerial level, and it's not the men's fault. Nor mine. I'm not a teacher like your smart alec friends. Nor am I a priest," he added cryptically.

"Come on Dad, you know that they could do the job standing on their head. Education is an opt out," he kept challenging.

"You don't listen, do you?" his father replied, exasperated. The huge frame tightened visibly, eyelids dropped over wary eyes. "I'm sure," the voice a warning octave lower, "you know the answer already. The English have always known what was best for us. That's for sure," he snorted.

"Don't be so childish," Colin struck back without thinking. "I asked a reasonable question and expected a reasonable answer, not an eruption of self-righteousness," he shouted. He knew he'd done it now. Shit!

The chair went first, pushed over by the table, which upset the tea-pot staining the tablecloth.

He rose to glare down at his son. His jowls fluttered. "Maybe my money was wasted after all," he spat back. Hurt. "You don't need to go to a bloody university to know a Protestant work-force will not take orders from a Catholic. Not even the Pope. Especially the Pope." He was shouting now. "You've been away too long, my son. This isn't bloody England. This is Ireland. Thank God. It used to be your home."

Colin heard the hall door slam, followed by the raking of the car's gears confirming his father's sudden departure. Jesus Christ, what had he done? He hadn't meant to question his father's judgement. It wasn't meant personally. Dear God, somebody had better start questioning something around here. Couldn't they see that time wouldn't stand still? It was running out!

He heard the creak of the loose stair board. Jesus wept, he'd forgotten about his mother. God, how he dreaded the forthcoming inquisition. The door handle turned.

"Colin! What was all that about?" his mother demanded.

"Nothing Mum," he lied, picking up the chair. "I'll make us a cup of tea. Sit down," he said, quietly patting the seat. "There's nothing to worry about." He picked up the teapot and squeezed her shoulder on passing. He poured what was left of the tea leaves into the sink.

"Have you seen this tablecloth?" she demanded.

"Sorry," he winced. "I'll take it to the laundry," he said.

"You'll do no such thing." She was positive. "Do you think money grows on trees? Was it money?" she asked.

"No," he replied. "I wish it was. No, I'm afraid it's more than that," he hesitated not knowing how to put it. "Well, to put it simply, Mum, I questioned Dad's judgement. About the works and he didn't like it," he confessed. He ran the tap to drown her reply, playing for time. "I'll apologise later," he shouted.

They drank their tea as he told her about the party. Careful not to mention Danny. She nodded her head listening intently as he unfolded his self-questioning of the previous evening and his clumsy search for answers this morning.

Colin didn't know how to approach his father. He wanted to put the necessary confrontation off as long as possible, so walked to the works. The yard was cold and miserable with an open gate. His father's office door was open. He knocked and entered.

"It's you then." His father stepped from behind the desk. "No need to sit down," he said brusquely. Colin's heart sank. "And before you say a word, your mother's been on the phone." The big hand rested on the door knob. "Well, your timing's good; I'll say that for you, five o'clock. Come on then, let's go across the road for a pint." He'd been forgiven.

Father and son drove homeward in silence. The match flared. Phosphorous and tobacco met. Colin listened to hungry lungs suck in full strength tar, seeking nicotine inspiration.

"It's my fault you know." His father spoke first exhaling through his nose. "I keep forgetting how little you know about the local rules. My own fault and I admit that," he confessed as if to himself. "When I think how careful I was to keep you away from our inherited prejudices. I sometimes wonder, did I do right?" he questioned himself. "You see, I thought that education would be enough. A new generation who didn't have to think about the old ways," he sighed audibly, wiping the inside of the windscreen with the back of his glove. He peered out into the evening. Colin felt the eyes turn his way. "There are some of us," his father continued, "who believe the border is a thing of the past. What with the new Common Market and her subsidies, wouldn't we all be damned fools to ignore that chance?" His chuckle was infectious, drawing them together. "Dublin's ready for sure and the farmer will take anybody's money. Economics is a powerful force. Maybe even strong enough to overcome religious and class taboos. But it's how we go about it? That's the question for sure." He wiped the window harder. "Wouldn't you think Dublin and Westminster could get together? Make Stormont an offer she couldn't refuse." He waved an unseen apology to the man on the bike with no lights. "Set up a United Ireland but within a United Europe. Not immediately," he stressed. "But evolved over the years. Say five, ten, more like twenty if the truth be known. It doesn't matter as long as we're all moving forward."

Colin opened the window a couple of inches. The cold air sucked the nearest smoke into the night. He wasn't ready to say anything. He couldn't believe his ears.

"Education, that's where the future lies. Integrated education, but it must come from the church; both sides must surrender their turf to the teachers and the teachers must be taught as one. Again, it will take time; I don't deny that and where to start? God knows?" He smiled for the first time. "I know you had to leave and I don't hold it against you. We'll work it out. Just you wait and see."

Colin waited for the car to come to rest in the driveway. He still hadn't said a thing. What could he say? It was the same feeling as at the airport. He was the piggy in the middle. Confused and abused by the logic and emotion of the Irish cocktail. Jesus, what a mess. What about Danny? His Civil Rights and the Charter?

He found his voice. "Thanks for telling me your hopes," he said. His voice choked. "You're right, I've been away too long," he apologized. "Maybe it's about time you taught me the Irish facts of life, I would like to help if possible. You never know, maybe I might return home sooner than you think."

"That's my boy." His father's face beamed agreement.

The drawing room curtain fell back into its fold. His mother smiled. Content with her men.

Children, really.

# CHAPTER SEVEN

## THE SPECIALIST – FORT BRAGG, USA 1966

"**COLIN, ARE YOU AWAKE?** It's for you." His mother's call was urgent. "A Mister Adjutant from Aldershot. Very English," she mocked. He could hear her already on the landing and advancing. "You didn't tell me that you were a captain now," she scolded. Now from just outside the bedroom door. "What comes next?" she asked. "Oh, never mind. Come along quickly," she insisted. "It must be costing the poor man a fortune." She led the way back down the stairs.

Colin fumbled, beginning to panic, with his dressing gown cord which had become entangled with the telephone cable. "Hello!" he said. Worried.

"Captain Monro?" His mother was right, very English. Funny how the old ear adjusts so quickly.

"Yes."

"Colin?"

"Jeremy?"

"How is God's country? Green as ever?"

"Jeremy, you do know it's only seven o'clock?"

"Exactly the same here, dear boy. No jet lag, what." He guffawed. "Dickie Fielding has gone down with mumps of all things," he declared cryptically. "Can't get his trousers on, never mind a parachute. Dare say you can work the rest out for yourself?"

"Jeremy, it is still seven o'clock in the morning and I don't know any Dickie Fielding, and it sounds like a very personal problem to me," he said pointedly. Colin could feel his body relax. It wasn't important. Just puzzling.

"Sorry old bean," Jeremy apologized quickly. "Took it for granted. He's one of them, Hereford and all that sort of malarkey. The thing is, he was down for a course in the States with John Wayne's outfit. The Green Berets no less, Mission Impossible and all that crap. Really is impossible I'd say hung the way he is," he laughed again. "So guess who is replacing him?"

"You're joking... aren't you?" he asked, checking the date on his watch. Not even the first. Colin knew that somebody had screwed up. "You know I'm not Special Forces trained," he tested.

"Perfectly true, dear boy, but it would appear that all the Hereford mob are fully committed to some party or other in the Middle East and can't possibly make it back in time. And believe me, they don't want to lose the slot. Apparently it's taken two years to convince our cousins we deserve the place. And besides, the old man says you're the only one available."

"When?" Colin asked.

"Got pen and paper handy?"

"You all right son?" It was his mother's voice. Colin felt the telephone removed from his hand. "You look as if you've seen a ghost. Anything wrong?" she asked.

He swept her into the air, spinning down the hall into the living room. His father looked up startled, missing his mouth with his last forkful of breakfast. "Good news I take it," he observed, returning the bacon to his plate.

"Good news. It's unbelievable," Colin shouted, lowering his mother to the floor, noticing her flushed face for the first time. Radiant in her joy for him. "I'm going to America," he burbled.

His mother straightened her dress, her eyes lowered, concentrating on the pleats and running her fingers down each fold. Carefully avoiding his eyes.

"When?" she whispered the word.

"When?" he repeated. "This afternoon," he continued without thinking.

"I'd better put the pan on then," she said. "Will I make you something to take with you?" she asked. The pan rattled and hissed to her first lonely tear.

"You always hurt the one you love," the words repeated, stuck in his head. Jesus, Barbara, not again, another cancelled promise, a week in Devon. Maybe next year? He didn't deserve her, four years on his personal roller coaster. He had offered her this trip, then Devon. He knew she'd refuse. His mother's principles still intact, but Barbara's embarrassment still burning from her first visit. "Not in my house, separate rooms it is until you make her an honest women and that's final." Maybe it was time to do just that?

Colin had explained the little he could to his father on the way to the airport. What HALO stood for in the parachuting world: High Altitude Low Opening. And how the Americans and they had been experimenting with ways of delivering a small team of specialists from a high flying aircraft. Men dropping in free fall, using oxygen and landing in a selected drop zone. The scheme was still in its infancy but the means and the men were available. Hence his trip to Bragg.

"Sounds daft to me and God help us if your mother ever finds out," were his father's parting words; suitably impressed.

— o —

The touch was light. "Welcome to Fayetteville." Her voice understanding. "We hope you enjoyed your flight. Have a nice day," she drawled. The Doris Day look-alike smiled her concern for his future. "What do you reckon?" His travelling companion nudged his shoulder. "A bit of alright," he smiled.

Staff Sergeant Desmond McCready, late of Banbridge in the County of Down, his appointed minder for the course, Paddy to his many friends, stood in the airport lobby grinning at everyone and anyone. The people all grinned back. The bloody man was infectious.

"Boss," he whispered the name but the call was urgent. "Listen carefully, no, don't turn round and for God's sake try not to laugh. Slowly now," he warned.

The voice was unmistakable. It hung on the Southern heat. English public school with a dash of colonial twang.

"I say you guys. I say, Captain Monro, over here."

Colin turned slowly. Paddy winked or blinked. The American fatigues had been hand-crafted. Most certainly in London. They fitted like a glove. The knife-edged creases were eased into calf length jump boots, polished to patent leather imagery. The slim waist supported a hand-stitched belt, its silver buckle a cameo of a screaming eagle. The battledress top was covered in every parachute insignia devised by the allied countries. The owner's name was emblazoned in jet black lettering on a white strip, visible from across the road. Mirrored sunglasses competed with dazzling teeth to reflect Colin's astonished face. Only the Red Beret and matching cravat remained of the original man. The bloody man had gone native. The apparition stood clapping its hands like a penguin at feeding time.

"Major Barbour, Christopher as in Wren," it introduced itself. "Welcome aboard," it enthused. "Liaison is my game and I play for the 82nd Airborne," it stated its mission in life.

Good God, it couldn't be real. Colin stared open-mouthed as Paddy grasped the welcoming handshake.

"Staff McCready Sir. Served with the General, your father." He warned Colin.

"Pleased to meet you. May I introduce Captain Monro?"

Colin accepted the hand. "Colin Munro," he mumbled, still in shock. Thank God for Paddy. He owed him one.

Action Man adjusted his shades, tucking his thumbs in the eagle's ears. "Marvellous to hear an English voice again," he said, slapping Colin's shoulder. "Do I detect a hint of the provincial Irish?" He asked eagerly. "My goodness, two from the Emerald Isle, your hosts will be pleased. They have a thing about the Green Mafia." The major removed his glasses. The eyes revealed a totally different person. Boyish, with a hint of embarrassment lurking in the corners. A pleasant face despite the public school mouth. He twirled his sunglasses. "Gum?" he offered.

The Pontiac slipped smoothly from cruise to control as they approached the giant statue announcing the home of the Screaming Eagles. Their host watched their reactions in the rear-view mirror, remembering his own arrival. How confusing it had been. Trying to absorb statistics of Texan proportions, fired in bursts by a youthful lieutenant so very proud of his country's achievements. "You have now entered the home of the 82nd Airborne which hosts Pope Air Base, whose airlift capability is second to none," the major went into his spiel. He was a natural mimic. "Right next door to Simonsfield where it's rumoured helicopters breed in the dark." The automobile, you couldn't just call it a car, berthed alongside a compound of wooden huts. Large men in green berets saluted the major casually but meaningfully. Their eyes recorded every aspect of the newcomers' arrival.

The lecture room hummed its promise of air conditioned relief from the body draining humidity. Colin and Paddy stood two paces inside the doorway. In front of them their assembled hosts waited. Gleaming from head to polished toe. Ramrod straight in their superior fatigues. Not a head turned to greet their late entrance. Flustered and sweaty, their shirts already stained by the simple effort of walking, they stood waiting... Embarrassed.

Only one pair of eyes looked forward. Recording their sin. The eyes directed them to sit. They sat... front row... nobody moved. They sat, cold sweat staining wrinkled shirts.

Roll call continued. Colin eased the armpits of his clinging shirt and adjusted the wilted epaulettes. Talk about the poor man's cousin. He wanted to hide from the John Wayne look-alikes.

"Captain Monro." It was a statement delivered in the husky voice of the Marlboro Man. "Parachute Regiment, British

Army," the voice continued to read from its list. The eyes lifted. Black pupils latched onto target.

"Captain Monro reporting for duty as instructed, Sergeant," he barked in best traditional manner. Coming to attention, stamping his right foot from on high.

The all-American cut-out bristled visibly. Its sculptured arm rippled an armful of personal achievement needed for Master Sergeant First Class. "Your movement orders, Sir," it demanded. The man didn't like Redcoats and took no prisoners.

Colin smiled nervously. He could taste the tension in the air. "I'm terribly sorry." He didn't know how to address the rank. "Sir?" he tried. "But we do not issue officers with movement orders in the British Forces," he apologized.

The room froze in a tabloid of pity. The words hissed through a single bubble of spittle clinging to the middle of the lower lip. "Are you bullshitting me? Sir?"

"If I interpret the question correctly, Sir?" Colin ventured again. "The answer is a definite no," he closed hurriedly. Colin watched the lower jaw go slack, exposing forgotten chewing gum.

Confused eyes searched Colin's face for even a glimmer of positive insult. The chair creaked under profound thought. "Okay Captain. Let's start again... Sir! All these officers and men have been given written, that is, typed written instructions." He shuffled the piles of paper before him. Visible evidence. "On how and when to get here. Got that?"

"Got that!" Colin agreed.

"Now you're telling me that you and your side-kick have moved halfway around the world and arrived here," he emphasised, his eyes rolling. "At Fort Bragg, on time... nearly," he checked his timepiece. The eyes cut off even the hint of a snigger from the assembled company. "Without any movement orders?" The lips formed a choirboy stress on movement, curling at the corners, anticipating the kill. "Not one written instruction, not even a copy? That's as I understand it... correct Sir?" he ended forcibly. He folded his arms willing to consider a plea of insanity.

"Quite correct, Sir. I can only apologize for the incompetence of our Washington embassy staffers who handled all our arrangements." Colin offered extenuating circumstances. Why annoy the man when he could pass the buck?

The chair groaned at the sudden shift of weight. Confusion vanished to be replaced by tightened eyes which glinted their understanding. The man stood ramrod straight.

"Sorry for any misunderstanding, Captain, but no bastard briefed us you were being handled by Washington. Sons of bitches," he cursed administration, scratching the back of his shaved head. "Welcome aboard Sir." He held out his hand. "You need help, anyway, anytime Captain, just ask." The voice was low and confidential and without a hint of humour. "You walk here?" he concluded.

Thirty all.

Game on.

— o —

The casevac chopper, or meat wagon to the initiated, circled the drop zone like some giant vulture. The landscape was dry and arid, stretching for mile upon mile. Continuous flat sand broken at intervals by clumps of incongruous pine trees. This was an American wasteland dedicated to those veterans who poured from the skies to liberate Europe in 1944. Saint Malo, Michel and Brieuc. Names to remember and deeds to imitate. Fit for airborne heroes.

Colin released the snap-hook retainers on his harness and dropped the remaining few feet to the desert floor. He had crashed through the upper branches of the pines, his arms covering eyes and face, praying for his canopy to snag, arresting his fall. He unbuckled his helmet and removed his goggles, wiping his forehead on his sleeve and sat down at the base of the tree. He flicked the zippo and lit the Consulate, inhaling the clear menthol into his still tense body and waited for the recovery party.

The last six weeks had been an experience of a lifetime. First the grooved repetition of new skills. Hands up, legs down, stomach forward, head back, hollow back, arms and legs symmetrical. Hold position. Hold position... Relax! Briefings, followed by more briefings.

They had been worked non-stop until they had become a part of their equipment. Equipment designed to cope with surviving a three-mile drop in free-fall. Suddenly they were ready to fly. That never to be forgotten first descent.

The long line of volunteers waddled like grounded ducks across the shimmering pan. Baked in sweat, throats cotton-wool dry. The line weaved into the welcoming shadow of the huge military transporter which was to carry them to drop height. Twelve thousand feet. Just below oxygen starvation.

"Stand – up… emplane."

Their deformed shadows cast a nightmare picture of hunchbacked gargoyles, as one by one they disappeared into the depths of the giant Starlifter transporter.

The men braced their feet as the aircraft banked into the sun. They felt the aircraft level out and noted the change of engine noise. Final run to target release point.

"Five minutes to run," the jumpmaster signalled.

Slowly, like the awakening of a sleeping giant, a yawning hole filled their vision. The whole back had opened up, a huge forklift platform stretching into an infinity blue pool… some dive. Dry throats sucked in fresh air. The giant's lower jaw shuddered and locked the platform into place. The transformation was complete.

Colin tried to swallow. Nothing. He stared at the jump platform. There was no escape. Checked the drill in his head. Walk to the edge. Pivot on the left foot. Head up and step vigorously into space... Step into space… Shit!

Checks completed, the line of men shuffled towards the ramp's edge. Feet trampled on feet. Hands groped for apology holds. Bodies swayed. Knees made compensatory adjustments. Muscles ached trying to cope. Eyes focused on... Nothing.

"Red on..." The jumpmaster pointed to the jump lights.

They stared.

"Green on..."

Colin was swept forward, helpless as an autumn leaf, falling, spinning, floating, turning over and over, alone in a scrambling crowd... Committed. Twelve feet from the aircraft and twelve thousand from the ground. There was no aircraft... No Earth... Nothing but blue sky and eternity... Concentrate... Bodies... Tumbling bodies... Everywhere tumbling bodies. A body doubled in doubt passed directly across his vision.

Concentrate... Push the stomach out... Arch the back... Push... Arch... Arms... Legs... Feel for the airflow. He closed his mouth as he felt his body flip over. He knew he was screaming but didn't know what. He gazed at the earth in wonder as he fell away with the army of rag dolls scattered on the wind.

It was magic... Pure magic... He was flying like a bird.

Check altimeters... Needles whizzing round.

Height seven thousand feet.

Never...

Falling like a stone.

Where's the handle?

Gone...

He dropped his head... Got it... He flipped over... Shit... Get back... Arch... He felt the handle in his hand... His fingers moved... Independently... Testing... He held on.

The earth... appeared... disappeared. He was on his back again. He watched as instructors zoomed in from nowhere snapping at their flock like worried sheep dogs. He flipped back onto his stomach.

Check altimeters...

Pull time coming up...

The handle was still there... He flexed his fingers... Still working... They itched to pull.

Not yet... Watch the needles... Wait for it... Coming to four. Look at the earth.

Nothing's... HAPPENING...

Sweet Jesus it's not working...

Lord forgive me.

Fire you bastard... Fire the automatic release... The barometric setting was wrong... Not working... Go for override... Go for manual pull.

Colin's fingers froze on the handle.

The ground... Look at the ground...

GOD GRABBED HIS ASS...

The bastard worked... It had bloody well worked... It had gone off on its own... He hadn't done a thing except panic.

— o —

The high whine of the buzz-saw pierced Colin's reverie. The recovery party was getting closer, tumbling the mislaid from the high pines. The branches parted as the recovery Sergeant broke cover.

"Hey Captain," he sniffed at the air, nose twitching. There were other hangers about. "We got your buddy down safely," he crowed. His smile evil. "Pity about his broken toe. Damnedest thing you ever saw. Kicked the tree trunk. Honest. Bad tempered son of a bitch," he wheezed breathlessly, blowing the ash from his cigarette, rubbing it into his absorbent vest. "I've called in the meat wagon. You're welcome to fly with him if you want. I wouldn't. Crazy son of a bitch. Keeps on about having the navigator's balls on toast," his voice puzzled.

"You guys sure talk a funny lingo. Crazy son of a bitch," he complained as the branches swung back into place.

— o —

# CHAPTER EIGHT
## THE DROP – SALISBURY 1967

COLIN HAD DONE A LOT OF THINKING on the long flight home. His career pattern was now established. The next step was possibly a staff appointment where life would be more static and socially orientated. He needed a wife.

The seagulls swooped over their heads dropping out of sight on the swirl of the cliff-top winds. He led the way along the sheep track following the contours of Hartland Point. Barbara had been quiet at breakfast. Moody even. But then some people were. The walk would blow away last night's cobwebs. They had paused to admire the forever changing view across to Lundy Island watching the prancing white horses of the North Devon coast crash onto the wreckers' rocks below. He looked upwards and outwards across the bay to Bideford and Appledore. Just like home. Antrim without the mist.

Barbara couldn't think straight. It was hopeless—there was no easy way to tell him; she didn't want to hurt him but enough was enough. She had enough of being an after-thought. Look at him, tanned and fit, full of bloody America. Good for him!

He squeezed Barbara's hand, banishing the guilt of lingering ghosts, drawing her closer to his side. Seeking security. She looked radiant. His fingers touched the small velvet box in his pocket as his arm encircled her body, drawing in the perfumed memories of the previous evening. He nestled his face in her windswept hair. He had made up his mind. He closed his eyes picturing their evening. He was sure

"I love you, really love you, Bar," he declared. He recognised the voice of his youth. It was a declaration of faith. His search was over; he was at peace with himself. "I mean it," he stressed, tightening his hold. "I want you to marry me," he whispered the proposal. He felt her body convulse within his arms. He heard the soft whimper escape her trembling lips. He turned her body, cupping her face in his hands.

He froze in fear and confusion. These weren't the expected eyes of joy and love but windows of pain and sadness. Her body struggled to be free.

"Don't," she exclaimed, turning away. The fear of rejection mocked his open declaration of moments ago.

She stood apart; alone, she felt the tears trickle from the corners of her eyes. She had to be strong. Strong for both of them. She had made up her mind. She spun on her heel forcing herself to face him. Why should she feel guilty? All those years of being taken for granted. She reached out. Their fingers touched. She lowered his hand and looked into his face. She recognized the crumbling lines of pain. She had experienced them all herself. No one could blame her. She would not accept any guilt. Her fists hammered against his chest.

"I'm engaged, Colin. Engaged to be married in two months' time. He's called Nigel. A widower. A bank manager with two young children. He loves me... needs me. They all need me," she sobbed. "You need no-one," she cried, "only the Army. The bloody Army!"

He caught her hands, pulling her back from the cliff-edge. She tugged away, slipping on the dry grass.

"Leave me alone. You need no-one. Only your bloody career."

His legs wouldn't move. He stood hands at his sides. A toy soldier with nobody to turn the key. He sank to the ground. "Sheila... Sheila." The cry echoed over the water as raucous witnesses circled overhead adding their own plaintive cries.

Ghosts didn't die.

His eyes watched the distant figure turn the bend below and was lost from view. He sat quite still. Fingers moved to pluck at the grass between his legs independent of any thought. They hovered over the small flower at his foot. Cold fingers sorted the mutilated debris which lay in the palm of his hand; still beautiful, the wood spurge opened its petals so delicately moulded but already dead. He cupped his hands to his face, inhaling the cocaine to the hurt and grief which bubbled in his mind. A numbness pervaded his body. He wept the bitter cocktail of loneliness and insecurity.

— o —

Colin's fingers touched the long sweeping wing of the MG as he stepped from the cockpit. Not quite as sparkling as a diamond ring but damned close and much more fun. He read the notice above the guardroom window. Knocked and waited. He knocked again. Louder.

Nothing moved. Sometimes these Brylcreem boys got right up his nose. How much longer could they continue to live off the tally-ho Spitfire image?

The orderly sergeant poured the boiling water into the delft teapot and stirred the tea leaves into a satisfactory whirlpool. He replaced the lid and covered the pot with the tea cosy. He always brought his own makings on weekend duties. Someone was in a hurry. He viewed his domain through the strategically placed mirrors. Officer, whippersnapper, Para, could be religious, expects answers on a Sunday. Five ten, muscular, built for endurance rather than speed. Irish plantation stock, topped with fair hair, possibly a Viking visit to the gene pool. Aye, blue eyes. The sergeant adjusted his battledress, checked his tie and brushed his flies with his fingers. Sliding back the window hatch, he looked the young Sir straight in the eyes.

"Welcome to RAF Abingdon, Captain Monro." He checked his clip-board. Joint Air Transport Experimental Flight; one of them. "We had expected you for lunch," he reprimanded.

Colin recognised a professional when he saw one. First blood to the old goat.

"Quiet, isn't it?" Colin looked around. "A wee bit like Ballymena in the rush hour. Been away long?" he asked, not waiting for an answer. "Sorry, I didn't quite catch your name?" he inquired pointedly.

The sergeant's eyes narrowed, retreating a fraction, measuring and judging. "Sergeant McCrystal, Sir." The response was immediate. Only the lips moved as the eyes and brain filed their conclusion. Monro, Protestant, Belfast, Queen's man and a bit of a smart alec... he concluded.

"Volunteered in forty-two," he replied to the first question.

"Would you like a cup of tea after your journey?" he tested without hesitation. The two men shook hands. Broad grins confirmed their common allegiance as brother exiles.

Nothing was too much trouble. The man knew everyone. Including Paddy and the storeman in the MG factory.

— o —

The days slipped into weeks, weeks into months as men and equipment became familiar. The boffins tested, adjusted and checked. Farnborough and Boscombes' cryptic calculations confirming their expectations.

They were ready.

There was a buzz in the air. Joe Soap, Paddy's nickname for the boss, slippery as hell and difficult to handle had called a meeting at short notice.

The colonel shuffled his papers as he peered absently over his half-moons. The voice was soft but clear with the hint of matured malt. "Good morning gentlemen, I'm delighted you could all make it at such short notice." The audience smiled knowingly. God help the man who was a second late. He adjusted his spectacles. "You will be pleased to know that I am informed by all concerned that we are as prepared as we will ever be. It was therefore most gratifying that we should this very morning have received some welcome news." He paused, always the actor. "That we are at last cleared to twenty thousand feet over Salisbury Plain." He waited, allowing them to settle. "Day and night using Decca Release," he emphasised. "And we have the authority to drop through cloud," he stressed, smiling for the first time. "We are directed to give a Command Performance." He read aloud from a well-thumbed signal pad.

"Place: Fox Covert...

"Time: Zero seven hundred hours...

"Date..." He hesitated, holding the paper at arm's length. "Yes indeed," he smiled hugely.

"The fourth... Tomorrow morning, I believe. Good luck gentlemen."

The Company stood as one. There was nothing more to say. No questions were needed.

The door closed on his back; the colonel listened to their end of term cheer. How he envied them their youth. Bloody youngsters!

— o —

The massive transporter ploughed its way towards the drop zone, playing hide and seek with the earth far below. The men were cocooned in a world of their own. Time didn't matter anymore. It had all been carefully planned down to the last second. Their masked faces sucked deeply on the life-giving oxygen from the mother console. Colin could feel his heartbeat imitate the rhythm of the pump. He inhaled deeply, consciously slowing the beat, preparing himself mentally and physically for the concentrated demands of the next twenty minutes.

The dispatcher signalled for attention. He pointed to the child's blackboard grasped in his left hand. No expense spared. The chalked message was clear and brief...

DECOMPRESSION – FIVE – MINUTES

DOORS OPEN – TEN MINUTES
PREPARE EQUIPMENT.

The men began their well-practised drill. They had learnt to ignore the dispatcher's anxious efforts to assist as he hustled his brood like a mother hen. Thumbs fumbled at unseen buckles. Heads lifted, feeling the pressure in their eardrums as the air pressure whistled its withdrawal. First a crack, then a gap, finally a chasm of blue lay exposed beyond the clamshell doors. Fingers of wind probed at loose clothing, finding chinks. Flapping success.

"CHECK EQUIPMENT."

The parachutists signalled everything okay. Their checks completed, idle fingers adjusted fitted goggles, anticipating the next instruction.

"SWITCH TO PERSONAL BOTTLES."

Gloved fingers disconnected the umbilical line to the mother console. Dry lips sucked deeply one last time until lungs overflowed. Hidden nostrils twitched, testing and confirming their personal oxygen supply.

"ACTION STATIONS!"

The final message screamed its chalked instruction above the mental turmoil.

Hen-toed, burdened by personal equipment and issue weapons, the two rows of three shuffled in mincing steps to the exit ramp. Calf and thigh muscles flexed and contracted as, legs apart, the men sought personal balance.

Mother hen pointed needlessly to the jump lights...

"RED ON."

Throats contracted. Hearts paused...

"GREEN ON."

The dispatcher's hand was still moving to the Green when he looked out into goggled eyes brimming with confidence. The men had entered their own private worlds of space. They were free as birds. Free, in free fall, miles from earthly problems. Free for a lifetime. Their legs and arms felt for the airflow, backs arched presenting the curved surface of muscular stomachs. Their speed increased to terminal velocity. One hundred and twenty miles per hour.

"Shit!" Colin breathed the word of relief into the rubber mask. Muscular aches and mental tension had vanished. He relaxed, lowering his head, resting his chin on his chest, eyes focused on the needles. Height confirmed, he turned slowly, adjusting his goggles to meet the airflow. Positions established, the team settled into their agreed stations. The circle of men closed in, their heads pointing inwards, together.

Thumbs-up.

Everything OK.

Their bodies floated in a landscape of Disney-like proportions, suspended in that hidden world above the clouds. Below them candy-floss mountains rolled away into hidden valleys where marshmallow plains stretched into infinity tinged pink by the sun's rays.

Height, fourteen thousand feet and falling.

The tableau of men and equipment lay motionless in free fall caught in a personal time vacuum. Without relativity. Only the growing shadows of their approaching bodies cast on the clouds below bore witness to movement.

Colin watched fascinated as one by one the falling figures were swallowed by their own shadows—suddenly engulfed in the reality of a bone-chilling white-out. The silence was complete. Eerie. Cotton wool filled his head. His eyes seeped with the strain. He felt his hand rub at his nose, irritable and itchy. He couldn't see a bloody thing. The goggles had misted into a white nothingness. He could see his fingers lift them away from his face. The perspex cleared but not his vision.

Suddenly they were out, clear of the cloud, flickering damp shadows indented on a papier mâché sheet. Sandwiched between two layers of cloud.

Paddy signalled to adjust stations. The team looked good again.

Colin sensed the adrenalin pumping freely into his veins. He watched his fingers rub at unwanted droplets settling on the altimeters. Hiding the needles. He pushed the goggles onto his forehead ignoring his streaming eyes. The needles were spinning.

Five thousand.

Check handle.

Going through four with three approaching fast. He felt the chute move on his back... Pain... beautiful pain. The buckles bit, bruising the flesh with their opening stress. He looked up into the olive green dome of nylon spilling the dank air from its huge panels. His cold fingers adjusted the control lines as cloud vapour swirled around his body. Numbed fingers pulled on toggles searching for confirmation of position.

Nobody.

Alone in a pea-souper.

He called out.

"Bastard," he bit his tongue. What an idiot! He fumbled to release the oxygen mask.

It fell free.

He inhaled the cold damp air into his lungs.

He wanted to celebrate.

Where were they?

No audible contact until the rendezvous; he remembered his own briefing.

Height?

Under a thousand and still in cloud.

He peered through screwed-up eyes. There, to his right, a flash of green.

Height?

Four hundred?

The needles were useless now.

Too low.

They had to be mad—even ducks wouldn't fly in this weather.

Colin stared at the soggy picture postcard spread out below. The church surrounded by gravestones. Cottages, some thatched. A cricket green. He spun the canopy violently, searching the terrain below trying to control the mounting apprehension.

Where the hell was Fox Covert?

The movement caught his eye. A car trundled slowly along the narrow road playing hide-and-seek in the hedgerows. A Morris Minor estate, or station wagon as he had heard the Americans call them. Most likely the district nurse. He heard the car's engine ease as it coasted downhill into the village.

One by one the huge canopies assembled, turning into the wind, the lead man selecting the landing zone. The remainder held upwind watching his approach, calculating and adjusting as they prepared to follow.

Perfect.

The large canopies lay in a loose circle like giant mushrooms squashed underfoot. Snap hooks clicked the quick release, freeing the body harness. Colin watched Paddy lumber across the field, a money box grin spread across his face. "Bloody marvellous, Boss, what a drop! Unbelievable. Team and equipment all okay. Man, I wouldn't have missed that for anything. Where are we?" he asked matter-of-factly.

"Exactly," Colin cleared his throat. "Exactly," he repeated. "What about the village? Did you see that Morris Minor? We nearly clobbered the district nurse. Can you imagine the headlines? 'District Nurse Attacked by Special Forces HALO Team'."

Paddy scratched his head, his own grin growing larger by the second. "I knew a nurse once and she would still love to be attacked by a Specialist Team or any team. Jesus man, is that all that's worrying you?" he asked. "Come on now, think about it. We've dropped blind, through cloud as a team and landed as a team. With our equipment intact and fully operational. Maybe somebody up there screwed up. Not us, man. We're fireproof," he crowed punching Colin's arm. "Would you look at that?"

The Wessex skirted the brow of the hill and turned up-wind sweeping to earth tail first in an operational landing. There was no mistaking the figure scuttling across the meadow as the chopper got airborne again. Pride apparent in every stride. The colonel halted before them, hands on hips. A successful coach of a successful team. "Well done, every man jack of you!" he shouted, actually excited. "Needless to say you had us worried for a moment or two. But a bloody impressive performance nevertheless; by anyone's standards," he added looking skyward. "The General is delighted. Gather in," he ordered. He sank to his hunkers; his index finger traced their trajectory in the morning dew. "Our calculations were spot on," he confirmed. "But unfortunately ground control fed in the wrong Decca lane. A parallel one. Boscombe Radar pinpointed this area within minutes once they realised the mistake."

The general's Wessex appeared from nowhere. They could see the pilot's grin as the machine fell away like a falling leaf behind the village. The colonel waved his thanks from within the circle of men. Wiped his brow and beamed at the expectant faces. "I can only repeat the chief's words. Today we have proved we can deliver a fully operational team from high altitudes using civil air lanes, through cloud and with pinpoint accuracy." His eyebrows rose to reveal twinkling eyes. "Congratulations to all concerned."

— o —

# CHAPTER NINE

## THE MARCH – DERRY 1968-69

TOM FELT CHEATED. Suddenly it was another July and there had been no contact with Danny. The charter had been looked at and accepted just like the weather as nothing new. He'd just about given up on his new-found conscience and settled back into the old routine when Danny had called to arrange a meeting. He sounded really bitter.

"They're killing the charter with kindness," he complained, "letting it lie there like a dead duck in the water. I still say we should go directly to the people. The question is how and where? We need to get on with it and stop walking around the bloody thing. I need your help lad. Now. I'll see you tomorrow," he finished abruptly.

No goodbyes. No explanation. You obviously had to be a mind reader to belong to this lot.

— o —

Tom relaxed in the back seat of the Cortina as it revved its way into the lush foothills of Tyrone. It had all been a bit of a rush and he'd have preferred to travel on his own from Cookstown but Dorothy had insisted on one car only, from Belfast. She looked uncomfortable sitting beside Alistair in the front.  He settled down to enjoy the scenery.  There was a tranquil beauty in the absence of man.

They had travelled along the industrial corridor leading south from Belfast turning right at Dungannon.  The car had passed through villages dressed in the full regalia of red, white and blue bunting fluttering its support for the man on the prancing white horse.  Women tended their beds of orange lilies on hands and knees.  Their slender fingers carefully tied the heads high, allowing the petals of hate to dance in the afternoon breeze.  Small children helped their mothers, anticipating the joy of plucking the stems and gathering the harvest of prejudice for their Orange bouquets.  It was an odd world right enough, when even nature wasn't safe from bigotry.  Tom looked back at the man on the white horse, his portrait suspended above every crossroads and couldn't help but wonder if he had even noticed how green the fields were on his way through to the English throne.  William, Prince of Orange.  King Billy to the likes of us.  A Dutchman chosen to safeguard the English heritage.  Confirmed and divined by the Protestant bishops in the name of God as their spiritual leader.  Those self-same bishops, still fearful one hundred and thirty-five years on of Catholic Mary's flames and Cranmer's fiery demise.  Fearful for their skins if not their souls, they had turned to the Protestant Mary and her Dutch husband for protection.  They'd held the white horse for Billy to mount.  The Catholic James wasn't to be allowed a second opportunity.  The battle for the soul of the English crown was fought for in Ireland on the banks of the river Boyne in July 1690.  There on the twelfth day in midsummer, a combined English and Dutch army under William defeated an Irish and French army under James II. And guess who carried the can?  Correct.  The Catholic Irish. They were to suffer as no other nation.  Deprived of every human right including the basic right to education.  Relegated to become second-class citizens in their own country.

The car turned yet another bend in the road.  Even the Romans would have had their hands full with this lot.  Mind you, they'd have earned plenty of wet time.  The brow of each hill revealed a patchwork quilt of vivid greens grey-hemmed by drystone walls. This was a different world. Up here Belfast didn't exist. This was his world and his people. But unlike the landscape which never seemed to change, its people were on the move. The young were asking questions. That small flickering screen in the parlour had shown them the harsh reality of their lot. The meek had had enough. Danny was right, it was now or never. The sudden silence broke Tom's reverie. He realised that the wipers had ceased their metronomic sweeps. Most likely exhausted. The car had turned off the main road at Creggan dropping back towards Carrickmore sneaking up on the village.

Alistair centred the car intrusively along the narrow streets of the village. "Shit," he cursed. The word clear, its meaning evident. The car's bonnet rested inches only from the baker's van, the rear doors wide to the world. Without a pause or look, Alistair's hand went straight for the horn. "Bloody morons," he cursed the thoughtless habits of the working class. Didn't they understand that he'd come to help them? He pumped the horn again. The dogs on the corner scratched and a cat in a sunny window across the street stretched. Yes, the sun had come out, but nothing else moved.

The baker held out his cup and saucer for a warm up of tea. It had to be strangers. "Just one sugar this time, Mrs Malloy, the figure you know," he reminded his hostess, patting his solid belly, a prominent advert for his wares.

Tom could see the pub on the corner at the top of the street. He tapped Alistair on the shoulder, making him jump. Serves the bastard right, he thought. He couldn't take to the man. Dorothy was wasted on him but then didn't everyone but herself know that for a fact.

"It's only up the street," he explained, pointing. "I'll go on," he said, quickly opening the car door and was two strides away before Dorothy could draw breath.

He ducked under the van's stable doors trying to ignore the aroma. No chance. Fatal, he peeked in on a harvest of soda farls and potato-bread. There they lay before his very eyes, row upon row covered in a coating of virgin flour, and, right at the back, his favourite mouth-watering custard tarts. He hesitated. There was even a batch of bags available suspended from a butcher's hook on the door.

"Take what you want son, you can settle in the pub."

The voice made him jump in guilt. How had he missed her? The huge arms bulged out of sleeves a size too small. Her strong fingers probed the duster into the tiny hidden corners of the window frame.

"I always do them in the shade, you see," she explained. Her head nodding towards the van's position as she adjusted her cardigan to a more modest position. Facing her task. "Finish them with last night's *Telegraph*," she demonstrated. "Gives them a great sheen," she explained scrunching the newspaper into an attack ball.

Tom smiled, studying his reflection in her work. "Better than any mirror." He beamed back at her through her own glass. He filled a bag placing the custard tarts on top, getting his hands covered in flour. It was everywhere. He clapped his hands together, dusting the surplus into the air well away from the cleaned windows. Unable to contain himself, he bit into the custard, gathering the overspill at the corners of his mouth. Careful to catch the crumbs.

"Get on with you now," she scolded lightly, pulling the cardigan tighter. "Real custard," she confided. She gathered the crumpled newsprint, shook the duster with the crack of a whip and closed her front door behind her. Her heels tapped her hurried path to the shaded window. Stretching on tiptoe she watched the nice young man push the last crumbs into his mouth before entering the pub. Definitely one of our own, she'd decided. She hugged her bosom. She could always tell. Mind you, the driver of the car worried her but the girl seemed nice looking. Her fingers touched the window netting into place.

The pub door nudged Tom's back, guillotining any intruding light. He stood uncertain in the semi-darkness allowing his eyes to adjust to the remains of reflected light.

"Nice morning, isn't it?" The voice was friendly enough. Tom guessed that it was the barman. Vague figures. "Can I get you something?" Definite question this time. He'd guessed right, same voice.

"He'll have a pint Patsy," Danny's voice came from behind him out of the shadows.

"Danny," Tom turned to the voice, and a feeling of relief passed over him for no obvious reason. "You're a sight for sore eyes," he gushed. "Been here long?" he asked.

"Long enough to manage without a white stick," Danny whispered. "Where are the others?" he asked, his eye on the door. "Come and sit down, Patsy likes to take his time. Isn't that right, Patsy?"

"Right enough," Patsy agreed.

"For the baker." Tom placed the coins on the counter.

"Thanks." Patsy swept the coins into the pocket of his apron, no questions, no explanation required.

Tom followed Danny back to the table explaining Alistair's predicament on the way. Silent figures listened to his explanation. The door opened again, turning every head. Dorothy stood framed in the outside sunlight, her flimsy summer dress revealing more than most could remember about their wedding night. Thoughts long dormant fought their way once again towards the confessional box. Sin was alive and well. Alistair eased past her, not pushing but near as damn it. Always keen to impress, our Alistair was. The door swung shut with a hiss as he advanced. Some will swear he stood on the animal's tail but who could tell in the dark? Some say fetch boy was heard but what with his screams and the dog's determined enjoyment, one will never know.

The small group sat in the back room trying to ignore Alistair's pained look as his naked ankle throbbed its iodine cure beneath the table. Danny had offered to fetch the doctor but Dorothy wouldn't hear of it. No need, she said as she painted on more iodine.

The room was small but spotless, used for visits from the doctor or, more likely, the priest. Oh yes, and Christmas lunch. Tom felt his head begin to nod with the tick of the clock on the mantle-piece, its persistent sound fading into familiarity as the voices droned on and on. Numerous proposals had circled the table, each one flawed in concept, containing an embarrassment to one or other of those present. He'd remained silent following Danny's lead, adding his negative vote to the chorus when required. Otherwise he was happy to watch Danny's remarkable range of facial expressions which formed his political mask of all things to all men. The mask winked at him conspiringly. Tom rubbed his eyes trying to disperse the shutters of boredom. Something was afoot. He arrested his slouching body movement and quietly slid his hips back until his spine pressed into the chair back.

"Dorothy," it was Danny's voice and the tone demanded attention. "I would like to take this opportunity of going on the record to say how grateful we all are to you for all your hard work and effort. And that includes your family's generous hospitality." Danny paused long enough for the others to nod their agreement. "The dedication and understanding that you bring to our cause is a lesson to us all."

Tom couldn't wait to hear what the old fox was up to. Danny was laying it on with a trowel.

The voice continued, all sweetness and light. "I can assure all present that the old brigade will not only lend her the moral support she deserves, but should the need arise our years of first-hand experience in fighting the injustice of imperialist laws out there on the ground."

Tom put his hand to his mouth, attempting to cover his smile. 'Imperialist?' The old bugger was playing with them, but why?

"Imperialist laws designed then as they are now to smother any aspirations of Catholic nationalism to equality and justice. Laws passed by Dublin," Danny's voice had hit the home straight, "and now by Stormont." The finger was in the air to emphasise. "But decreed, as always, by Westminster, our ancient enemy. An enemy who continues to ignore our proposals. An enemy who will only listen to force and conflict." Tom watched the faces around the table twitch their unease. Danny had paused taking a sip of tea, now cold, from a china cup. He rested his hands on the polished surface leaning towards the occupants ready to continue. "And that force and that conflict," his voice was low making them lean into him eyeball to eyeball, "can and should be a passive force. Remember Gandhi," he declared dramatically.

Danny sat down to a silent table. He had planned to enlarge the Gandhi theme but had decided it was all wasted on them. He didn't bloody care anymore. He didn't give a tinker's curse what this lot thought. They were getting nowhere fast and his time was running out. Dublin was pressing him for action. It was all a bloody game to these people. A middle class crusade. He sat studying their faces What in hell's bells did these middle of the road Protestant do-gooders know about anything? Had they shared their beds with brothers and sisters? Had life forced them to listen through thin walls to their drunken father trying to satisfy his lust and please the church at the same time? Privacy. Now there was a joke. Not even a privy indoors. Queue in the rain. Queue for space. Queue for the dole and queue for God. Sweet Jesus save us from the champagne socialists. He ticked them off mentally, Alistair and Dorothy, he a tight-lipped schemer, she a guilt-ridden dreamer. Tom an innocent thinker who needed guidance. But Tom's time would come. He would see to that himself. Danny forced a comforting smile. Danny Boy, maybe you're going too fast for them. God, he could throttle them for their ignorance. He maintained his smile knowing that he still needed them. They had the clout to organise and penetrate the Orange corridors of power, but in the end he knew in his heart of hearts that it would be the ordinary people of Belfast and Derry who would hold the key to the future. Careful man. He had allowed the mask to slip. He would have to be more careful. Give them what they wanted to hear. Bloody Ghandi... Would you look what happened to him! He adjusted his mind and tapped the table for attention, ready to continue.

"Peaceful conflict," he reassured them.

Their faces relaxed. Peace to mankind. They understood peace.

"A peace movement right across class and religious boundaries. Maybe a rally to begin with, even a march of some sort. The answer lies with the people. A march, yes, but not a local march, a people's march. A march by the people and for the people. A march which will unite two cities. A march from Belfast to Derry sucking in the media and sponsored under our demand for civil rights." He smiled at them as if he was surprised at his own cleverness. He'd floored them just as planned. Now they could talk to their hearts' content. They couldn't think of a reason for refusal. It would become their idea. "Can I have a seconder?" he asked. "Thanks Tom," he confirmed. "A show of hands?" he counted. "Carried unanimously," he declared.

— o —

The car trundled downhill casting its lengthening shadow under a watery sunset. Black and white heifers slowly folded at the knee, bedding down in the lee of protective walls. The land was at peace with itself. Danny had offered him a lift, provided he drove, knowing full well he didn't want the experience of a return journey with Alistair at the wheel. Tom thought that the march was a great idea and told him so but this wee man worried him sometimes. Nobody had noticed or if they had, had chosen to ignore Danny's offer of stewardship for the march. His so-called lads would provide all the protection needed, he'd said. Where did the lads come from? And who was protecting who and with what and from whom?

"Good of you to drive," Danny said quietly. He sounded tired. Suddenly he looked old. "I'm a wee bit tired," he confessed as if reading Tom's mind. "You know how it is. All this mental work. I can't keep up." He squinted his eyes against the last rays of the day. "Education must be a wonderful thing and wouldn't I be able to cope with all those mental gymnastics and superior people." He glanced sideways, a smile twisting the corner of his mouth. He shuffled his arse to sit up straight. "Mind you, a good pint would be some sort of compensation. I could murder a pint. How's about you?" he asked, slapping the back of Tom's seat. "Mind you, and mark my words, one day they'll put the likes of us in prison for that," he said without a hint of a smile.

Tom braked hard, pumping the pedal as the car slid into the side of the road. Danny straightened his cap and eased himself back from the dashboard, grinning hugely, his eyes twinkling with pure devilment. "Now isn't language a wonderful thing right enough. When even a simple statement like that can be taken the wrong way," he said. "Get on with you, lad, I only meant that one day they will be able to arrest you for driving a car away from a pub."

Danny laughed aloud.

"No chance," Tom replied. "How would they do that?" he asked, puzzled.

"They'll take your breath away," Danny predicted.

They drove on in silence, each man now content with his own thoughts, the social conversation completed. The car twisted and turned through the evening shadows as shrinking fields rolled themselves into darkened corners. Danny pushed his cap forward over his eyes. "Give me a shout when we get there," he said as he slid even lower into the seat.

He closed his eyes. Wasn't history a funny thing right enough? What would the likes of Tone, Casement and Russell make of today, he wondered? All men of vision flawed only by their trust in others. All of them betrayed and executed. Betrayed, Tone by the French, Casement and Russell by the Germans and always executed by the British. He shivered not from the cold but memories, memories which would never go away. The bastards had had him once. Slammed up they called it, in the jug. Evil he said, pure bloody evil. A hell on earth. He rolled with his thoughts remembering with each bend in the road those cold dark stinking nights. Nights when he lay on the hard boards of his bed, nights caged like an animal with his own excrement festering in the corner. He had studied, worked and planned to keep himself sane. He'd vowed there and then that never again would some be-wigged and bemused buffoon pass sentence on him not knowing or caring why Northern Ireland existed. There would never be a next time. The world would listen this time. And wonder, wonder what injustice made men fight for so long and for so little. The Brits thought they had finally won in the early sixties. The superior bastards. They'd won and no wonder. Hadn't his own people released that quisling statement? He could still repeat it word for word. Jesus man, those responsible were lucky he was locked away at the time. He toyed with the words buried in his psyche:

> *The Irish Republican Army Council announces that all arms and other material have been dumped and all full time active service Volunteers have been withdrawn.*

It still hurt, all those years of sacrifice and one mealy mouthed sentence scuppered the lot. Five long years he had served his apprenticeship of self-education; Marxism, Communism, even Unionism, any bloody 'Ism' would do provided it served the cause. On his release he had cultivated intellectual idiots and kissed tight-lipped Protestant cheeks, drank with drunks and threatened violence with violence. But it had been worth it and now he was ready. The movement was ready for a new push ready to go public under the Civil Rights Charter. His people were in place. Not many, but enough to control the do-gooders if push came to shove. Enough in case it went wrong. The defenders of the past were ready for the future. The lull of the sixties was over. A new army was ready to take to the streets not with guns and bombs but with leaflets and words. Not in back alleys but along the corridors of Protestant power. A new civil army with right on its side. They had everything to gain and nothing to lose. The Charter cried out for justice on votes, housing, employment and equal opportunities within the Six Counties. It had to work this time. His people would never get another chance. This was their last shot.

"We too can have a dream," he mumbled aloud.
"What's that?" Tom asked.
"Are we there yet?" Danny lied.
"Just about," Tom replied.

— o —

The revolver dug into Danny's side no matter where he put it. He was embarrassed to call them an army with only five hand guns between them and those had been buried for years in the old graveyard at the top of the Shankill. Hidden under the Protestant wreaths of plastic flowers encapsulated in their glass domes of faded colours and past memories. He'd argued against their resurrection but he had to agree in the end. Didn't the hard men need their comforters and hadn't they agreed to try it his way first. The guns were only there as a precaution, they'd promised. Danny rolled over onto his back and stared into the cold blackness of the New Year's sky. The remains of a headache lurked at the back of his skull self-inflicted from student socialising. He'd forgotten that they had youth on their side. Bloody students. A total of seventy students in all and eighty Peelers to protect them and those bastards all on overtime. No complaints there. Tom had agreed with him that there was no need for this march but Alistair's mob had thought it novel. You could say that again, bloody novel isn't the word. The stupid idiots had allowed this shower of dickheads to kidnap the original proposal when they no longer needed it. And now it had become a march too far. Time had overtaken their original July planning. How could you plan for the past months? Hectic wasn't the word. He'd kissed the ass of every committee in the North and even some in the South. Their original plan had been good. Start small and build. Rally support, letting the marches grow naturally into the ultimate marathon from Belfast to Derry.

## Colours of Prejudice

The first march had been in August in Dungannon. A real flop. Who was going to travel all that way? And for what? And to crown it all, didn't it bucket down on them? Two thousand wet souls had straggled through Dungannon on their own. Jesus, he could have cried.

Then came Derry in October. Who the hell marches in October? The rain doesn't fall in October, it comes in sideways, straight off the Atlantic. Sheets and sheets of mackintosh weather. But no, they wouldn't wait. The committee said yes. And then guess what? Bloody Stormont put a ban on it. A public order ban. The result was that only a few miserable souls had defied the Duke Street ban. Wet and miserable, they'd shuffled their way towards Derry's city centre and a bowl of hot soup. Their heads low with anoraks tied at the chin, the dejected band of men and women just wanted it to end. They accepted that they were beaten before they'd even started. Then it happened. He still couldn't believe it. The marchers were surrounded by a swarm of Peelers with their truncheons at the ready. The bastards were spoiling for a fight and they had the excuse to enforce the establishment's decree. Nobody would believe that even those bastards could be so stupid. What were a few verbal insults from tired youngsters or even a placard or two thrown in frustration? Moses couldn't have asked for more. It had been a bloody miracle. Despite the presence of a reluctant media and several MPs, Fitt and McAteer amongst them, and the already obvious defeat of the ragtag and bobtail army awash at their feet, the Peelers had taken the insults personally. They had sandwiched the marchers into the middle of the street and hosed them with water cannon and smashed them with baton charges. On top of all that they had pursued those that managed to escape into the heart of the Bogside, and searched shops and hotels in the city centre for any refugees. They had beaten the shit out of them. Fenian bastards, they swore with each swing of the truncheon. All on camera. You wouldn't believe it but isn't it all there for all to see?

The media had loved it. Television had beamed their brutality and hatred around the world. The public had been horrified.

Glory be, Civil Rights Centres blossomed overnight. Fifteen thousand marchers had taken to the streets and at last the Catholic voice was heard in political circles for the first time. Captain Terence O'Neill, that archaic hangover of colonisation, was forced to sack Craig, his bully boy of a Home Secretary in December. There were rumours of plots and counter-plots and to be honest nobody really knew what was happening. It was self-generating. Even UDI was on the menu according to some. Another Rhodesia. Westminster was forced to look at the province in a new light. Stormont had used the truncheon of state for the last time. The need for reform was accepted at the highest level. Hardliners were sacked from public office. The old mould had been broken for good.

Danny shifted his position, massaging the pins and needles in his left leg. He smiled a grim thought to himself. If they had won all that, what in hell's name was he doing lying here freezing his balls off? And another thing, there was definitely no need for this silly gun. He pushed at its discomfort. There was no need for armed challenge. Why give the Prods a chance to confuse the issue? He believed that last night was a one-off. Okay, the village below which was to have been their original resting place for the night was now a shambles. Its shops looted and its homes windowless. But he knew what they were up to and who the bully boys were. And he wasn't playing their game. That's exactly what they wanted. Some idiot to fire his pistol. They'd be covered in peelers in the wink of an eye. Wouldn't those peelers just love an excuse to withdraw their official protection and to leave the village hall below exposed. Wouldn't they be really popular if they could supply the Fenian kebabs for the Protestant barbecue? And that's why he was lying here. Just in case. He wrapped his coat tighter. You didn't catch Alistair up here, nor any of his friggin' committee. No fear. Bloody know-alls ignoring the need to consolidate their success. Offering themselves, no, not themselves, us, bloody idiots like himself as a four-day, moving target for every Protestant hothead who wanted to take one last poke at the taigs. He'd told that bloody know-all bastard, that they needed time to organise; gather their supporters around them to keep the people on their side. Only fools and bigots needed this march and both were present now. Jesus in heaven, why does youth yearn for martyrdom? He tucked the front of his shirt down between his legs and closed his eyes to the stars. His lips moved in silent prayer.

— o —

The bedraggled band snaked its way through the mist-shrouded pass dropping down from the Sperrin Mountains to the hinterland of Lough Foyle, Derry and dispersal. It was the 4th of January, a Saturday, a New Year. Their enthusiasm had been reduced to hot food and dry clothing. Danny admitted that he was knackered after three days on the road, and what made it even worse was that bastard Tom looked as fresh as a daisy. Danny tried to match Tom's stride but his legs were sore and his feet blistered, and if the truth be known weren't his legs only half his size? He tugged at Tom's coat.

"Slow down man, aren't we nearly there," he panted. "And they're open all day," he promised, his face showing a sudden grin of anticipation. "I could murder a pint," he threatened through dried lips.

Tom smiled in agreement, his fingers probing the lining of his jacket pocket. "Here you are," he exclaimed, offering the packet of mints. "This should keep you going. Suck on the hole first, that way it lasts longer," he advised. "Only five more miles to go and it looks as if we're in for another quiet day," he said cheerfully.

Danny popped the stupid sweet into his mouth, tasting the relief. He swallowed gratefully. "Is it my imagination or are the Peelers a wee bit edgy today?" he asked.

Tom checked their escort. "You could be right, there's less than yesterday, and they're keeping their distance."

The marching column broke stride. He gazed over the anoraked heads in front to see the reason for their hesitation, remembering the small bridge marked on the map. The front ranks were already forging across as the remainder closed up. The backlog was funnelled naturally by the high banks on both sides.

Tom stopped... listening.

It was a peculiar sound, a sort of whistling, coming from overhead. He ducked instinctively as the screams drowned the impact of broken glass. Catherine wheels of splinters tore at damp leggings slashing through to bare skin. Terrified girls covered their faces sinking to their knees as men stumbled, cursing their panic, searching for a way of escape. Danny spat the last of the mint out onto the ground, scared he might choke. He could only shake his fist at the rows of gloating faces ranged along the tops of the grassy banks.

"FENIAN BASTARDS."

"CATHOLIC GITS."

"POPE'S POOFTERS."

The vitriolic abuse poured from their foul mouths and was carried on the wind. Tom swept his anorak hood back from his face to reveal the gallery of florid-faced bigots, their arms pumping stones of hatred. His mind tumbled at the hideous scene spilling a nursery rhyme into his consciousness. He felt his lips form the words. "Sticks and stones will break my bones but names will never hurt me," he mouthed. It was his mother's voice he heard. Her childhood advice of protection against life's bullies. He wanted to laugh but couldn't. He could feel the tears trickle down his cold cheeks. His legs wouldn't move. A body crashed into him forcing him to stumble and fall. He watched the girl behind him fall over, heard her bone crack like a corded whip. Not a sound escaped from her frozen lips. Her face melted into the dancing feet.

"BASTARDS!" he screamed the obscenity at the top of his voice:

"FUCKING BASTARDS... PROTESTANT BASTARDS!" he howled.

He felt the foot on his hand but there was no pain. He grasped at the owner's trouser leg, using it to pull himself upwards. The leg kicked back. "FUCK OFF!" it shouted. Suddenly terrified, he sucked at his damaged knuckles. The cauldron of fear bubbled and hissed its hatred. He shook both his fists in the air. "BASTARDS... BLOODY BASTARDS... PROTESTANT BASTARDS!" His scream echoed inside his skull like a stuck record. He could hear the deep hatred in his own voice. He sank to his knees. Helpless. Rivulets of blood diluted by the soft rain seeped through his muddy fingers. A discarded mitten lay severed from its hand, red-stained and alone. He searched for the other. What the hell for? Fucking mitten, red hand, fucking Ulster. He needed a weapon. His frantic fingers closed on a rock, its sharp edges cutting into his palm. He eyed his target, a saliva-dribbling cretin succoured from birth on hate and prejudice. He forced himself upright. New words had joined the echo in his head. He listened.

"Tom, for God's sake man, will you put that rock down!" the voice ordered him. "Do you want to be arrested?" it asked.

Arrested!! He tried to shake loose from the man pulling at his jacket. How did the man know his name? The tugging was more insistent.

"Christ, Tom, come on lad, there's nothing we can do here. Have a look at the bridge, man." Tom felt the hands grasp his head. "We can't fight those bastards as well."

He looked towards the bridge. The traffic jam of human bodies continued to push and shove trying to gain a foothold to freedom out of the valley of Hades. He watched the truncheons snap desperate fingers.

"Come on, you stupid bastard, we've got to get out of here."

Tom recognized Danny's voice...

"Danny... We..." he felt the protest die in his throat as the mist engulfed him, felt his fingers clutch at consciousness.

Danny hoisted his young friend onto his shoulder. He'd never manage. He heard Tom's toe caps trail a furrow through the litter of hate. Jesus, how his shoulder ached. He couldn't do it. He tried to shift the weight of his burden. It was hopeless.

He turned away from the bridge leaving the lemmings to follow the path to its bloody conclusion. Danny shifted Tom's weight once more, easing the numbness in his shoulder. He felt the small droplets of sweat trickle at intervals from under the rim of his cap. He shook his head, exhausted. Where the hell was the follow-up car? He had told the driver to keep it out of sight, not make it disappear. His step quickened as the road sloped towards Claudy. Coloured flecks of exhaustion flashed before his eyes, dancing to the throbbing in his head. "Jesus and Joseph," he cried, calling for help. He felt Tom's body begin to slide from his frozen grasp.

The young volunteer panicked, searching desperately for the knob to turn the radio off, his brain in neutral. A clawed hand grasped onto the right windscreen wiper. There were two men lying across his polished bonnet. The nightmare slid from his view. He crossed himself quickly before scrabbling for the door handle. The bodies lay sandwiched, their limbs grotesquely twisted. He stood still. An arm moved followed by its hand which then disappeared again beneath the coat. He saw it grasp at its find, struggling to tug it free.

The dark metal matched the grey sky. He couldn't speak. Only pray. He closed his eyes waiting for the shot. Danny summoned the last of his remaining strength, tugging at the cold evidence of intent. The lad was crying, praying for their souls no doubt. Well, he wasn't dead yet. He reached up until his fingers touched the driver's cheek. The wee bugger was crying right enough, his eyes closed. He'd give him something to cry for in a minute. The boy looked into the pale face. Its eyes bored into his soul telling him of the pain, the exhaustion and the forgiveness. He lowered his head to receive instruction.

"If you don't move your arse fast and right now, you'll get my boot in it as soon as I'm able," Danny promised. "Take it... Now... Get it out of sight," he ordered.

"Well done lad." Danny praised the lad's efforts. Tom was folded into the back seat.

"Now, just help lend me your shoulder. That's just fine."

Danny grimaced with the pain. He fell into the front seat, his legs following with some assistance. The lad had stuffed the gun well out of sight under the carpet beneath the seat. He felt the car vibrate into life. Danny patted the back of the driver's head.

"Good lad," he encouraged. "Now listen carefully. Slowly, you know what that means, don't you?" he emphasised. "Slowly turn the car around and take the back roads into Derry and remember that we're in no hurry. Good lad," he nodded. "Let's go then," he finished.

Danny allowed his head to fall back. He could do no more.

The driver eased the car out onto the road. He checked both ways. Nothing, sure nobody used this road anyway. Jesus, wouldn't he have a story to tell his children's children.

— o —

Tom's fingers tested the bruised tissue, tracing the extent of the swelling. It really hurt.

Where was he? He allowed his eyes to focus in the half dark. The double bed filled most of the floor space. Only the crack of light from beneath the door confirmed that there was other life. He grasped the headboard, pulling himself upright against the pillows. A shaft of pain settled in the nape of his neck. He groaned aloud.

The door opened immediately.

There was no mistaking who held the handle.

"Danny," Tom said relieved. "Thank God."

"You're a lucky man God knows," Danny said. "You know what?" Danny crossed to the bed. "A few inches lower down and it would have been curtains right enough, that rock would've crushed the base of your skull like a grape so it would. At least that's what the doctor said." Danny sat down on the bed. He felt Tom's forehead. "He's a nurse really," he confessed, "but we call him Doc. Funny job for a man being a nurse; mind you, he'd do anything to help. Walks funny as well. Never mind. A good soul right enough."

Tom tried to untangle his legs from the bedclothes. "Here, let me help," Danny offered. He eased the patient upright. "Your trousers are here but you'll have to wait for your shirt. Mary's still trying to get the blood out." He pushed a bundle of clothing into Tom's arms. "There's an old pullover of mine in the meantime," he offered. Tom pulled his trousers on gingerly, slowly raising each hip careful to avoid large movements. "Mary says your trousers are ruined but you'd never get into mine so she just dried them for you."

"They're fine, thank Mary for me." Tom buckled the belt. "Where the hell are we?" he enquired. His head really thumped.

Danny had crossed to the window anticipating the question. Like a nosey neighbour he carefully parted the flimsy curtains. "Come and see for yourself," he said. He stepped back, offering Tom his arm. "We just need those two fiddlers Lynch and O'Neill and we could all watch Derry burn," Danny said quietly.

Tom steadied himself on the edge of the window-sill. Together they gazed out on the Dickensian scene. Row upon row, street upon street of small terraced houses stretched forever into the night, slated roofs shimmering in the glow of random fires as wood sparks and exploding plaster rent the night sky. Tom found it terrifyingly beautiful in its ugliness. Bonfires dotted the black map of tribal dominance. He stared in disbelief. These were no July bonfires. These where houses. Catholic houses in Derry in January. He turned bewildered, weak and confused, feeling the fear of reality begin to rise. He was frightened to ask.

"What's happening Danny?" he whispered. "What does it all mean?" he sobbed.

The laugh was forced and cynical, the bitter words filling the flickering darkness of the small room. "What does it mean?" Danny repeated. "Simple lad, they decided to make a job of it and rub our noses in it," Danny said. "The arrests were the signal." He kicked the wall, rocking the Man on the cross above the bed.

"Arrests?" Tom cried. "Because they arrested those cretins at the bridge?"

"No lad," the voice broke the face dark. "Not those idiots. The marchers; you see, they arrested the marchers; the injured and the innocent herded them into vans and took them away. Resisting arrest, they said, disturbing the peace, that's what they said. At least the Gestapo were honest. A Jew was a Jew." Danny pointed his finger out into the night. "Those cretins as you call them are now running wild, stoning, clubbing and burning unhindered." He grasped Tom's shoulders. "You want to know why?" He paused to draw breath on a convulsed sob. "Because those Protestant bastards at the bridge were B-Specials out of uniform and in cahoots with our so-called protectors," he accused. He crossed the tiny room and sat down on the side of the bed, head in hands, his sobs pitiful.

"Danny, what can we do...? Tell me!" Tom cried.

"Do, lad?" The voice strong again. "We go right back at them. We have been fighting the bastards for fifty years and nobody has listened until now. You didn't believe it yourself. It was all a political game played by Stormont and Westminster. Always has been. But this time I honestly believed we were getting somewhere at last." He crossed to the window, rubbing the glass pane. "Stormont is scared and Westminster embarrassed. The people on the mainland have seen the face of the bigot on their screens. Witnessed the injustices carried out in their name." He turned back into the room. "But this... I just don't know. It's clearly organised. The backlash I dreaded." His voice was tired. "God help us Tom, we may have undone all the good of recent months. The hard men on both sides are manning the barricades of history. We may have stumbled at the last fence."

"Too little, too late, too much too soon," Tom observed.

"Crap!" Danny retorted, the voice hard and cold. "The gun or the ballot box? That's the question? Aye, that's the real question. We'll see how the bastards answer that one...?"

— o —

# CHAPTER TEN

## THE CRISIS – DERRY 1969

**TOM FOLDED** the *Belfast Telegraph*, the trumpet of births, marriages and deaths, and placed it on the kitchen table. He didn't need to look at the date to know it was August in Derry. You only had to listen. And today's news wasn't good. Both sides had run for cover since January after Burntollet had been laid at the door of history. But no one would admit to being responsible for that history. His own people had turned to the traditional protectors and who could blame them after the fires of Derry? Burntollet had given the hard men the chance to slice the cake. It was dog eat dog. So nobody was surprised when the Orange fist descended, culminating in the marching season of July and August. He shivered despite the summer warmth of the small room. Eight months, that was all, and he didn't know who was who anymore? Talk about coming out of the woodwork. Liquorice allsorts they were. Nobody agreeing on anything. The so-called hard men wouldn't listen when Danny had told them straight. "You don't point your finger at Prod history unless you can afford to lose it." The result was as he had said. The Lambeg drums thumped the message of danger, calling the faithful onto the streets. Protestant women listened once again to the slamming of doors as feet pounded wet pavements. Dogs stepped gingerly around stern-faced men as they stood on street corners waiting for the word. Adding their pennyworth to daily rumour.

112  *Colours of Prejudice*

The word was handed down. "No Surrender," hit the streets. Enough was enough. It was time to call a halt. The men in suits sat back in a halo of Orange, their minds made up. They began by dumping O'Neill in April. The sympathiser and appeaser with a doubtful name. The Captain was replaced by the Major. Superior rank, double-barrelled, Chichester-Clarke was wheeled out. A pure mainstream anglophile with his old school tie, old charm and old ideas. The Major had spent Easter inspecting his injured troops, dishing out morale and massaging the masses. The long innings had begun but nobody had noticed the rules had changed. Violence bred violence as frightened men, on both sides, justified their actions. Policemen became fair game and hooligans got what they deserved. The age of the body count had started.

Despite everything, Danny had tried desperately to apply some logic, trying to convince the trouble-makers that Westminster was listening. That Stormont's days were numbered. In despair he had gone to Dublin in June. But to no avail. He sensed that there was something going on down there. A hidden agenda. A political agenda, and he wasn't part of it. He'd often wondered who was putting the lead in the hard men's pencil. Then it all began to fit. It became obvious, when he was side-lined in July as too liberal. Him too liberal. Those dopes from the South wanted it all and now their agitators had played on the old hatreds and prejudices and with never a dickybird from the pulpit. The people fell for it. And who could blame them? Fear and rumour filled the vacuum of missed opportunities.

Tom peered through the crack in the curtain at the ancient walls of Derry, so English in their dominance, towering above the Bogside and its people. There they stood, legs apart on their ethnic ramparts, tossing their traditional pennies of insult into the serfdom below. Those same smug faces of Burntollet gloating in the August sunset. He marvelled at their audacity.

Didn't they realise they had left his people no choice but to defend themselves as best they could? The barricades were in place and the milk bottles full. Even the children had helped to carry the heavy petrol cans to the rooftop assembly lines. The Bogside was ready. Ulster's Alamo was ready. The Catholic people were ready. The notes of promise from the Castle were long overdue. The gentlemen in suits had reneged, screwed up. There were no gentlemen out on the streets tonight. Although some did say the police had a few military advisers tucked away in civilian clothes. Tom couldn't help but smile at the thought. It would take more than mufti to hide the Prince of Wales Own with their county check and brown brogues. Didn't they stand out like a boxer's balls? When would they ever learn?

Danny had left for Belfast earlier in the day, determined to keep the hotheads under control... If possible. He'd said that it was touch and go; they could lose it all. His parting words had been clear and to the point. "Believe me, son, you can do anything you want with a dog, but hit it twice in the face... The second time it'll have your hand off. And we've hit the bastards twice. Full in the face. We could lose our arm right up to our necks," he warned with that still cynical grin of life.

The defenders had repelled the first police charge, their barricade defying the weight of the armoured car, its burnt-out wreckage a testimony to the dormant skills of unemployed builders. Tom looked at the anxious faces clustered around the map.

"We have to hold Rossville Street at all costs," he said, circling the tiny street with a child's red crayon. "If they break through there we're done for," he stressed.

The circle of men looked at each other, fear evident in their eyes. Their hands were blistered and their backs sore, but most of all they were scared. These were ordinary men, with ordinary problems, like no job and with no chance of a job. No hopers. They had dug trenches, lifted manhole covers and ripped up paving stones.

The man on Tom's left spat on his hands. "Let the bastards come, we're ready for them."

"Bloody right!" they all chorused.

The attackers came in force... Determined. Up Lecky Road into Toxs Corner they came, their armoured Land Rovers in the lead followed by the footsloggers. Abbey Street was shaky but Rossville Street held. The attackers paused for breath. The defenders cheered... they'd held their ground. They'd dented the Castle. Stormont was hurt. Her authority had been questioned in the open and found wanting. The battle lines defined, the attackers withdrew as darkness fell.

Fires lit the night sky but this time it was fires of their own making, camp fires for the weary defenders. Fires to warm their hands, to tell their stories.

Tom felt self-conscious as he inspected the damage, trying to hide his surprise as the weary men responded immediately to his words of encouragement. He returned the smiles of toothy grins in sooty faces. The hands on his watch were clearly visible in the red glow.

Well past midnight.

"We've beaten them," the voice was high; its face radiant, eyes ablaze.

"They've had enough," Dorothy proclaimed.

"Dorothy?" He'd forgotten about her. He'd warned Danny, said his piece about women on the front line. "If her own husband didn't care, why should he?" Danny had replied.

'Oh Danny Boy...' the opening words of the gramophone record broadcast the tenor's provocative emotional words on the clear air. The simple words were immediately chorused by the men on the barricades to the weary police awaiting new orders. Tom felt her hand in his. They stood together, joined by a common emotion.

The first canister of tear gas exploded to their right. Tom grabbed Dorothy, pulling her away from its menace.

"Tell the men to hold on here as long as they can," he shouted above the panic. "Get them to use their handkerchiefs, shirts, anything to cover their nose and mouth. Tell them to stop breathing if necessary."

Dorothy nodded. A frightened smile clung to her open mouth, her eyes already streaming. Tom watched the clouds of defeat drift over their heads. CS clouds. There was something wrong, but what was it? Then the penny dropped. Jesus and Mary, the clouds were drifting the wrong way. They were going backwards. Back towards the walls. Then he saw her, in the midst of it all. He called her to join him. He wanted her near but she couldn't hear. He jumped down, keeping low, noting her last position. He grabbed her ankle, pulling her down as she clambered over yet another railway sleeper. People turned, sensing his excitement.

"Dorothy... Look... Can you believe it? The silly bastards haven't allowed for the wind," he cried. "There..." he pointed. The Tricolour fluttered confirmation. "The bloody stuff's drifting back into their own advance, back up their own noses. Can't you see?" He lifted her bodily. "The thick bastards aren't even wearing masks."

She slid down his body keeping her arms around his neck, their lips touched, pressed then opened to personal needs.

The defenders peered over the top of the barricades, some more brave than others clambering on top. Standing upright their feet began to dance... A victory jig of relief right there and then... On top of the barricades. Nobody paid any attention to the young couple leaving the scene of triumph. Hand in hand.

The Police Commander picked his path along the ramparts stepping carefully over the rubble to avoid scuffing his highly polished shoes, a streaked dawn sky making visible his first defeat. He knew he couldn't ask his battle-weary men to face that rain of missiles once again. He also knew that his decision wouldn't be popular in the Castle, but he could do no more.

The gentlemen in mufti waited, well mannered. The Commander didn't need to speak, they understood his tired nod for help.

"I understand Sir." The army officer's voice was sympathetic. "But as you are well aware it will take time to get the necessary permission."

"Thank you," the Commander replied. The swagger stick slapped green barathea. "This won't happen again," he promised aloud.

Danny switched the radio off. He'd managed to hold the Belfast hotheads back from the brink, but for how long? Sure, how long was a piece of string?

The Major had declared his hand from the steps of Stormont. The B Specials, his Protestant old guard of part-time bully boys in uniform, were to be mobilised. All eight thousand, five hundred. They would be used to the full, not for riot or crowd control, but to relieve the regular police—RUC.

Danny lifted the telephone. "Tom, is that you? Good man. How's it going? Did you hear that idiot Chichester-Clarke on the radio? What a prick! Thinks he's bloody Churchill. You've got to hold out for another twenty-four hours Tom, until the Army is called out. Westminster can't walk away from this one. Yes. We're ready here. Let me know when they arrive. The Army, you idiot. And the same to you. Good luck lad."

"That was Danny," Tom explained needlessly. Dorothy had been dozing in the chair when the phone rang. "He says that he needs twenty-four hours or until the Army arrives. Try to get some sleep," he suggested quietly. "I'll stretch my legs and do the rounds; better make sure the boys are keeping the pot stirred." He tucked the blanket around her. "We'll see what today brings soon enough. Sweet dreams... I love you," he whispered to closed eyes.

— o —

The Home Secretary stood before the dispatch box, adjusted his reading glasses, timing the pause to perfection and read his decision from the prepared text in a suitably sombre voice; peering over his glasses in emphasis when necessary.

The House listened with foreboding.

> *The General Officer, Commanding Northern Ireland (the GOC), has been instructed to take all necessary steps, acting impartially between citizen and citizen, to*

*restore law and order. Troops will be withdrawn as soon as this is accomplished. This is a limited operation and during it the troops will remain in direct and exclusive control of the G.O.C, who will continue to be responsible to the United Kingdom Government. The Ireland Act of 1949 affirms that neither Northern Ireland nor any part of it will in any event cease to be part of the United Kingdom without the consent of the Parliament of Northern Ireland, and the United Kingdom re-affirms the pledge previously given that this will remain the position so long as the people of Northern Ireland wish.*

Finished, the tall man slumped into his seat. "Bloody Irish," he muttered to himself.

— o —

The colonel of infantry smiled at the irony as he read the instructions once again. He did wonder, was there a joker in the house? "Proceed to Waterloo Place, Londonderry." The order was clear but this was no joke. He grated his teeth and grasped the handle on the dashboard of his Land Rover as his driver crashed the gear box, determined to lead the charge.

Tom reached for the telephone. He could see Dorothy through the window talking to the troops who had erected their flimsy barricade, in reality a control point between the two sides. The cavalry had arrived thirty minutes ago in a cloud of burning rubber scaring the hell out of the already nervous B Specials. Large men with bullfrog voices barked rehearsed orders, pointing with brass-tipped sticks to exact locations.

"Danny? Tom... John Wayne's arrived," he joked. "Of course they're armed, they're bloody soldiers, aren't they? You'll kick yourself for missing this one. The last of the Specials have just filed through the Army checkpoint... You

No kidding. The whole area's clear... Yes... Only the soldiers remain, and Danny, the bastards have gone home."

Danny replaced the telephone, cursing at the empty cigarette packet. Wouldn't it be grand to be so innocent? They'd won a vital skirmish, that's all and in the outback. No mean feat but the real battle was yet to come, here in Belfast, out there on the Falls and the Shankill where both sides hummed with rumours of war. "The B Men were out of control... The Micks were taking children hostage." The mental barricades were manned on both sides. He sensed that the Shankill was waiting but waiting for what? The bastards were taking their time, playing the old game of nerves. He checked the clock. It was after one in the morning and black as a coal bunker. Danny ducked instinctively.

"Mother of God!" he prayed aloud. They couldn't... They wouldn't. He listened to the echoes but there was no doubt, the bastards were opening up with heavy machine-guns. Heavy calibre bullets hammered death and destruction into the night. He could hear the ricochets bouncing off gable walls into the maze of alleyways that separated the two communities. They were using the weapons of war. All-out war.

"They're coming. God help us they're coming..." a voice yelled its fear from the dark.

"Shut your gob," another voice replied.

"Do you think we're bloody deaf?" yet another voice. All frightened as hell.

Danny noticed the man next to him cross himself before tossing a cocktail of defiance into the dark mouth of the advancing mob. The flame burned instantly bright, illuminating the thrower's retreat as he melted into the night. The noise was terrifying. Getting closer and closer... Like flotsam on the crest of a wave, the Protestant mob poured out of the eerie glow. The beast was abroad. Spent petrol fumes attacked its nostrils, gagging its throat, quickening the pace. The beast advanced on its steel-capped shipyard boots, crunching the broken glass underfoot, protected behind a wall of dustbin lids on which it hammered its message of hate, in rhythmic chant. "Kill the

Micks... Kill the Micks," it growled in unison. Danny felt the elbows of panic dig into his ribs as men pushed back preparing themselves to join the retreat.

Danny ran for his life, pushing and cursing until he could run no more. Finally exhausted and gasping for breath, he fell to the ground. He felt his fists plug repeatedly into the damp earth, hammering at the face of fear. "All for nothing... All for bloody nothing," he sobbed, mesmerised by the horror unfolding before his very eyes. Wormlike, he pressed his body into the earth, biting into his lip, feeling no pain. He watched the beast's progress, praying that it had no use for the rubble lying on the waste ground where he lay. He wasn't aware of the blood dribbling down his chin; his body was dead, unable to function. Fascinated, he continued to watch man's inhumanity.

The first wave of shield bearers had passed; he was safe for the moment but not for long.

Then came the rattlers. Two lines of men, one to each footpath, they ran in line astern down each side of the street, their bamboo canes gripped tightly in both hands. The tipped ends rattled their message of destruction, breaking parlour windows, showering shattered glass into best kept rooms. Then the second wave appeared tossing their petrol bombs through the gaping windows. The explosion and flame were as one, igniting curtains, engulfing unpaid furniture, illuminating the occupants' ghostly white faces at upstairs windows.

Danny wanted to run but couldn't. They were at the bottom of the street now, regrouping, laughing. Satisfied, they moved on, searching for prey... Catholic prey.

Tom listened to the radio in disbelief. Street after street of houses had been attacked in Belfast. They said that some were still burning. Stormont had left the Catholic populace to the night mob, only sending in the army at midday. Now Belfast was cut off from the rest of the province. Isolated. The phones had been out of action for hours. Nobody knew who or what to believe.

The shrill ring filled the room. "Yes... It's Danny," he announced to the crowded room. "Are you all right? Thank

God... We've been worried sick... Right, got it... I'll be with you as soon as I can. Yes... Don't worry, I'll drive carefully."

— o —

The room was small, the size of an American wardrobe. No living thing could grow naturally in its shadowy recesses. Plastic flowers did their vulgar best to remind the inhabitants of a real world. The only window, small and ill-fitting, its sash cords long frayed, rattled in the gusts of summer rain. Danny stared out at the man-made clouds of destruction suspended over the small white-washed backyard. Bridget picked at her balled jumper. She was nervous—weren't things bad enough without the biscuits being stale and not a shop left? Hadn't the world gone mad? The tray was ready, its contents checked for the guests. She would have preferred them in the parlour but the rattlers had done their work. Her lips moved in silent prayer. "Please Lord, let them all burn in Hell. Thank you Lord." Feeling better, she did up her neck button from the draught. Her curse complete, she stepped down from the back kitchen.

Tom jumped to his feet offering his help, glad to do something.

"There's a wee tray for now," she offered, touching the curl at her ear. "There aren't many gentlemen in these parts," she said to Danny, smiling at Tom. "Nothing much, mind you," she apologised. "The explosion damaged the biscuit barrel—can't keep them fresh. I'm just popping next door for a wee minute. Knock on the wall when you're ready." She stood, arms folded. "Now take it before it gets cold," she scolded Danny. "God only knows what he's living on besides his smokes," she said to Tom. "He was alright to start with, then he decided that it was all his fault, silly bugger," she explained as if Danny wasn't there. "Just stares out the window and sucks on those bloody Woodbines. Can't be good for him—you ought to hear his cough in the morning; rattles what's left of the window, it does."

The window rattled in Danny's ear as Bridget slammed the front door, compensating for the bent hinges. He added another spoonful of sugar to his cup. The match flickered at the end of his cigarette. He drew deeply.

"Have you seen what those fuckers have done?" he asked, knowing the answer. "Three nights they've been at it doing their damnedest while the British Army sit at the end of the street. Have you heard the radio? Ten dead and sixteen hundred injured." He took another drag. "Homes and factories gutted." He looked at Tom for the first time. "Would you tell me, are those radio announcers crowing or commiserating? And have you seen the walls?" he demanded. "The gable walls... Have you seen what our own people have written on our walls?" he cried.

"IRA... IRA... I RAN AWAY..." he spat the words out.

"They're right; you know, that's what really hurts... I ran away... That's the awful thing... they're right!" he shouted. "I ran away... I was scared shitless by those heathen bastards." Danny knuckled his eyes. "Smoke," he explained. "They can't say I haven't tried. As God is my witness I've tried," he declared, attempting a smile. "You know what went wrong? We didn't consolidate. We moved too fast. We had no structure, no command and no weapons. They had heavy machine guns, bloody Vickers, for Christ's sake." His eyes turned to the window half expecting to hear the noise! "I ran away right enough... But never ever again... I swear by all that's Holy that one day no matter how long it takes, those Protestant pigs will get their just desserts... Including that toffee-nosed git of a major," he paused, noticing Tom's questioning look. "No, not their precious Prime Minister. No, I mean that English wanker at the end of the street. The bastard wouldn't talk to his dog like he talks to us." The cup and saucer rattled with his pent up anger. "Public school wanker," he finished.

Tom fidgeted, embarrassed at the older man's hurt and visual hatred. But Danny wasn't finished yet.

"All we need is time and to be left alone." He waved his finger in Tom's face. "The barricades must stay," he warned. "We mustn't allow the Army to become the protectors of our people." He sat forward. "I need someone I can trust... Completely," he emphasised. "Someone to keep me informed of honest criticism and listen to my counsel." He paused. "You're the man," he confirmed, grasping Tom's wrist. "What do you say?" he asked. Danny watched Tom's hesitation. "Remember Burntollet," he struck. "We need each other, Tom." The two men embraced their commitment.

Next door Bridget replaced her cup and saucer carefully on the polished table and nodded knowingly to the wall. "I'd best be getting back," she said. "The boys are ready, God bless them."

"Aye indeed," her friend agreed.

— o —

# CHAPTER ELEVEN
## THE INVITATION – B ELFAST 1971

COLIN LOWERED *THE TIMES* and reached for the glass at his elbow. He savoured the words of the Belfast street philosopher. "Anyone who isn't confused here doesn't really understand what's going on," it reported.

Well, he for one was confused and beginning to get really worried. He had listened in tight-lipped disbelief to the horror stories told by returning comrades. It was unbelievable but the army had been in Belfast for two years and still there was no sign of a settlement. He had volunteered to go but no one seemed interested. His turn would come, they informed him. It had been agreed that he could remain at Hereford pending his selection course and Paddy had been showing him the ropes. They had bonded into a two-man team, understanding the needs of the other. Now this overnight summons from Aldershot. Out of the blue, just like that, as Tommy Cooper would say and from a brigadier no less.

The small bald pate was chameleon-like blending its perfect camouflage against the polished hard wood of the large desk. Man and desk went together and both showed their years of hardening in the tropical sun. The knotted muscles of the forearms led to short stubby fingers which supported paper, pad and pen in the classical prep school formation. The nose was directly in line with the pen, sharp and pointed, leading to a shortened chin. The man didn't look up. Carefully selected memoranda patterned the green leather desktop placed in exact locations, memory filed and instantly reachable. A naked power hung in the air.

Colin felt uncomfortable. He shuffled his feet. He felt threatened. His eyes settled on the paperweight. Black veined lines criss-crossed the bleached white dome and trickled into the hollowed eye sockets. There was no nose. Just an empty skull.

"Do sit down," the voice acknowledged his presence. The eyes continued to follow the written word. He spoke to the page in an exasperated voice. "Forget the sword, it's the pen that counts these days." The pen was replaced without the need to look. The eyes loomed large, stared directly at him, then settled back. "You come highly recommended," he complimented.

It was a large man's voice. It didn't belong. "Now you're comfortable." The eyes focused on their prey. The man obviously had a sense of humour; pity was that he didn't know it.

"You have been reading the papers." It was a statement. "Your fellow countrymen invited us to their punch-up, that is, to their most recent, in the August of 1969 to be exact." There wasn't even a hint of a smile. "A date politicians and widows will remember." His fingers rubbed at a lurking headache.

Colin watched the man rise from his chair and cross to the window. What was this all about?

He listened as the voice continued from afar.

"One side saw us as a support arm there to help them as Catholic bashers. The other side hesitated in judgement but not for long; Catholic bashers we were, they decided. I think it is possibly the only time that both sides have ever agreed on anything." Colin searched the face for a hint of humour. Nothing. "We on the other hand could not agree on anything. We simply panicked in historical blindness. That is to say, Stormont passed the parcel and Westminster dropped it." The man had resumed his seat.

Colin waited; it was as if he wasn't there. The man was somewhere else. The short fingers continued to massage the brow, easing the skin around the eyes. "The Army was ordered to pick up the parcel," he explained, remembering Colin. "As a neutral referee… Neutral… A word that is possibly unknown to your fellow countrymen."

Colin tried not to smile. Why was he being told this senior officer's opinions?

Colin found himself reading the man's lips.

"Call it what you will, it had long been forgotten as a problem at Westminster. Granted there was a minor skirmish in 1921. However, the iron fist of the Black and Tans was mostly successful and we were forced to hang a few trouble-makers. Under the circumstances we achieved a skilful withdrawal leaving the natives to their internal punch-up."

Colin closed his mouth. This wasn't real. This bloke was out of the ark.

The lips moved on. "I will endeavour to be as brief as possible in deference to your background. Now where was I? Ah yes, 1921. We left them to their Civil War and a new Republic. Sinn Fein emerged the victors but weakened and not strong enough to challenge Ulster. The result was confirmed as Home Rule for the twenty-six counties, now a Republic, and the six remaining counties accepted by all the parties concerned as the Province of Ulster. Then came 1939 and the Second World War. The Republic remained neutral but always a back door threat for German intrusion whilst the Province volunteered en masse, as they had done in 1914. Ulster became recognized in military circles as the breeding ground of the white Ghurkha." The voice was respectful. "Conscription was never necessary, nor National Service; you see, we couldn't train a possible threat to the status quo."

Colin couldn't help but be fascinated; history had never been like this at school.

"The Province was justly rewarded for those services and everyone seemed content," he explained. The eyes returned to Colin's face. Questioning? "Yes," he answered himself, "you would have been a schoolboy then. You should remember the Coronation in 1953, followed by the royal visit in 1956." The face was transformed. Young again, its worry lines banished.

The voice was lighter. The hands restful. "That visit is still quoted in the Foreign Office as the perfect overseas tour. People accepted their place in society with an innocence we shall never witness again."

Colin shifted his weight. The lesson was fascinating but his bum was numb. Overseas?

"What we didn't know nor care to know until now was that the store-keepers had misused and abused, some would say those very powers granted in order to rule." The brigadier checked his watch. "Coffee?" he asked abruptly.

"Please," Colin answered quickly, startled at the sound of his own voice.

The door opened immediately. The sergeant steward dispensed the coffee with the assurance and finesse of a professional.

Colin declined the sugar. No, he couldn't be? Bloody hell! He glided across the boards. He didn't walk. Christ, wait till I tell the folks! He tried to avoid the steward's obvious efforts at a confidential smile. The brigadier blew his breath onto the hot coffee. Colin smiled to himself picturing his mother's comment on such practice. She was a dreadful one for so-called etiquette.

"They are the most loyal of men," the brigadier confirmed. Colin kept his eyes on his cup. What did he mean? The brigadier smiled, thinly. "My father always had one good man protecting his back," he explained. The brigadier's eyes studied his guest's reaction over the rim of the cup. "An old Indian custom," he added cryptically. This was educational in every sense of the word. The door opened and closed without a sound, no click of a latch, no rattle of tray, just a knowledge that a presence had departed.

The man was refreshed. His caffeine level renewed. "We have tried appeasement. Guaranteed the enactment of all the original Civil Rights' demands and confirmed Constitutional Sovereignty for the majority. We have inaugurated the Ulster Defence Regiment to replace the B Specials and sacrificed one prime minister," he continued. His fingers numbered each point on the desk top. "Meanwhile, the plant of Irish nationalism has rooted itself in local carnage flourishing on the daily sacrifices of bombings and shootings. It is already becoming a way of life. A tragedy of Shakespearean proportions with no winners. Eventually the plant will become a common weed choking any new seedlings of hope."

Colin leaned forward to catch the final words. The voice was low, thoughtful, the eyes inwardly painful and distant. The fingers reached out and stroked the paperweight as if seeking comfort.

"The Mau-Mau, in Kenya, believed in the supernatural," he stated. The voice strong again, his eyes steady, challenging Colin's. "I have always regretted my friend here could not be convinced that compromise was the more powerful magic," he confessed. "Survival is the name of the game, political survival." The lips smiled at the obvious indiscretion. "Our political masters have a limited choice. One, release the dogs of war. Hardly, too difficult to identify the enemy and too close to home. Two, seek and destroy. Difficult to achieve without good intelligence. We would need our own people on the ground. Three, disinformation. Possible, but not immediate. For the future. Hearts and minds. Win over the local populace—Catholic and Protestant—and isolate their leaders. Four, train the local force in Two and Three from whom we would select our new leaders, both civil and governmental."

He paused. "Let's begin with the civil force," he declared. "Our eyes and ears. I'm not going too fast?" he asked suddenly, not bothering to wait for an answer. "Their local police are ignoring us because we took their B Specials away. Their Special Branch believe they are special and won't talk to anyone. MI5, ah yes, our very own, the so-called ghosts who never materialise. They are determined to withhold any helpful information from military intelligence, who I must confess, at this present moment couldn't pass the local people's eleven plus," he confessed. This time the smile was real. The brigadier leaned back in his chair. "Perhaps you read the recent article in *The Times*? A very clever piece of journalism which sums it all up in one sentence. Puts it in a nutshell, so to speak. Couldn't have written better myself. How did it go?"

Colin listened to his own voice quote the report word for word. "Anyone who isn't confused here doesn't understand what's going on!"

"Exactly, word for word, they said you would have no trouble understanding and appreciating such pearls of wisdom for their true worth. That's why we need clever Belfast men listening and reporting."

"Sir!" Colin heard his own voice again, strangely high. He felt sick with apprehension. He couldn't help it, this wasn't his sort of game. He was a soldier. Not a bloody reporter, a snitch. The brigadier had got the wrong man.

"Let me finish before you judge," the man overruled. The eyes commanded silence. "Belfast is a sea of rumour and counter-rumour, some of it true and some false, but all of it useful in the right hands. Naturally we have our own people at the coalface. Learning how to dig the American way. The Bragg way. You will be aware of their Black-Ops?"

Colin sat upright, his jaw slack.

"Yes, I believe you have been there quite recently," he revealed. "Mine was a different course but the same people. The problem is that it all takes time and the aims are long term with the results often hidden. In the meantime we continue to antagonise the Catholic populace. Ransacking their homes in out-dated search and destroy missions with the token Protestant forays thrown in to create meaningless statistics, simply to satisfy Stormont's needs. We have lost any credence as independent brokers. The military have become the coconut shy, available for anyone and I stress anyone, including our masters, to throw stones, bottles or if you will excuse that very appropriate word... shit at!" Colin had never heard the word pronounced in quite that manner before, the resonance perfect. He knew that he was listening to a master player. A second smile. Was he human after all? "I'm nearly there," he promised, "but it is essential that you understand exactly what I'm asking of you. The preliminaries are now over, the safety-catch is off and we move on, to the widows' war. The war of fatherless children, of crippled bodies and minds where there can be no winners. There is no doubting that we can contain that war but at a terrible price. The first instalment will be internment. It's all Stormont can see in the short term. It worked for them before but unfortunately for them the world has moved on and they have not. We must try to educate both sides, give them goals. Time goals with long term aims. And we must spell out the consequence of failure. You must understand that we haven't much time and they have even less.

"Internment is on the cards, we know that it will not work on its own; at best it will contain the alienation to small pockets of embittered elements. Those people already beyond the hearts and minds programme. The internment operation must be carefully planned and implemented. Arresting no more than fifty of their top men quietly and skilfully using good local knowledge. We need time, time for the politicians who are prepared to talk, to meet, and that includes the South. Especially the South. And time to evolve, otherwise we are into entrenched warfare for the foreseeable future and God help us all if that happens."

Why me? And what for? Colin asked himself, but the brigadier answered the questions as if he had read his thoughts.

"Why you?" the brigadier asked. "Simple. You are Belfast born. You would appear to be highly motivated and capable of independent thought. Essential qualities for the task ahead."

Colin knew the brigadier was wrong. He wasn't capable of any thought.

The raised eyebrow stopped any embryo protest. The man put both hands onto the table.

"My invitation is simple and before it is offered I must stress that you are entitled to refuse. Naturally a refusal would be nothing more than a question of judgement, my judgement," he stressed. His face tightened in a mortician's smile. "You would be my eyes and ears, supplying me with legitimate criticism from three sources—Protestant, Catholic and Military.

"Whether you accept or otherwise, you are not to reveal any content of this meeting to anyone, including your colonel. Should you accept you will never attempt to contact me direct—my steward is available in an emergency. You will attend me only at my request and answer to the code name of Romulus. Finally, you will be withdrawn from your present holding post immediately and report to your old battalion now in Palace Barracks, Holywood."

The brigadier stood. The meeting was concluded. No questions. The handshake was brisk the fingers strong.

"Thank you sir," Colin replied, accepting the hand of command. Had he accepted? The steward held the door. "Good luck Sir," he said, knowingly. He'd accepted!

— o —

# CHAPTER TWELVE

## DEMETRIUS – BALLYMURPHY 1971

COLIN SAT IN THE BACK of the cold personnel carrier so aptly known as a Pig. He listened to the driver arm wrestle the gearbox into submission. The noise was enough to awaken the dead, never mind the sleeping natives. Three o'clock in the morning but it sure wasn't Crystal Gale time; no, it was collection time on an August morning. The ninth, to be precise

The convoy was proceeding as the police would say on the last leg of its journey along the Ballygomartin Road. The gearbox whined its continued protest climbing the steep hill towards the Black Mountain. The embattled Shankill lay below and behind them now, a simple row of city lights stretching into the heart of Belfast.

The troops rocked shoulder to shoulder as the convoy pulled off the road, coming to rest in the shelter of a hawthorn hedge. Combat-booted soles kicked the rear doors open releasing the smells of operational troops. Colin stepped down grateful to breathe God's clean air of the early morning. The Pig stank! He relieved himself against the warm rubber of the tyres lit by a pale moon. Finished, he sank to the squat position to check his orders.

The single word declared their importance:

SECRET
CODE NAME: OPERATION DEMETRIUS
DATE: 9th August 1971 [Monday]
TIME: 04.30
POSITION: SH (Sierra Hotel)

There hadn't been a word. Not a single word. Nothing from the brigadier since his initial briefing in Aldershot and now internment was about to happen. Four hundred and fifty men were to be lifted. Quietly and skilfully and using local knowledge, the brigadier had promised. They didn't even have room for that number in the conventional prisons. Crumlin Road was already overflowing. Where the hell were they going to put them? That was, provided anyone was still at home. Ah! He smiled to himself. Stormont had lots of rooms. Who needed local knowledge to find four hundred and fifty front doors? Colin looked at the size of the feet surrounding his squat position. Didn't they realise that these men in camouflage jackets, bulging with bullet-proof vests, were frightened of the dark and bogeymen just like anyone else? Especially Provo bogeymen hidden in upstairs rooms with machine guns. What the hell did they think his men were going to do after all the rumours and the dummy runs in July? Knock on doors? Only Stormont and Westminster could believe internment was still a secret.

Experienced troopers rattled hard-boiled sweets against their front teeth, nervously fingering their fag packets, checking their lighters wrapped in a dirty hankie. They knew the score.

They had been into Ballymurphy before. They could still hear the cacophony of dustbin lids, whistles and female-shrieked obscenities. Then the heart-stopping fear of tripping over children lurking in dark recesses. The wee bastards waiting to coax their mongrel hounds into the mêlée of confusion. A hushed voice asked the time and was told the impossible. Gloved hands pushed back restraining cuffs.

Omega watches pointed to 0400. Thirty minutes to get in position.

Colin was nervous. He looked at the faces before him, checking their names in his head. "Okay Sergeant-Major, move them out," he ordered. "Quietly and skilfully are the buzz words, Sergeant-Major," he explained, enjoying his private joke. "Let's do it," he ordered, tapping the man's shoulder. The group set off in single file, the Sergeant-Major leading with Colin and his radio man in the rear. Combat boots crunched the loose chippings underfoot. The moon was brighter now, showing the route. Whiterock cemetery lay across the way. They hadn't far to go.

— o —

Quiet as the graveyard they had passed.
In position.
Two minutes to kick-off.

The door was cheap, the lock cheaper. One kick did it. She filled the hallway, her bosom uplifted by folded arms. The advance was quick, sweeping them back into the street, whilst disclosing a command of barrack-room jargon which drew reluctant admiration from the troops. They put her door back on its hinges unasked.

The second attempt revealed folds of Guinness wrapped in a vest and pants. They must have the wrong man... he'd said. Ask the police... he insisted. He wanted his fags with him... he continued despite the thickening lips.

This was their third. Colin didn't like it. This bastard was underlined... Rourke was a known name. And every man and his dog knew what was happening by now. He nodded. The rubber-soled combat boot kicked the door into the hall, its crash drowned by the incessant barking of the street dogs.

"Fuck it..." the first trooper cursed aloud, barking his shin on the exposed hinge as the second hit the stairs at a run, followed by the third crashing to the floor in the stairwell to cover the other two. Pieces of plaster fell to the carpet, gouged by the butt of his rifle. The first upended the table as he crossed the living room in two strides, hitting the far wall of the kitchen before stopping.

"All clear downstairs," the first confirmed.

"Got you... You bastard... He's up here... Under the bed... In the back bedroom!" yelled the second. "I've got him covered," the voice was high and excited. "Get the man with the cuffs up here fast," it demanded.

"Where's the fucking copper?" relayed the third.

"Jesus, I'd be quicker making them myself," the complaining voice of the second. "Get your arse up here quickly, Paddy, or I'm sending him down un-cuffed," it threatened. Colin smiled in the darkness, ignoring the screams from above as the arresting officer took the stairs two at a time.

He turned away, crossing the hall in two strides and entered the living room. The woman sat half hidden by the upturned table. She looked cold even in her flannel nightdress. Folded into her side was a terrified child just old enough to walk. Jesus... Old enough to tremble. The woman's eyes stared vacantly at their blackened faces. They held no hatred, no questioning, and only an emptiness reflecting life's defeats. Colin recognised the self-denial of the untouchable, a soul lost in a maze of self-doubt when all hope had gone. He recognised Sheila... His Sheila.

The light from the torch made her blink as she reached out feeling for the child drawing it ever closer. He watched her hands cover the child's ears trying desperately to smother the noise of the invading warriors arresting and abusing his father upstairs.

Colin raced from the room. The front door hinge twanged unnoticed as he crashed to his knees on the concrete path. It came in a lump, an ejection of fear, spewed out from his heart onto the remains of her trampled begonias. Begonias in Ballymurphy? They had always been her favourite. Why hadn't he been told? Why hadn't he asked? He felt his stomach muscles contract matching the heaving shoulders of his dry retching.

"What happened Sir? What did the bitch do?" The sergeant-major's khaki-clad knees appeared beside him. "I'll make that bastard pay for this," he threatened, turning away.

Colin couldn't move. He watched from all fours like a wounded animal. The grasp for the prisoner's throat followed by the raised rifle butt and the crunch of yielding flesh, then a moan of painful despair. He forced himself upright clinging to the neglected fence.

"Stop..." he shouted. "Sergeant-Major. Stop... That's an order," he declared, knowing that he was already too late. He spat out the last of the bile. "The woman had nothing to do with it!" he shouted, clutching his crutch. "It was a self-inflicted injury," he groaned aloud. "I walked into the table, got me right in the balls," he confessed.

The Sergeant-Major lowered his weapon and eased the sweat-stained headband of his beret with his thumb. "Resisting arrest," he confirmed, pointing to the prisoner. Liam touched the stumps of his broken teeth with his tongue and tried to lick his ballooning lips. He flinched at the sharp pain. His eyes flashed in the darkness recording the outlines of every blackened face. One day those bastards would march to a different tune, he vowed. They would know the Funeral March by heart. They would all be on their knees like that one in the begonias; not that they mattered, they were the only things the bitch showed any affection for, those and Colum their son. He would make sure that the boy grew to recognise the man in the begonias for what he was.

— o —

# CHAPTER THIRTEEN

## ANOTHER FINE MESS – LISBURN 1971

**C**OLIN'S BOOTS squeaked his passage on the polished floors.

Lunch smelled good.

The white-coated corporal bit his tongue as he watched the overgrown schoolboy approach. It was okay for him, he didn't have to polish the sodding floors. Boots in the mess. I ask you! Operational dispensation. What a load of balls.

"Telephone Sir," he called respectfully.

"Thanks Corporal," Colin replied with a smile. "I'll take it in the hall." He liked the corporal, always thoughtful and respectful. "Captain Monro," he identified himself.

"Romulus!"

Colin recognised the voice immediately.

"The Stagecoach car park on the Lisburn Road, tomorrow night twenty hundred."

The click confirmed the end of a brief one-way conversation. Colin kicked at the skirting board in frustration. Lunch didn't smell so good any more.

The corporal inspected the damaged woodwork rubbing the bruised paint with a spittle finger.

— o —

Twenty minutes he'd been waiting. Colin checked his watch again, looking up at the mackerel sky flecked red against the setting sun, adding its own backdrop to the rose garden. He watched wandering couples reluctant to leave as they strolled amongst the fragrant beds. "Shit," he cursed aloud. He'd been watching the car park. The casually dressed figure approached on foot and strolled towards the rose garden. The brigadier was walking and alone. Why not? He looked like anybody's gardener. A small weather-beaten man with a slight hunch to the shoulders. Colin watched him disappear into the sales office.

The eyes lifted from the newly acquired catalogue at Colin's approach. "Ah! There you are. Truly beautiful are they not? I expect it's the soft rain," he ventured, reaching out to touch a bloom. "Mine never mature like this," he commented. "Peace, I believe," he named the rose. "This is a beautiful place and the friendliest people. Always so helpful. Shall we find a seat?" he suggested, looking around.

Colin followed in the man's short steps.

They settled in a quiet arbour.

"And now to business," the man opened immediately. The catalogue lay forgotten. "If you would cast your mind back to last March, the tenth to be precise, when we had the three Scottish soldiers murdered and dumped in a ditch. Goodbye Mr Chips, they said, only it was spelt Chichester-Clark and hello Mr Faulkner. Hello indeed," he emphasised. "The change in Stormont was quite dramatic. We could control the galloping Major but this new incumbent," he paused, searching for a word. "Canny," he tested. "Yes indeed, most appropriate. Canny in thought but headstrong in practice. Always a dreadful combination to control. Take today for instance," he opened his hands in despair. "The man wants yet more arrests despite the recent debacle and he has asked us to consider the introduction of concentration camps. This man's history stopped with the Boer war for God sake," he exploded. The brigadier paused to allow a strolling couple to pass. The girl smiled and the young man said hello. The brigadier touched his cap in acknowledgement allowing Colin to return the greeting. He waited, checked that they were out of earshot. "And that's not all by any means. The man wants the introduction of compulsory identity cards along with curfews and more seek and destroy missions. Oh yes, and possibly the death penalty," he sighed.

Colin noticed that as he spoke his eyebrows had become separated. The handmade brown brogue kicked the nearest pebble into the bushes.

The tired businessman jumped at the noise as he searched his pockets for the car key. He was late as usual. He'd had to buy his round. He repeated his excuse in his head.

"Sod her," he said aloud. Why bother? Couldn't she smell his intake from the garage door? The ignition fired, always a bloody relief with a Ford. He turned the steering wheel for Lisburn, clocking the two men in the arbour. Harmless enough looking. Just two rose growers with not a worry in the world. How he envied them their contentment.

The brigadier noted the car's number from habit. "They're all mad, you know," he explained in a matter of fact, upper class and English accent. "Your fellow countrymen are clearly certifiable," he confirmed, adjusting his tie. "However, that isn't why I asked you to attend me tonight. No, you will recall that I stated on our first meeting that what I needed was the truth," he said, drawing Colin's eyes to his own. "The whole truth, no matter how bad. I now need to know what it was actually like out there on the ground. Take your time but please, exactly as it was. No cover, no frills."

Colin tried to keep his briefing to a minimum. He described the cock-up as it happened. Listing their mistakes and emphasising the open hatred of the Catholic populace. The man listened, his eyes closed, storing every word on mental shelves. He asked no questions, allowing the younger man to express his true feelings unhindered.

Finished, they sat in silence, each with his own thoughts.

"Thank you for your efforts." The voice was tired. The eyes open. "And a most enlightened viewpoint, well-structured and informative. Funny world," he said. "Never mind, we will endeavour to be more selective next time," he promised. "Oh yes," he emphasised, "believe me, there will be a next time." His index finger traced the trough line in his cord trousers.

"The good news is that despite everything, we did net a few interesting fish, but will we be allowed to gut them?" he asked himself. Suddenly he'd perked up. "We need their knowledge and I don't care how we get it, but get it we must before we are forced to throw them back. The problem is we don't yet know their interrogation learning curve and how long we can hold them." The strong fingers rolled the catalogue into a tight baton. He stood, tapping his thigh, his free hand searching his inner pocket. "Nothing secret but nevertheless very interesting," he said, holding forth a carefully folded document. "Makes interesting reading."

Colin's eyes scanned the listed names and addresses of Northern Ireland Civil Rights activists. "Some of the names could be helpful," the man suggested. "Goodnight," he closed and was gone before Colin could get to his feet.

Colin found himself torn between the list of names and the man's exit route. The brigadier turned left at the entrance to the Stagecoach Inn striding out towards Lisburn. There... a car, moving slowly. Colin was immediately alert, his hand moving automatically to the Browning tucked in his waist band.

A blue Ford had eased forward, obviously in no hurry, the driver's head searching in all directions watching the man's progress intently. Colin's weapon was clear and ready as he jumped the rose beds. He stopped, feet astride, left hand supporting right, he aimed at the driver's face. The sergeant steward smiled back at him, touching his right index finger to his nose as the car moved out onto the main Lisburn road. The little bugger wasn't alone. His back was well covered. Old Indian habit, he smiled to himself. Jesus, sometimes he was really naïve. He could really kick himself.

— o —

Colin rang the doorbell and stood back, nervous. He didn't like this, he was a soldier, not a detective. The list had three addresses highlighted for his attention: O'Neill, Hall and Rourke. Rouke he knew about and was no surprise other than to see it in print; likewise Hall for which he read Dorothy, whose family had supported the underdog forever and a day. But the first name hadn't registered for some time. His brain and memory unconnected.

O'Neill was a name that you'd expect on such a list and carried three possible addresses for pick-up. Thomas Edward O'Neill, his Tom, his blood brother. Same address in Cookstown but had made himself known in the Malone Road and Ballymurphy. Now that took some doing. Champagne socialism right enough. What was his game? He needed answers. Answers to his personal jigsaw. He was fed up being treated like a mushroom, kept in the dark and fed on shit.

Dorothy stood before him obviously startled, even frightened. He was becoming conditioned to that look but surely not with her? He ran his fingers through his hair. No beret, no uniform. Just a social call. A cup of tea in your hand as they say.

"Dorothy, how are you?" he asked, feeling bloody silly. What else could he say? "Long time no see," he continued, hearing his own accent strong and faultless. He'd been home for a while now.

She had recovered her composure enough to glare at him. "You'd better come in then," she invited, grudgingly. Turning her back she led him down the hall. "Alistair is out," she said over her shoulder. "Then you most likely know that already," she said accusingly.

He wiped his feet carefully, thinking wasn't it nice to be civilised. The door closed behind him, intact. "Thanks," he called after her. "It's you that I wanted to see," he stated. He'd decided to ignore the jibe. This was a no-win situation for sure.

"Coffee?" she asked, already filling the kettle. Old habits die hard.

"Thanks," he replied, relieved. "Black, no sugar," he advised, to her back. He waited for her to turn round. "It's a funny world..." Their words clashed shattering the nervous aura surrounding his presence. "You first," he offered. "I don't know where to begin. I feel I'm a stranger in my own land," he confessed.

The aroma of fresh coffee percolated its presence as Dorothy lit a cigarette. Her hesitant fingers flicked nervously at the unformed ash. They sipped their coffee, quiet for a moment, intent with their own thoughts, simply two old friends in no hurry to be alone. She needed to talk and he needed to listen. "You know that they forced Alistair to resign. After everything we had done for them." She spat the words out, all pretence gone. "He had a run in with the southern cowboys. Then you would know all about that, wouldn't you? I know he's never been popular but he tried his best. Danny hung him out to dry and that bastard Rourke put the boot in." Her voice stopped dead in its tracks.

Her eyes full of hurt.

"I know all about Sheila," he said quietly.

"I'm sorry Colin, really sorry. Why she married him God only knows! Bloody Florence Nightingale! We have learnt to ignore it but he's a dangerous piece of work, an evil bastard. Huge ego but with plenty of balls." She bit her lip looking for a reaction. She had said too much already.

He leant across to touch her shoulder. "It's okay," he told her. "Really, I'm fine now. If anyone's to blame, it's me and my bloody pride. Maybe if I hadn't left? Why didn't she join me? Oh, who the hell knows? Who knows," he repeated, reaching for her hand. "Life's full of mistakes." He waited, giving her time to meet his advance. "Tell me about Liam Rourke," he encouraged, releasing her hand.

"Sure he's nothing more than Danny's gofer. You know the wonderful Danny. Top of your list I would imagine," she challenged. "He's always running back and forwards between Derry, Dublin and Belfast." She stubbed at the smouldering end of the cigarette reaching for the packet. "Alistair's feelings were hurt at first, but we are as well out of it all now. Things have changed. The original aims have been achieved. One man, one vote and an end to gerrymandering with equal opportunities in work and housing. We have even accepted the Ulster Defence Regiment in place of the B men. Harmless bastards." She stopped. Catching his look, she laughed, "No, not the B men, not those morons, they were never harmless. No, I mean the Mickey Mouse Army. The UDR, they're harmless, provided they're controlled by their English officers," she corrected. She sighed deeply, taking a deep drag on her second cigarette. "And then what happened?" she asked accusingly. "Don't your lot go and introduce the bloody Special Powers Act? Exactly what those hotheads of Danny's wanted." She paused. "Don't your people know that their present policies are a recruiting campaign for the Provisionals? Volunteers are flooding in." She stabbed at the pile of ash. "We can't match words with the glamour of the balaclava and the gun. The Official wing is dead, killed off in Dublin when they wanted to recognise Westminster. Good as committed suicide, Danny said. But make no mistake, someone, somewhere recognises the Provisionals, otherwise where are they getting the guns and ammunition, pouring into the Falls and the Bogside unhindered."

Colin stopped his hand reaching for the coffee, scared to move in case he interrupted her flow.

"The Provos have a brigade staff with three battalions and over fifteen hundred volunteers," she confirmed, pride in her voice despite the personal hurt. "Tom says..." She stopped immediately, suddenly unsure, and obviously flustered.

Colin felt his eyebrows lift.

"It's no secret," she challenged. "Your lot know all that already." Her eyes darted to his at the sound of the doorbell. Her coffee splashed into the saucer.

"Hadn't you better answer it?" he said, smiling.

The *Belfast Telegraph* hit the table in front of him. "It was the paperboy," she stated the obvious. Dorothy's nail bent under her emphasis as she read the bold black headlines aloud.

"Cross Border Talks at Chequers. Can you believe it?" she fumed. "Lynch and Faulkner in the same room. God help Heath, that's all I can say. Those two would argue a black crow is white or green or orange." She paused for breath, pouring the slopped coffee from the saucer back into her cup.

They both laughed at her words.

Recovered, she went on. "Those two will talk in circles forever," she declared. She smiled broadly. "Our only hope is that they both disappear up Heath's arse," she finished.

Their laughter was real in common appreciation.

Dorothy touched Colin's arm this time. "I really enjoyed our chat," she said quietly. They had reached the front door.

Colin paused on the path, half turning back just before the door closed. "Oh, I nearly forgot what with one thing and another." He stepped closer, fumbling in his top pocket. "Could you do me a favour?" he asked innocently. "Could you get a message to Tom from me? Tell him it's about Sheila. He stays with her sometimes when he's in town, I believe. It's a small world right enough. He can contact me on this number. Regards to Alistair," he finished, turning slowly, enjoying her confusion.

Dorothy stood in the doorway until Colin's car had turned the corner. She could feel the perspiration damp on her forehead. Smart arse, she fumed at herself. Sucker... She'd done it again. That was her trouble, she talked too much. Jesus, just how much did those bastards know? Did they follow Tom? Did they know about Portnoo? Would they tell Alistair?

She closed the door and picked up the hall phone. Her finger dialled one hundred. Wasn't life a bitch? Colin wanted to talk to Tom about Sheila's problems. Well, she needed to talk to him about her own. Their own! Her fingers touched the tightening dress at her waist. "Yes please... Yes... I would like a Buncrana number. Yes... Buncrana, Donegal."

— o —

# CHAPTER FOURTEEN

## OLD FRIENDS – HOLYWOOD 1971

THE MESS CORPORAL ushered Colin to the telephone. He held the door open with his foot, reaching Colin the receiver.

"Yes?" Colin queried. The corporal's foot was still in the doorway.

"Excuse me Sir," the corporal requested, brushing against Colin's leg as he bent down to run his finger over the bruised skirting board.

Colin watched his performance with bemused annoyance. The man never stopped cleaning things. Okay, pride was one thing but this was bloody stupid. He closed the door forcibly but the corporal was quicker, controlling the speed with the handle.

"Colin?" He recognised the voice instantly despite their years of separation.

"What's you doing?" he asked.

"Nothing now," Tom replied, quick as a flash.

The two men laughed into the phone, suspended for a fraction in time, all those years ago. "Colin, it's good to hear you. It's been a long time. Dorothy said you wanted to talk... about Sheila, she said."

"Well, you haven't changed that way then," Colin observed.

"What way?" Tom asked.

"Straight in at the deep end, still no messing."

"Sorry," he apologized, "bad habits hang around." Tom hesitated. The silence hung on the wire. "We should meet. I can't say that I'm happy on the phone—you take the point I'm sure."

"Anytime you say, Tom," Colin offered openly.

Tom's reply was slow and carefully worded. "This is just between you and me and no one else. Do I have your word on that and that I won't be lifted?"

"For God's sake Tom, what do you think I am?"

"I know who you are and what you stand for; the trouble is, do you? I have your word then?" He insisted, his voice hard, emotionless.

"Of course you have my bloody word for fuck sake," Colin replied.

"When and where?" Tom asked.

"It's up to you." The voice at the other end lost its distant edge for the first time. "There's always Hannigans?"

"Hannigans it is… when?" Colin asked.

"Two hours okay," Tom offered.

"No problem, see you soon."

"That's fixed then, and Colin?"

"Yes"

"You have my word also."

"On what?" Colin asked, puzzled.

"On not being lifted," Tom laughed aloud, putting the phone down.

The corporal watched the captain stare at the receiver. Why didn't he put it down if he'd finished? Bloody officers. Colin listened carefully for any hint of interference but there was only a faint click. There always was. How the hell could you tell? I mean, they weren't going to make it obvious, were they? He recognized the signs; paranoia was setting in, or was it? His foot tapped the skirting board, deep in thought, as he replayed the call in his head. The voice in his ear was positive and slightly aggressive. He stared at the receiver still in his hand.

"Shall I replace the telephone, Sir?" the voice asked. It was the thoughtful corporal.

Colin smiled his thanks and squeaked his way down the corridor.

— o —

Colin breathed in the drinker's ambience of spilt stout mixed with damp coats and clinging tobacco. The peaceful fug hung in visible layers. He ordered a pint of Guinness. He never tired of watching the detail of preparation involved in dispensing a pint. It was as if he had never been away. Satisfied with his work, the barman released the pint to his customer's keeping. Thanking the barman and having answered the questions of the day, he took a corner seat, away from the door, back to the wall.

He sipped at his pint content to wait. In no hurry. Hadn't the barman pigeon-holed him as soon as the door shut behind him? He was different, not one of them anymore. It was an animal thing, survival. Jesus, he was becoming paranoiac.

The company spoke in whispers.

The barman wiped his counter down. "He's in the cubicle round the corner," he mouthed, satisfied that he was alone. He nodded towards the back as he strangled a pint glass to a high polish. Colin nodded back, inspecting the church like pews, available for private sin.

The drinkers' eyes followed Colin's progress in the large Bushmills mirror behind the bar.

The booth door clicked open as he neared. Tom half stood bending over the centre table. He looked thinner than he'd pictured him, his facial muscles tense. "You look good, fella."

"You look alright yourself," Tom replied, offering his hand, drawing him into the booth. Colin slid naturally into place. Their eyes met briefly.

The barman placed fresh pints on the table unasked. "I'll keep an eye out," he volunteered. The door clicked closed.

"I hear that you still can't get the real stuff over there then?" Tom raised his glass to the dim light.

"No chance," Colin confirmed.

"They say that it doesn't travel, whatever that means. And sure they wouldn't know a good pint if it bit them," said Tom. "You're glad to be back then?

"Yes and no, if you see what I mean," Colin hedged. "I'm sure you understand. We're not everybody's cup of tea."

"What the hell do you expect if you go around kicking people's doors in? Did you say hello to her? Did you apologize?" Tom demanded. "Did you?" he pressed home.

Colin bristled, straightening his shoulders. "I didn't notice your feet move but I've got a terrible pain in my ball's," his voice hard and tight. "But you're right, no, I didn't," he confessed, "And I'm deeply ashamed of myself. Christ, Tom, what was I to do? What would you have done? Sheila in Ballymurphy."

"I'm sorry, you're right, I wouldn't have known what to do either. Jesus, what a fucking mess," Tom confessed, looking directly into his old friend's eyes.

"Thanks for that anyway," Colin accepted. "I'll try and be a bit more diplomatic in future."

"I thought you'd have been briefed that diplomacy is old hat around our neck of the woods. No one trusts anyone. Not anymore, Sunshine." Tom took an angry swig of his pint. "We tried talking nicely before you arrived. Some of us even signed petitions. Remember Civil Rights? When your lot patted us on the head and told us how deserving we were. Told us to be patient. Everything would be delivered. All crap, just playing for time, always playing for time," Tom paused. "That's how they met, you know..."

"Who?" Colin asked, completely lost.

"Who do you think? Sheila and Liam. She volunteered to sit on one of our social committees. Social as in need not as in sherry. She said that she was the token Protestant and a nurse. It was one of life's little twists and turns, their meeting. It wasn't my fault, I'd nothing to do with it, honestly," he stressed.

"I know it was nobody's fault—I'm the one to blame if blame's the game. I should have come home when she wrote that silly letter but not me, too proud. Stupid bloody pride, that's all it was. The male ego."

"You should never have left us." Tom drained his glass.

"Maybe you're right," Colin agreed quietly. "Tell me about Sheila. Sorry," he apologised, lifting the empty glass. "Can I get you another?" he offered.

"Please." The smile was friendly.

Colin listened attentively for the next half hour to Tom's story. There was no need to interrupt, just listen. It was all so simple, understandable. "Fate, call it what you like, had brought them together. Liam hadn't even been on the march. Too important. He'd waited in Derry over the New Year. Waited for the march to end. When they heard the news on the jungle drums about Burntollett he'd gone out to see if he could help Danny. Sod's law really, he'd run straight into the B men coming the other way, their blood riled. Well, I suppose that you can guess the rest and to be honest with his accent he's lucky he's still alive. They had pulverised him and left him dumped in a doorway. He'd ended up in hospital with broken ribs, a fractured skull and the usual toe cap bruising. You can guess some of the obvious. The liberal nurse and the wounded warrior, white uniform, white bandages; it was all there for the romantic. Sheila had moved him into her cottage on his discharge. The tongues wagged of course. Bad enough no ring, but him from the South and her from South Belfast. But they were in love and didn't care. Anyway, no sooner were they together than Liam was needed in Ballymurphy. Sheila had insisted on going with him and her already pregnant. She refused to be separated. It was a dreadful mistake but she wouldn't listen. You know how stubborn she can be. They didn't have a snowball's chance in hell and Ballymurphy was her hell. Liam had tried for a while but with the new baby, the wee house and his night work for Danny, he was never home or always in a rush. Then to top it all he started drinking—it went with his job. Always busy. With no visible support from Liam, Sheila was shunned by the locals. She became an outcast. Spat upon if she ventured out."

The two men's eyes met in the painful pause.

"I'm really sorry, Colin." Tom stopped, reaching across the table.

Colin drew back at Tom's touch, unable to stop himself, numb. He felt the grip tightened on his wrist.

"Colin... Listen man, I tried. Honest to God, I really tried but she wouldn't listen and she wouldn't go back to Derry. Jesus and hell.... I'll try again," he offered. "Maybe she'll listen now she's on her own. What with Liam being lifted and she and the child alone. He's nearly two now and becoming aware."

The two men sat in silence, each man suffering the other's failures.

"How much longer can you hold him?" Tom spoke first.

"How long do you need?"

"Christmas should do it!"

"I'll make it the New Year," Colin promised.

Tom raised his head over the divide, signalling to the barman for replenishment. "Good health." Tom sipped the fresh glass. "Now then, maybe we can do each other a favour," he said to his friend. "Would you tell your men in Lisburn to keep their off-duty troops off the streets and away from pubs for Christ's sake? Don't they understand that there's too much hatred for us to control where drink and guns are involved?"

The old friends eased their glasses into the centre of the table, having found common ground.

"I'll try, I promise you that, but with Faulkner in charge of policy I wouldn't hold your breath. He'd rather see the bodies on the street than show any possible sign of weakness. They say he has No Surrender embroidered on his pyjamas."

The two men laughed at the shared quip.

"Now you can do me a favour," Colin suggested.

"I'll try," Tom replied.

"Tell me something? Why have you of all people, a reasonable and logical man, turned on the very people who came to help in the first place? The British Army." Colin waited. He watched his friend tussle with his thoughts, finally emitting a deep sigh of frustration.

"Is it any wonder? I sometimes feel like walking away from the whole bloody mess," Tom declared, running his hand through his hair. "What hope is there of your English friends ever understanding our problems when the likes of yourself can't or won't be bothered to listen," he chastised, his voice rising. "I'll say it slowly so that you can remember what to tell your English masters. We're not taking on the British Army, we are taking on Stormont... Stormont... STORMONT and its lackeys, and everything that it and they have stood for in the past fifty years of misrule. Can't you see it for yourselves, man? You have replaced the B Specials. You administer internment on Stormont's behalf. They couldn't do it without Westminster and Westminster couldn't do it without you. They think that we will just go away, but not this time, Colin. I'm telling you, not this time," he stressed. "Tell them Colin... Honest to God... Not this time..."

Colin watched the hatred washed by a wave of frustration, softening the deep lines of bitterness etched around his friend's puzzled eyes and twisted mouth. He realised that the bar had gone deadly still, Tom's final words filling the hollowness of arrested conversations. He edged forward in his seat holding Tom's eyes as his hand felt for the butt of the Browning. He watched Tom's lips move, forming new words.

"Tell me," Tom's voice was quiet, stretching the ears of the men at the bar. Colin could feel his own sweat trickle down his back. "How many Protestants did you lift in August? How many of the Orange bastards' doors did you kick in?" Colin was aware of the beast at the bar, moving, shuffling its feet. "Terrifying wives and children. How many?" Tom demanded.

The private booth had suddenly become a pulpit. A hand opened the door.

"No idea? Well, I'll tell you for nothing. Not one... Bloody none. Demetrius! Is that what you call British justice?"

Colin knew his heart had stopped. Maybe for good. His right hand eased the barrel of the Browning free. He felt his thumb finger the safety catch.

"That's right," the voice had changed again. "That made you sit-up," Tom crowed, smiling his enjoyment at Colin's discomfort. "Demetrius... A classical cock-up with pieces of paper everywhere. Lisburn confetti we call it. The only name they got right on their list was their own codeword... Demetrius... Mickey Mouse would have been better," he finished.

Colin's mind raced to grasp Tom's words. Was he playing with him? There was no escape if he was but he'd promised. The whole bar had erupted in laughter easing the tension. They were laughing at him, at the British Army. They were laughing.

The bar comedian seized on his chance. "Isn't that a good one right enough?" he opened, making his mark. "Did you hear that? MICKEY... Mouse," he emphasised. "At least we'd know whose side he's on," he waited and waited.

"Sit down you eejit," they chorused. "MICKEY," he explained, lighting another cigarette. The whole bar joined in the fun.

Colin stared into Tom's laughing mouth. He had a gold filling. What's that about? They're all bloody mad, he thought. The brigadier was right. They're all bloody certifiable. Every one of them. He withdrew his hand from the sweaty metal pushing the catch back, releasing the captured beads of sweat trapped in his armpit. He laughed the loudest. The bar settled down to its own business. The door closed.

"It's good to know you can still laugh with us," Tom said. "I only wish you had been here for the marches. Experienced the hope of a new era. Jesus man, it was right there in our hands one minute and gone the next. All gone. Shattered at Burntollet. The beating of the drums and the organised violence. The crushed dreams. Then you might begin to understand the fear on both sides. There are no spectators anymore. You see, we really did try the conventional way. We asked for a political voice. Men, like Fitt, Hume, Devlin and others, all of them tried. Tried to promote friendship and understanding between the North and the South," he paused, recognizing Colin's Ulster smile. He smiled back. "Okay, granted we had unity in mind but long term and only with the consent of the majority."

"Come off it Tom," Colin responded. "I was with you until you got to the majority bit. Which majority do you mean? Ulster's established and legal majority, or some pie in the sky overall majority to include the whole of Ireland, an ill-conceived and illegal majority?" He knew that his tongue was running away with him but it had to be said. "Don't you realise that you're talking treason. Man, that's some negotiation technique," he said, smiling. "You know how they negotiate here, don't you?" Colin continued. "Always by the book, the Holy Book, the Bible, an eye for an eye and a tooth for a tooth. You dig up the Falls... They dig up the Shankill... You barricade the Bogside... They barricade Sandy Row, and so it goes on and on until everyone's so deeply entrenched nobody can climb out. Can't you see any further than your own noses? Can't you see that you're digging your own graves? Good God man, you've all got to sit down and talk. Talk now, not tomorrow but now, before it's too bloody late."

Tom sighed openly, suddenly tired. "Maybe it's too late already, Colin." His finger's fiddled with the glass. "You see, we have our own ways of talking to each other. Haven't you seen our gable news sheets... Our walls of information? Ulster's score boards of death. Tribal score boards... US—THREE... THEM—TWO... Us and Them; until killing has become a game. We're all to blame. Your lot as well," he accused, pointing his finger. "We could have sold the people internment if you had sacked Stormont at the same time. What a golden opportunity lost forever. Just think, man, how the plotters on both sides would have been exposed for what they were and left powerless. But we couldn't see any further than our selfish noses. And didn't Westminster miss her chance?

You see, they thought that they had a military solution. Silly bastards. Look at them now. Your lot are piggy-in-the-middle. Your backs exposed to both communities. You know that the military can't win and neither can we." Tom stared into his glass. "You're right and I agree we need to talk and soon," he admitted. "Let's hope that we can go on from here. You talk to your people and I'll talk to mine. Fair enough," he finished.

They shook hands as friends, recognizing that a bridge of hope still existed between an ever increasing gulf.

Colin closed the booth door and forced himself to walk at a normal pace looking straight ahead, feeling the multitude of eyes watching. He heard whispered words, felt his waistband warm and wet, the Browning sticky, bulky, and so obvious. The front door slammed shut behind him as he sucked in the beautiful air. He was alive. He needed a pee. He needed to tell the rose grower that they were willing to talk. Tom was willing to talk.

— o —

"Captain Monro, telephone," the mess corporal indicated the hall booth. The voice was unmistakeable; the rose grower had wasted no time. "I'm delighted to hear that you are renewing old friendships," the voice continued, obviously pleased with itself. "I would of course be delighted to discuss any conclusions you may have reached but unfortunately tonight is impossible. Perhaps you could put pen to paper. Nothing complicated of course, the simpler the better. Say one side of A4 should do. My driver will be in the motor transport yard at Holywood in an hour's time. You will recognise him of course."

The line went dead in Colin's hand. He looked out through the window to the lough shores below, so beautiful and so peaceful. The twinkling lights of a passing ship reminded him that it was nearly Christmas. He replaced the receiver and crossed the hall to the dining room.

The evening *Telegraph* showed shoppers laden with presents, determined to forget the massacre at McGurk's bar on the fourth of the month. Fifteen people had been killed and they were the lucky ones. The injuries of the survivors had all been listed in the local newspapers, where personal grief had become public knowledge. Public columns of sorrow. What kind of person, Protestant or Catholic, could leave a bomb ticking away amongst all those human limbs? Did they watch the results? Did they gloat? Would they like the pieces? Colin marvelled at the resilience of the people. He folded the newspaper.

"More beef Sir?" The meat was blood red, its fat done to a crispy perfection. He chewed on the pliant fodder, savouring the animal juices in his mouth. "Ashtray, Sir?" The corporal rearranged the table in front of the doctor, tidying and wiping, making his disapproval obvious.

"Much too clever for his own good that chap," the doctor observed. "I see that nothing has come out of the tripartite talks," he commented, rattling the newspaper, putting his cigarettes away. "Wilson's fifteen-year unity plan isn't much better when you read it... Fifteen years," he shrugged his shoulders. "It's a drop in the ocean to these people."

The doctor pushed his chair back noisily. "Must go," he said abruptly.

— o —

Colin groped for the bedside lamp; nothing, only empty space, it had gone and so had the bed. He was lying on the floor. The silence was total, his head hollow. He covered his ears with his hands, conjuring up memories of childhood seashells, allowing the retreating tide to ebb in his head. His eyes focused slowly, recording the devastation, trying to make sense of it all. The curtains flapped angrily in the breeze shredded beyond repair, whipped by dangling sash cords hanging from empty window frames. He shook his head listening to the peculiar noise of minute particles of glass cascade from his body, forming a circle of glass.

"Bastards," he cursed in pain, quickly withdrawing bleeding fingers from his ruffled hair. He felt his ears pop. "Fucking bastards," he swore. He could hear distant voices. Men's voices, giving orders.

"Bring some light..."
"Anybody hurt?"
"Get the doc..."
"How the hell did they get in?"
"Over here..."
"There's a body down."
"Where's that bloody torch?"
"That you, Doc?"
"Thank God."
Mixed questions.
Mixed voices.
Mixed emotions.

He noticed his door had gone. The corridor was full of bouncing figures, hurrying here and there. Pencil shafts of guiding light stabbed awareness into the scene of apparent chaos. New voices sang out, authoritative voices; demanding information. The tableau froze, captured in a cascade of instant light. Men stared open mouthed at the sparkling hall chandelier tinkling its complete defiance.

"Well done Corporal," the doctor's voice acknowledged. Command was established.

"Over here Colin." He obeyed the order, joining the gaggle of officers on the mess steps. The doors, or what was left of them, hung outwards, completely useless. The Second in Command put a match to his pipe.

"Did anyone," he puffed away, "see anything?" he asked.

"Show's over, chaps," the doctor announced. "Nobody hurt, the odd bruise and the usual lacerations," he announced matter-of-factly. "Silly buggers placed it under a Pig in the MT yard. The armoured plate absorbed most of the blast. Bloody lucky," he informed them, full of information.

"How it got there is more to the point," the major stressed, peeved by the doctor's interruption.

The doctor stood on the bottom step, black bag in hand. "Are you there, Corporal?" he asked, peering into the darkness. "I know that you're lurking somewhere close, so listen up. I want the bar open in fifteen minutes," he ordered. "Must do one final check." he said.

Colin watched the retreating figure return to the scene of combat. He looked for something to do.

A black bag lay among the debris. He knew instantly what it was.

He felt his stomach turn over, his legs tingled empty of blood, logic began to form putting the pieces of information together. The ruse had worked but the second bomb hadn't.

The gaggle of officers had been the main target, not the bloody stupid Pig. He flew up the steps, kicked the door to the telephone booth to one side, stumbled, kicking at the detached skirting board. His fingers fought to match the emergency number pasted before him.

"Ops… We need the Bomb Squad!" he shouted into the phone. Jesus... It worked. "There's a second bomb," he gasped. "Yes... Positive... The bottom of the Officers' Mess steps. Yes... I can see the fucker from...." his voice froze in his throat.

"Is that you, Colin? Are you still there Colin?" the Duty Officer shouted. "Colin... For God's sake answer me."

"Fuck it," the corporal cursed, tripping on the steps, brush in hand. He lay, sprawled on the ground, the brush shaft broken, pieces of gravel imbedded into his palms. The black bag stared him in the face. "Bloody officers," he swore. "Always leaving things at their arses," he growled aloud. He pushed himself to his feet. "Bloody hands," he swore. "Jesus," he cursed aloud, picking at his hands. "Bloody thing," he continued, kicking out at the offending briefcase, watching it slide away beyond the light. Still cursing he followed it into the darkness. "Bastard," he muttered.  It lay on its side.  The cause of all his pain.  He picked it up and sniffed at the shiny black surface.  "Well, well," he crowed, his pain forgotten.  "Would you believe it," he asked the night as he sniffed again.  "Plastic," he confirmed.  "Cheap plastic and that old bugger of a quack guarded it like it was the real McCoy."

He raced after the doctor.  He hadn't got far, the silly old goat.  There he was, deep in conversation with the colonel.  The corporal waved the case above his head in triumph... He heard the noise and felt the heat but there was no pain... No awareness... Nothing.

Colin drew back around the corner.  Just in time.  He had seen the case waved above the man's head, had sensed the flash as the hot air engulfed his body penetrating his nostrils, forcing his mouth open.  He screamed aloud knowing that he didn't want to turn the corner again.

Colin read the last line of the citation aloud.  "Did knowingly and willingly sacrifice his life in order that others might live."  He added his signature below the doctor's as the colonel spoke a few well-chosen words to the widow.  The padre joined them on their walk back to the mess.  He had noticed that the doctor was quiet, unlike him, withdrawn even, constantly touching the plaster above his right eye.

"Colin," the doc's eyes were questioning, his voice puzzled.  "You know, I can't get it out of my mind, it's been there for three days now," he scratched at his chin this time.  "Scottish, wasn't he?"

"Yes, from Glasgow.  Dreadful," the padre intoned.

Colin couldn't decide if he meant the place or the loss?

"Thought so," the doc smiled, excited.  "They don't play much cricket up there," he exclaimed, triumphant.  "That explains it.  That most peculiar throwing action of his, no wrist movement at all, no wrist, more like a wave.  Strange fellow altogether," he confirmed.  Happy at last, he looked forward to his gin and tonic in peace.

— o —

Colin still didn't believe he'd made the call but he had to, he had to know. He watched the car come to rest in the golf club car park. The driver turned this way and that, trying to avoid the puddles. A real challenge in December. Well, this was it, he thought, shit or bust. The man himself was waiting. Colin tapped on the window and shook the drizzle from the coloured umbrella. He smiled weakly, unsure of his reception. What was he going to say? He clambered into the front passenger seat pushing the wet umbrella behind the driver's seat. He waited but not for long.

"I'm not used to being given orders by my peers, never mind junior officers, Captain," the voice was low and obviously miffed. The face like thunder.

Colin felt his own hackles rise. He could still feel the wind of death in his lungs. "I apologise for any misunderstanding, Sir," he opened, hesitant. He wasn't as brave now but he didn't bloody care. The rumours were rife. "But as you are well aware, there are some very ugly rumours surfacing in the barracks regarding who really did plant the bomb in Palace Barracks." There, he'd said it. He could feel the man's breath on his cheek as he turned to reply. He'd had garlic.

"Rumours?" the brigadier returned in a controlled voice, the mask of authority still in place.

"They say it had to be one of our own men," Colin insisted.

"My steward, for example?"

Colin felt his stomach heave. Jesus. Doc had been right... There was no way an outsider could get into the MT yard. The Pig. His steward. Yes... It all added up; except the gaggle. The second bomb. It was impossible. No logic. But who, and how, and why?

"You're quite right," the Brigadier confirmed. "It was one of our own. Correction," the man continued, "It was in fact one of your own men." The lips parted, "Born on the Falls Road, a cook, now a deserter and hiding in Dublin. We do believe the best friend of the brave but dead hero. Whom I am informed was a Glaswegian Protestant. Ironic, is it not?"

"Jesus Christ," Colin blurted out, flustered, guilt written all over his face.

"Quite. A salutary lesson if nothing else. Nothing is ever what it seems in this place. Do you think it will turn to snow?" he asked, looking out the car window. "I do hope so; these poor people could do with a White Christmas. A time of peace and goodwill to all men. Would you trust O'Neill?" he asked, suddenly.

"Yes," Colin replied immediately. He didn't have to think.

"Good." He turned, back into the car, his eyes penetrating. "He would appear to be our only hope of progress. He must be made to understand that Stormont will not accept the No-Go Areas for much longer and that we are being pressed to make an example of somebody, anybody." He lifted one shoulder ever so slightly. "I have reluctantly agreed to recommend military action but not before Christmas and then only in a limited form. Tell him that we recognize the need to avoid the alienation of the Catholic population any further than we must." The gloved hand wiped at the window. A passing figure head down against the wind waved back. "It would appear that your friend O'Neill is a reasonable and intelligent man," he said. "That's according to his friend Rourke's interrogation report."

The figure returned, pulling a trolley. Head still down. "How can they play golf in such weather, never mind enjoy it?" the brigadier asked, moving on immediately. "Perhaps intelligent enough to consider an offer." He allowed time for the words to penetrate. "An offer of a phased withdrawal rather than a head-on confrontation."

"It's Derry we're talking about. Isn't it?" Colin asked, shivering involuntarily. Someone had walked over his grave. "Let me get my head around this," he said slowly. "You want me to ask Tom to do a deal and it's the Bogside you're after?"

"Merely a testing of the water and those who swim in it. Derry will come later and hardly a deal, more a friendly proposition." The reply was smooth, prepared. "You see, we believe that your friend is having the same problem as ourselves. The populace have had enough of the street rabble and it's costing the merchants money. The rabble on the other hand are enjoying the game. It's costing them nothing. They can't lose." He smiled. "Funny old world when one stops to think that we actually subsidise the players on both teams. Pay them British benefits, whilst they refuse to recognize the hand that feeds them. They pay no rent or services and declare a Free Derry. Free... Most appropriate, don't you agree?" he chuckled. Colin smiled back. The wee man's humour had gone native. "Tell O'Neill that it's the trouble-makers we're after. The ones who are of no importance to either side and therefore dispensable at this time. We must be seen to achieve order. Stormont wants heads on platters. We may be able to stall them until the end of January at the latest." He sighed openly. "Who knows with Stormont? What I do know is that the civil authority must be seen to be obeyed, otherwise the end to No-Go areas will be swift and painful," he predicted, the voice tired.

The rain was heavy again. It drummed on the car roof. They watched the figure dripping and sexless in its rubber protection trudge wearily onwards down the fairway.

"Explain the following scenario to O'Neill." The brigadier turned to look directly at his companion. He was determined that there would be no misunderstanding. "A battalion, possibly your own."

Colin knew it was fate and he couldn't escape it.

The voice continued. "Will lie up close to Derry, in all appearance as a support company in reserve. In reality they will enter Derry on a Sunday morning when all law-abiding citizens are abed or at Church. Early Chapel, I believe they call it. The troops will penetrate an agreed distance within the barricades, where snatch squads will lift all hostile hooligans in that area, known and otherwise. The rabble will be delivered directly to special courts on Monday morning. In return there will be no attempt to search or challenge their core areas.

"O'Neill's lot will take no part in the action. It is a face-saving exercise to both parties. We must be seen to clear the streets on our own and unchallenged. Otherwise Stormont will have her way. The squads will use speed and batons only. They will however be covered by armed guards who will be under strict instructions to keep their safety catches on. O'Neill has my personal word on those orders. We will not shoot first," he stressed.

Colin's mind raced around the implications. The streets would be cleared under common agreement. The British Army was recognizing the Republicans, recognizing the Provisional IRA as a force to be reckoned with and therefore negotiable. Unofficial, yes, but the beginning of the end. A sleeping partner. The man was waiting. Jesus, what was he supposed to say?

"Tom doesn't have that sort of power," he replied.

"Quite so, but he does have the respect and the ear of the man who does," the brigadier stated calmly. "As you do," he smiled. "We must try every avenue open to us," he charged.

"I'll do my best," Colin promised.

"I know you will," he said, touching the young officer's sleeve.

The Brigadier watched the figure turn and half wave before entering the other car. His own son, Toby, would have been the same age as Monro had he lived. He'd been tall for his age. The restrictive gene had missed his generation. They had been so proud of him, everything was perfect, Jordan, the job, military attaché to the Embassy and to the crown it all a place for Toby at his old prep school, then Eton. He was to have started that September term. His wife, Catherine, was to have flown home with Toby at the end of summer. New school uniform, new friends, for life.

He tightened closed eyes, squeezing the memories. Their final walk in the hills, he couldn't spare the time, work, career. Toby had wanted to say goodbye to the dog. The forgotten landmine of Middle Eastern hatred.

The shattered bodies.

The body bags.
The cedar wood coffins.
The nightmare flight home. Alone with their shattered bodies and scattered dreams, all nailed down in those awful wooden boxes.

He had never remarried and the pain had never stopped. Time does not heal all. Work had helped but he would always be alone.

Colin watched the second car take up station. The man's caddy was never far away.

He watched the two cars exit the car park.

— o —

Christmas had passed Tom by in a flurry of dirty snow but the New Year had brought good news. Liam had agreed to a trial separation on his release and he'd convinced Sheila to return to Derry and the cottage. But he hadn't mentioned Colin to Sheila yet. She needed time. He walked slowly, feeling the wind on his back. He'd arrived early for their meeting and had taken the opportunity to walk the harbour wall. He climbed the hill to the hotel.

Colin watched his friend's progress from the hotel window, sensing his enjoyment of winter's elements. You could see the wind rush the hill, leap-frogging the grass embankment just below the crooked railing, rattling the scenic window of the Bayview Hotel. He heard the porch door slam yet again.

The barman took a sip from his steaming mug of sweet, four sugars, brown tea. He blew on it, his eyes searching for the milk bottle. "Wouldn't it burn the bake off you?" he said aloud in disgust. He added a dollop of milk. The man at the window had put one in the barrel for his mate still to come. Wasn't it as quiet as the grave and just as miserable? But then wasn't it only halfway through January? He lifted his head from the

Australian racing form as its pages rustled from the wind of the open door before the bang announced his next customer.

The two men were terribly serious right enough, speaking low and stopping altogether when he brought them a fresh order. Jesus, he just hated people doing that, sure you had to do something. Even listening was better than nothing. You could go nuts and no one would notice. He could catch the odd word every so often but it was useless to try and make any sense of it. What with that bloody window rattling and the door slamming. And nobody appearing for God's sake. He watched the seagulls' battle to rise, and, exhausted, fall back into the harbour. He wondered how they kept warm at nights. You could tell the clever ones, weren't they walking? It could snow again he decided. He poured himself a warming glass of Powers. "That's great stuff, right enough," he complimented the distiller.

The two men looked his way.

He smiled back at them through the whiskey glow. The one who had been doing all the chin-wagging looked different. He could tell that they were nearly finished talking; it was a sort of gift he had.

"Well there it is, Tom, and I still can't believe it myself," Colin said, feeling the burden lifted.

"You know what you've just offered us, don't you?" Tom insisted.

"For sure," Colin nodded.

"Jesus... What an opportunity," Tom said, elated. He drew circles with his glass on the table top. "Maybe it could work. It has to work," he said positively. He paused, his face troubled. "Just pray to God nobody and I mean nobody leaks it."

— o —

Danny lit another cigarette, playing with the box of matches. A week to go to the end of January and time enough for things to go wrong. The debate had been going on for two hours. He stubbed out his previous butt, its dying smoke curling around his nicotine-stained flesh. The ash overflowed. They'd a hung vote and now it was all down to him. The buck stops here, Harry Truman had said. "I say we go with Tom's proposals; we've bugger all to lose but God help any man who breathes a word of this outside these four walls. He'll answer to me personally," he stressed, threateningly.

The men exited at agreed intervals, each one taking a different escape route through the maze of factory corridors. Danny turned away from the door, crossing to the cabinet in the corner. The humming neon heightened the staleness of the room. He tugged hard at the cabinet drawer cursing its reluctant runners.

Tom heard the clink of a trapped bottle and glasses.

"To success," Danny said. Their glasses touched. "You're going to have to be careful, Tom," he warned. "No, not with Colin," he anticipated. "I'm not worried about him at all. No, it's those English spooks in Lisburn and their disinformation. Good word that, American they say, but can you believe it?" he questioned. He eyed Tom's reaction. "It's the way I tell them," he joked. "Tell you what," he offered. "What if I get the boys in Dublin to prepare the usual press statement? Brutality, over-reaction, innocent bystanders... that sort of thing. Just in case. You know the score. We can always spike it," he promised, pouring another drink. "Provided they keep their word," he concluded with a wink.

"CYA... Cover Your Ass, Colin calls it," Tom explained, holding his glass out to the fresh drink. "American."

"Isn't that a good one?" Danny agreed. "I'll remember that one for Boston," he said. The eyebrow rising. "I'm sure, I told you," he quizzed. "No matter," he admitted. "Yes, it was arranged ages ago. Visiting rich relatives," he winked. "So the store's all yours."

— o —

# CHAPTER FIFTEEN

## BLOODY SUNDAY – DERRY 1972

COLIN LAY ON THE SOFT, DAMP, BED of meadow grass listening to hidden birds compete with the distant peal of church bells. For January, it was spring-like and peaceful. Only a few fields away he could hear cattle lowing their relief as familiar, horny hands slapped their rumps, shooing them back to the fields from milking. Work done and the gate secured, God-fearing men returned home to struggle into church boots and their Sunday best.

He rolled over onto his side and looked down towards the city, lying still, beyond the meandering waters of the Foyle. Londonderry, Derry, the tribal names of a divided society.

A dog barked its message of need, disturbing the slumbers of restless men. Female hands tidied away used socks and discarded shoes out of sight, before they added the heaped spoonsful of sugar to mugs of tea as they stirred a new day. Up the hill and out of sight young men waited, tin mugs in hand, before the stainless steel tea urns of war. Young faces with hard eyes, licked dry lips, sucking on the last dregs of loosely rolled tobacco. Eyes that had seen the severed limbs and torn flesh of comrades. Heard the promise of death, spat on by the female spittle of Irish hatred. No lines of compassion wrinkled their young faces. These were the battle-hardened warriors of the Belfast streets. Men stretched to their limits of endurance again and again until they never wanted to see or hear of another bloody march.

The men checked their watches. Fags out. Their heels ground the tension into the damp earth. It was time to go. Down the road into the city.

— o —

Colin looked out over the barrier at the sea of defiant faces. There was a carnival atmosphere. Women and children waved their tri-coloured banners, parading their defiance of foreign authority and their God-given right to enjoyment. Maybe he had worried for nothing. The crowd was well-behaved. Tom was right. He knew what he was doing. He watched his men turn aside the jostling body of the marchers as they approached the barrier. Watched its tail snake to the left, passing round the corner and out of sight. Thank God it was nearly over. He allowed himself a smile of relief as he nodded his new found confidence to his men. Tight lipped, they stared through his smile, wiping their palms on bulging smocks, adjusting their weapons, flexing cramped fingers. Smith was chewing at his nails but then Smith always chewed at his nails, he spat a defiant piece of quick onto the barrier and gripped his rifle with meaning.

The revellers had returned. The women and children had gone. "Jesus Christ," he heard his own apprehension. The crowd shook itself, moving faster, with a purpose, suddenly a surging mass of elated faces were racing towards the barrier. Smith's barrier! Faster and faster, until as if at a signal the lead ranks wheeled away spilling the parasites of society from its body onto the side-lines, leaving them in the open. Exposed. The trouble-makers stood still, forlorn and unsure, the stones of scorn heavy in their hands.

— o —

The man knelt at an awkward angle to the old stone wall. He found it difficult to remain both concealed and comfortable. "Better the bloody cramp than no feeling at all," he reminded himself through twisted lips. He shuddered at the thought of being discovered on their ancient ramparts. The bastards would tear him apart. Bloody animals. He held the scope in his hand like you would a telescope. The SLR rested against the wall, its mount carefully protected within the soft folds of the oiled cloth. He'd known it would be a waste of time. The people he hunted didn't appear in daylight and definitely not amongst the common man. He scanned the crowd to pass the time. Youngsters, mostly boys, with a few girls. The boys' hair as long as the girls' and just as attractive. More so in some cases. He focused on the image filling the scope. There you go. Ponytail, high cheek bones and the remains of acne. The new man.

"Jesus!" he swore aloud. The sudden movement jarring his knee on the rough stone, he cursed again, catching hold of the falling rifle by instinct. The shot had come from his right. Right bloody beside him... where no one was supposed to go. They couldn't even organise that.

"Jesus," he swore again, scrabbling on his hands and knees, no longer worried about the rifle, the scope or its mounting. Only his own skin mattered now.

The wee man stood nervously at the bottom of the steps. He'd never liked it, not for one minute. He'd asked questions and wouldn't any man. And a lot of good it'd done him.

"None of your bloody business," they'd said. "Just make sure that nobody touches the bike and return the package he gives you to us."

He held the bike at arm's length. What did he know about bikes? His body betrayed his embarrassment. He half turned, footsteps. He felt the tension rise in his body. Wasn't he confused enough? One lot approaching, the other fading, going away. And then he was there, his man, all in a rush. The eyes blinking like a ferret in daylight, with hunched shoulders, no neck and the collar turned up. They didn't speak. The package passed from hand to hand. Bloody lumbered again.

"Get out of the fucking way," the ferret hissed in his face. He jumped backwards as the engine burst into life. Then he was alone. Except for the package.

The carnival was over. The token volley of stones whistled through the air. The troops stood still. The marchers stood back. The throwers turned away. The command radio crackled its message of impersonal speech. The general nodded his head in agreement and replaced the earphones.

"Now's our chance... Go get them," he ordered.

Coloured smocks sprang from the earth, eager as beagles to please their master. Personal war cries of attacking troops mixed with the crowd's screams of fear. The retreating stragglers turned to look. Colin kicked at something in his way. A body rolled into the gutter. He stumbled, corrected, and was swept along with the pack, his body pumped by massive surges of adrenaline. He tripped again, going down under a welter of feet, brown, white and black, surged in confusion with khaki puttees. He felt his fists punch at human flesh, trying to free himself from the mass of limbs blocking his recovery. His fingers grasped on handfuls of clothing, pulling himself upright, ignoring the wriggling limbs and panic punches. His fingers froze on motionless limbs. He recognised it instantly... A single shot... The second shot released the tumbling bodies of professional soldiers instinctively going to ground, shouldering their weapons. Searching for the enemy. Local youths and men stood thunderstruck in the mêlée. Stunned and confused, the crowd stood its ground, upright and exposed. Completely defenceless.

"Lie down... Lie down, you silly bastards... Lie down before you're knocked down!" The voice was hysterical, high pitched, verging on the feminine and coming from close by... Colin sobbed aloud, recognising it as his own. The crowd imploded, terrified by reality.

Caught in the open.
Exposed to retribution.

Men and boys ran for cover.
Headless chickens.
Trapped in their own coop.
Colin lunged at the soldier beside him, knocking the rifle barrel skyward. A look of hatred bored back into Colin's face. Their eyes locked.

"I'm okay Sir," Smith said, his thumb returning the safety catch... The flame subsided.

"Ceasefire, you idiots... Ceasefire..." he yelled. "Identify targets... Identify targets," he commanded, shrill, his voice trailing off into a penetrating silence.

Rifle covered rifle. The mêlée died. Terrified youths caved in at the knees; sinking to the ground, they clung to the dead and dying. Colin pointed the pistol towards the persistent movement to his right. The target was clear. A man in a dark suit, down on one knee with his right hand raised... Colin aimed. A red and white flag fluttered in the breeze, falling limp, it stuck to the man's cuff. A handkerchief, a bloodstained handkerchief. The man fumbled with his other hand, moving his lips as words tumbled to falling beads, and dropping onto a dangling cross. Jesus, he was a priest!

"Help that man!" he shouted, his voice was under control again. "The one with the bloody handkerchief... Kneeling down... The bloody priest!" he screamed. "Move it, you idiots... Do it!" he ordered.

— o —

Danny sat sucking the white meat out of the red crab claws. He licked his fingers clean and belched quietly, feeling the injected bubbles of the American beer rise in his throat. His hosts were too excited to notice his appreciation. His sticky fingers continued to flick excitedly through the multitude of newspapers lying on the table top. Headlines leapt from their front pages... "Bloody Sunday... Ireland's Sharpeville... Army

Run Amok... Paratroopers Murder Thirteen." Four days of world-wide condemnation and all crowned by this morning's latest offering. "Dublin – Twenty Thousand Burn British Embassy. Irish Government Declare National Day of Mourning." Danny raised his glass of cold beer aloft; he winked at his hosts across the table, his eyes crinkled above a wicked grin. "God bless the British Army," he proposed. The glasses clinked. "Always dependable and forever predictable. From India to Aden." The laughter was loud and appreciative. "And you lot wanted to pay a public relations man." He touched the side of his nose. "Man alive," he chided. "Don't we have the biggest PR firm in the world and with a Queen at its head?" His stained finger stabbed into world opinion. "One shot. One shot, that's all it took. Just one bloody shot and their house of cards is ready to fold. We have them by the short-and-curlies and no amount of troops can prop their beloved Stormont up for much longer." Danny stood, swaying gently. "Long live the Republic and Long live its Army." His eyes moist. "To the IRA," he proposed the toast to his hosts, watching the honest round faces, alive with historic brotherhood raise their glasses. Cheers ran around Jimmy's Restaurant as they felt privileged to drink their Bostonian beer in such illustrious company.

A part of history once again.

— o —

The brigadier sat stiffly to attention in the anteroom, its windows overlooking the most theatrical parade ground in the world. Horse Guards Parade. He had never quite forgiven God for his restricted growth. Only a quirk of nature, some dormant gene, had prevented him from commanding his Sovereign's scarlet multitude. To have followed his father and his father before him in a family tradition. Inches, bloody inches and a military manual. Regulation inches. It wasn't fair. He pondered the use of the English language. Words, their origin and their meaning. Words, such as those of the report nestling in his briefcase, like one of their own ticking bombs. Each word carefully crafted, syllables articulately used and finally transcribed into a two-page synopsis. Last Sunday's disaster. He had read and re-read his classic innuendo of non-identifiable responsibility. Quite brilliant under the circumstances.

The dulcet tones of the senior civil servant interrupted his self-congratulation. "His Lordship will see you now Brigadier," he informed, condescendingly. The pale fingers held the door open. How he despised these manicured guardians of the men in suits.

First the eyes, then the head and shoulders, followed by the trunk and finally the legs unfolded upwards into a towering presence.

"Nigel, how good of you to make that dreadful journey and at such short notice." The hand absorbed his own. "Do have a seat," he offered cordially. "This was your father's office I do believe, holds fond memories I dare say. Sherry?" They raised silent glasses, testing the smooth liquid. Neither man spoke.

The brigadier watched the colossus return to the sea of leather, sinking into its comfort. He was too old a campaigner to fire the first shot, even in self-defence. He waited...

The minister took an appreciative sip of his sherry. There had always been wariness about the man before him, a tendency to be a loner, even at school, he remembered. He'd looked ridiculous in the frock coat. Dreadful about his wife and child. Never married again. "We have read your accomplished report with obvious interest and, dare I say, relief." The minister had opened the batting. The tricky problems had been dealt with in an efficient and civilised manner. The blame pointed mostly downwards. He had survived. Others, less fortunate, wouldn't. "To re-cap," the minister's speech had quickened. He had been running twenty minutes late to start with. He looked over his glass. "The Lord Chancellor will appoint an appropriate judge to head the inquiry. No one will be sacrificed in public," he emphasised. "Your officers and men will be sure of their facts," he stressed. "We cannot afford the slightest misunderstanding." The hand rested on the open file. "You will move forward immediately, using every means possible to prepare the ground for a possible truce leading to confidential talks and direct rule by Easter," he stated. Finished, he closed the file.

"Thank you Minister." The brigadier stood. "I appreciate, your concern Sir, and will personally supervise all future contact," he confirmed. He returned his empty glass to the tray and collected his briefcase on the way to the door.

"Ah! Yes."

The brigadier stiffened. There was always a catch. "Nothing to worry about really. Nearly slipped my mind. There will be a file on your desk, awaiting your return, self-explanatory really. Deliberate and planned agitation amongst our Boston cousins apparently." He folded his bifocals into their crested case. "Strange how quickly one bad apple can ruin the barrel," he confided. "Messy business; crushing bad apples," he explained. He patted the departing shoulder. "Something to muse upon as you cross the sea. How to crush without leaving a stain? Delightful to see you once again." The handshake was brief. "Perhaps we may have a reason to celebrate next time."

The door clicked shut on the hidden world of power, dumping the brigadier into the reality of the outside world. He dismissed the offer of a guide, knowing his way; he asked for his car in twenty minutes. The brigadier strolled the corridors of military history savouring the pure indulgence of childhood memories. Each painted face, an old friend. Dead heroes, dead horses, now disturbed only by a feather duster. He recognised the pain immediately, sharp and persistent, followed by the tingling in his left side. He pushed his back to the wall and squared his shoulders. It passed as always. Heartburn.

— o —

Colin stood, chilled to the bone. It wasn't only the cold March wind whipping through the mangled gaps of death; it was the whole cursed thing. The hypocrisy itself, viler than the lingering smell of scorched flesh. Limbs separated from torsos, their brains clinging to walls. Everyday furniture buried in corpses. Young girls, without legs, the tattered remains of a wedding dress stuck to the expensive carrier bag. Fucking bastards, animals... He wondered how his men kept going. Bloody Sunday hung over their heads. They were accused and condemned by the world media. Branded wild animals. He was sick. Sick of trying to understand. Sick of the bastards' excuses. Sick of their bigoted blindness. Sick of their self-righteous abuse. And sick of picking up the bloody pieces. Sure, soldiers made mistakes. They're human, not like the bastards who did this. The Abercorn Restaurant packed with shoppers, until there was standing room only for God's sake. Anyone's mother and sister. There had been no warning. Nothing! Only the sudden impact of vicious shockwaves, followed immediately by an unimaginable destructive energy released in that confined space. A fucking bomb! Why couldn't they make the bombers clear up their own mess? Like they did in Belsen. Drag the bastards down from the Maze and rub their noses in the carnage. Let them vomit as he had. Retching until empty and then some. Then shoot the fuckers! Even those bastards wouldn't rush to claim this one. This one was beyond the pale even for them. His head hurt. He felt his tears trickle down dirty cheeks.

Only policemen of a certain age and experience wore medal ribbons. He stood motionless, a rock of sanity in a mindless world. He had watched the young officer take control of a bloody mess in every way. He knew it was his reality time. He moved closer to him, slowly and carefully. He reached out.

The hand was warm and comforting, like his father's used to be, the accent local. The fingers kneaded into his pain and tense muscles. "Makes you wonder about God, never mind his bloody Church. No country, even God's is worth this..." The fingers dug deep. "I'm really sorry, son."

"Captain Monro! Radio message." It was Smith the quick. "You're to ring Lisburn ASAP... The brigadier…" Smith was impressed.

The large policeman removed his hand from Colin's shoulder, suddenly embarrassed. "I hope it's good news for a change, Captain. Good luck son," he added.

Colin returned the comradely salute. Suddenly he felt warmer.

— o —

The switchboard had promised to return his call. It was times like these that he missed the helpful corporal. "I have the brigadier on the line Sir... You're through, Sir."

"Congratulations Major..." the pause was deliberate. "Your Colonel kindly permitted me to be the first with the news." Major? Was this someone's idea of a test? Promotion? What for? Derry? Hardly. The Abercorn? Who cared? And what about his men? They were still scrubbing soapy hands and forever tossing in restless lager sleep. "Surprised?" the brigadier's voice.

"Yes Sir."

"Well deserved, my boy." Jesus, this was unreal. "We need to meet," the voice was real. "Tonight sharp"—an order, more like it. "Things are moving very fast indeed. Too fast. My car should be with you shortly. Informal, obviously. Now I would like to speak to your Colonel." Conversation over.

Colin flashed the switchboard.

He didn't like this man. This so-called driver.

They had arrived. The security was impressive. "Talk about Fort Knox!" he tried small talk.

"This way..." the pause very deliberate before the, "Sir." The man was light on his feet. He even walked like a bantam. There was no hint of the rose grower here. Everything smelt of Mansion polish. Colin felt uneasy. Alone. The corridors empty of life. Only the spillage of squeezed light from office doors confirmed that spooks were present. He was alone in the last colonial outpost of a once great empire. Lisburn. And close by, Hillsborough. Home of the garden party mentality.

"Do sit down, Major!" The brigadier signalled, opening his desk drawer. His hand held a small box with velvet covering of deep blue. "I do hope you will accept these as they are intended," he said quietly. He pushed the box across the desktop. "I know that you will wear them with the same pride as I did and my father before me." Colin watched dumbfounded as the fingers released the catch. "Obviously, I have no further use for them myself and it would be a pity if they lay hidden from mess life forever." History sat smugly in satin comfort. Two sparkling crowns, regal and inviting. Colin could smell the Raj.

"I don't know what to say," he mumbled. He watched his own fingers reach out to touch the box. Lifting it to gaze... Entranced.

"Thank you, will do," the voice sincere, the smile human. "It's been a long day for both of us, but I'm afraid this problem wouldn't keep. Do put them away. There's a good chap," he finished softly. "I have studied your section report of our cock-up in Derry," the man and voice had returned. Colin hadn't noticed the file on the desk. "And I'm sorry to say it, but you appear to be the odd man out." The brigadier's hand selected the marker flag. "Perhaps we could go through your evidence one more time. Sometimes, the most simple of facts can be misconstrued in written statements."

Colin bristled. The small box dug into his flesh at the sudden movement. He had told the truth. He had not seen any flash, nor could he tell purely by the sound from which direction the opening shot had come. Jesus Christ, hadn't he been trampled over, down on the ground, struggling to get upright, never mind achieve command. He repeated his statement, word for word. Every line indelibly written in his memory.

"Thank you." There had been no interruptions. "Exactly, as I had expected. Concise, logical and honest. Would that all concerned in this pathetic event could be as honest," he confessed. He closed the file. "You see, we have reason to believe, from reliable sources as they say, that the first shot was planned."

Colin bit his lip, but it was out before he could stop himself. "By which side Sir?" he asked.

The brigadier simply rested his hand on the file. "That, Major, is why you and I are here tonight and why the Lord Widgery is deliberating so long and carefully before delivering judgement."

Colin felt foolish and ungrateful.

"Do I make myself clear?"

"Sir." He needed to explain. "My men and I have spent most of the day mopping up the Abercorn. I'm tired, and full of self-doubt, and what is so sickening is the hypocrisy of the media. Okay, we may have made a tragic mistake in the heat of battle. Derry was an accident waiting to happen. Why can't we tell the media that?"

The older man crossed the room, bringing the whisky decanter with him. "I sometimes forget what it's like out there," he apologised. "Believe me, when I say that never have I seen such wanton destruction of civilian life. Even in Africa. Today's massacre was evil. Such crimes can never be justified. They should be condemned from every pulpit in the land and by every editor in Fleet Street. Condemned by the people. Their own people. Condemned until there is no hiding place for their leaders. Condemned, as one would a mad dog."

Colin knew they had found common ground at last. Two frayed warriors searching for explanations.

The brigadier settled back into his chair, replenished glass in hand. "What I am about to tell you is for your ears only," he stressed. "Bloody Sunday is history. There is enough evidence available to satisfy the truth." The free hand slid the file into the desk drawer. "We move on," he said, inhaling the whisky fumes deliberately. "Westminster has had enough of these Irish peasants. We are condemned by world opinion as you so rightly say, despite our initiatives and good intentions. Well, their time is up, our political masters have decided that if they are going to be blamed and held up to ridicule, they may as well be in control of that ridicule. Stormont's days are numbered. We must be able to talk to the Catholic minority unhindered by Orange bigotry. We must have a dialogue with the Catholic moderates. And I need you to maintain contact with your friends to achieve this."

Colin couldn't believe what he was hearing. The man understood. He was giving them another chance.

"It will be difficult," the brigadier continued. "Some would say impossible, not to be misunderstood. One side may see it as a weakness. The other as treachery." God Almighty, how he envied this young man's innocence. "The initiative must come from PIRA. Otherwise we will be accused of condoning violence as a means to an end. I suggest the offer of a truce as a beginning." He savoured the malt. "Talk to your friend. Explain our dilemma."

Colin fought desperately to slow his mind. Tom and Danny, would they understand? Would they want to understand? Would they trust him after Derry? A tattered wedding dress floated through his mind...

"I'll try Sir," he said, suddenly weary of it all.

The brigadier drained the last of the malt. Sometimes he wished that he was dead. At peace with those he loved.

— o —

# CHAPTER SIXTEEN

## DANNY BOY – LONDON 1972

TOM THUMPED THE TABLE unconcerned as the stale butts spilled from the heavy glass ashtray. He had had enough; enough of Danny's twists and turns and his avoidance of issues. Danny's reaction had really frightened him. It was as if he wanted the bloodbath to continue… Regardless.

They glared at each other, horns locked, the old and the young. Each determined to win. Both righteous.

"For God's sake Danny, we can't keep on blowing people to pieces!" he shouted. There, he'd said it. He looked around the table for support. "We'll lose any sympathy we've gained. Our own people can't take much more. Even you can see that," he pleaded. "Isn't it as plain as the nose on your face, haven't you been saying so yourself for four years, ever since Burntollet, that it was a march too far. Well think about it, how's about a bomb too far?" he challenged. He watched Danny's chest heave; he had struck home, heard the smoker's wheeze of anger. Had he gone too far? It was the first time he had disagreed with Danny in open forum.

Danny felt the bile churn in his stomach. He'd been warned by others about Tom's precious conscience, but this was different. He'd gone soft. Become a fellow traveller, but with no belly for a real fight. Then what did he know? Could he have mobilized world opinion? Raised the American dollars? Convinced Rome? Pushed Stormont to the brink? Embarrassed Westminster? Secret talks my arse; there was nothing secret about Westminster's predicament. They were running scared, their money on the wrong horse. He leaned forward. "What about Aldershot?" he asked. "Was that a bomb too far?" he challenged, smiling round the room.

"What about it, for Christ's sake?" Tom cried, on the edge of his chair. "An empty mess... Seven non-combatants. You want me to list them?" He raised his left hand and began to count. "Five canteen women and a gardener; and wait for it, a Catholic chaplain. It could have been anybody's mother or father in that bloody room, but to crown it all, a priest, one of our own. Tell me," he shouted, spittle flying, "how did you explain that score at your Boston tea party? Jesus, sometimes you make me sick; and talking of sick... now there's a thing. Nobody but nobody has admitted to the Abercorn madness." He heard their feet shuffle. "Would that be too close to home? Now, would that have been the one too far? Too fucking far to claim it? I'm right, Danny, I'm right and you fucking know it," he spat out the words of condemnation. He was exhausted but he'd come this far and he might as well finish. "Tell us Danny," his voice low and tired, "tell us we haven't lost our way? Tell us before our own people do," he insisted quietly.

You could hear a pin drop.

"It won't happen again. It's been taken care of," Danny promised, his voice quiet and authoritative, never taking his eyes from Tom's. Tom lowered his eyes. "You have my word on that," Danny emphasized.

"Thanks," Tom replied.

The room settled, realising the moment was past.

"There's a strong rumour," Danny continued, "that the Shankill have agreed to a truce already. Scared fartless in case their Paras come looking for them instead of us," he joked. The smiles were back. "Maybe we should get in first, right enough, and stick their olive branch where it belongs," he proposed. Laughter filled his ears. They were his again but it had been close. He brought them to order. "Do I have a proposal?" he asked. "A seconder? Hands... Carried," he declared. "But I'm warning you here and now that any ceasefire will be on our terms," he stressed, looking directly at Tom.

"Aye, that's for sure," licked Brown Nose Jim, wiping around the stray ashtray, cupping his nicotine stained fingers, returning the spilled butts, finishing the job on the seat of his trousers.

— o —

Tom sat bemused in the back of the camouflaged Andover of the Queen's Flight. It had all happened so quickly once Danny had agreed the meeting. Danny had insisted on a full delegation, including prisoner representation. The flight had been what they call uneventful except for the bumps. They had all wondered why the Queen would choose to use a wee thing like that to travel in; most likely for the corgis.

"Ten minutes to touchdown," Colin called into Tom's ear. Tom nodded his head, gripping the seat's arms. The bloody thing was all over the sky. Tyres squealed, engines howled, the charabanc had arrived at RAF Northolt. "Reverse thrust," Colin's voice again, "Sort of acts like a brake," he comforted.

"Sort of?" Tom queried, looking out the porthole window. Men stood with umbrellas at the ready, lined in front of wartime huts. Jesus, talk about 'Reach for the Sky'.

The convoy turned left out of the gates following a well-rehearsed route into the city; White City, through Earl's Court, over the top of King's Road and along the Embankment into Chelsea and Cheyne Walk.

Everyday sightseers, cameras loaded, ignored the men in anoraks as they crossed the pavement to be greeted by more men in suits.

Colin crossed and re-crossed the black and white chequered hall for the umpteenth time. He slouched into his sentinel chair. Most likely Chippendale, he thought. They had been at it for three hours, give or take a comfort break and a trolley or two from Harrods. He had counted the dark veins on the glistening new leaves of the giant cheese plant many times. The count different each time.

"You couldn't even afford to feed that bastard on your salary," the voice echoed, as in chapel. "Tom." Colin was on his feet immediately. "How the Hell?

"Man, there's doors everywhere in this wigwam," Tom answered the query. "They don't need me in there anymore," he said, his eyes taking in the surroundings. "Your lot never bloody learn. Do they?" he challenged, his voice hollow. "What a place to bring us Irish to," he stated, spreading his hands. "Tell me something. Did they intend that all this opulence would impress? Overawe? Jesus man, can't they see that it's like a red rag to a bull. Can't they understand that we see it as our own Liffey water that paid for this and the bastards had the cheek to sell it back by the pint glass? All this and more from Paddy's Guinness. I don't suppose he even comes to Ireland, just collects the dividends down the road. Nice work if you can get it."

Colin couldn't help but smile.

"I suppose you have to admit it, he's charming, didn't ask us to wipe our feet, but condescending. Jesus man, they're all condescending, they don't even know it. No wonder we carry their chip on our shoulders." He kicked gently at the Italian pot plant, like his father used to inspect the worth of a car. "I'll tell you now for what it's worth," Tom said, looking directly into his friend's eyes, "there's no chance of anything coming out of there except misunderstanding. Here," Tom offered the folded paper, "this is for you, your own personal copy. I wanted you to see it before they emerged from in there. Tell them they have until midnight to answer," he said, resignedly. "Otherwise they can read all about, it in the morning papers." He turned away. Back to where he had come from.

Colin stared at the typewritten statement of intent, so obviously prepared in advance.

"But you promised," he stuttered, "you promised to try. You can't just walk away, Tom. Please," he pleaded. The retreating figure halted, hand on the door handle, turned. "Believe me Colin, I really tried." He patted the inner pocket of his open jacket. "We even had the second envelope all ready but you must be the last of the innocents if you think they wanted discussion. Grow up man, we can't change those bastards; they're too entrenched in their own importance to history. They really thought they could scare us, put the frighteners on us; the Arrogant English Bastards!"

The double doors opened abruptly. Colin could only stare at the mass exodus with Danny in the lead as it swept past him along the hall and through a hurriedly opened door to the pavement beyond. Security, caught unawares, squawked urgent orders to sleepy drivers, milling around the silent party of angry men, standing in a united group on the exposed pavement. Nobody spoke. There was no need. They had been prepared this time. Danny's second option had been agreed beforehand. There would be no divide and rule this time.

No Michael Collins.

No English semantics.

Tom joined the group.

The car doors opened.

Men ducked their heads.

Car keys turned.

Hope pulled away from the pavement.

Colin locked the toilet door, placing the chair closer to the light and read Danny's declaration of war.

> *One. That the Irish people as a whole should decide the future of Ireland.*
>
> *Two. That the withdrawal of all British troops from Irish soil should be completed by January 1975.*
>
> *Three. Pending withdrawal all British troops should be withdrawn from sensitive areas.*

*Four. A general amnesty for all political prisoners, internees and persons on the wanted list.*

Colin sat stunned at the audacity of the demands. They'd shoot any man who agreed to these proposals. They'd shoot the man who suggested them.

— o —

The small car pulled off the potted road, inconspicuous until now; it bounced its way into the vacant field next to the golf club car park. He was early. Colin slid the Mini's window open listening to the thunderous pounding of the Atlantic rollers breaking on the deserted sands below. He shielded his eyes against the setting sun. The black headland of sculptured basalt glowed its unique beauty at day's end. Man wasn't needed here. This was God's work. It was hard to believe that all this beauty belonged to two troubled tribes whose people took it all for granted. Who allowed their young men and women to go to their wet grey graves without the chance to appreciate their real heritage? Both tribes were out of control. Westminster had had enough. This was their last chance. He was the final messenger. There was no need for a letter of intent, the message was simple and precise…

Derry and Belfast were to be cleared of all barricades. Tanks from Germany and seven extra battalions were on their way to implement Operation Motorman. The operation was an open secret, fraught with unsolvables but it had nevertheless been given the green light. Time had run out…

Come to the table or face open warfare.

The brigadier had stressed that he must get it across that Westminster was willing to accept over one hundred dead. Bloody Sunday would be a picnic in comparison. It was not a bluff. He was to obtain an immediate answer from this meeting and for that reason Westminster had insisted that Danny attend with Tom. Danny was the man with the scythe.

Colin checked his watch once again. They were late. Where were they? He turned in his seat. The place was deserted, well, almost; a hacker was stuck in the nearby bunker, frustrated but determined. Sand exploded everywhere. A car reversed out of the car park, turned neatly and slowly picking its way back through the potholes. It stopped, waiting for a second car coming from the main road. The evening sun glanced sideways into the interior of the first. Colin recognized Tom. He knew the driver of the second. They followed each other into the field, Danny leading. They parked on the shore side. Close together. Windows open.

Tom stepped from the car first. "Make me an offer," he called to his friend across the car roof. He looked younger, fitter than their last encounter. He smiled broadly at Colin's questioning expression. "Golf, you silly bugger, how many strokes will you give me? It's you who's the bandit I'm told."

They met in the middle ground between the two cars, embracing, slapping each other's backs. It was going to be okay!

"Don't you believe all that you hear," Colin laughed openly. "Even that hacker could murder me," he protested, his eyes searching for the lone golfer over Tom's shoulder.

The scream filled his head—Tom's scream of anguish. He could see his throat move; follow the spittle on his chin, tiny bubbles clinging to red flesh. "No... No... Holy Mother of God... Noooo!" Tom's last 'No' was held long and pained, not willing to die, not willing to meet the final truth...

Colin spun away from his friend's terror, ducking instinctively, his eyes searching, hands groping. Recognition was instantaneous; the hacker, the bunker. Danny trapped, half in, half out of the car... The rifle barrel... The flash... The report... Danny breaking free... Standing... The implosion of the head; then the speckled red line of flying tissue... Brains spattered on a car roof, inside and out... Dallas, Kennedy... Slow motion, the man on the knoll; the fucker in the bunker.

"You fucking bastard, you fucking stupid English bastards!" Tom's words, yelled in his face, fists striking anywhere they could find. "Danny had agreed to new talks, he knew he was beaten... You had won... Sweet Jesus, you don't know what you've done..." the scream sobbed. "You don't know what you've done! You'll all suffer for this, all of you, every bloody one of you."

Colin felt the pummelling stop. He watched Tom stumble to his car, never once glancing at Danny. Both knew Danny was beyond help. And Tom was gone, leaving his final words hanging in the air: "What did they pay you? How many pieces? How many promotions? Judas... Judas... You're fucking dead!" The words pounded and the waves broke.

Colin turned to face the bloody mess. My God, he thought, is that all there is to life? The noise was a nuisance, then an intrusion on his senses, a high pitched intrusion, a whine, a high ratio whine. The motorcycle was airborne, fleeing along the old tramway track heading towards the Causeway. He didn't need to see the rider's face. The face like Tom's words would be imprinted on his memory forever. The obedient servant! The Lisburn golfer!

The small gathering was instant. "Could you take a drink son? Who's the dead one? Jesus, what a mess. When's it going to stop? God help us. I don't think he's a member? Hard to tell."

Colin walked past the gathering crowd of club members unaware of their presence. Their eyes followed his path down the fairway to the nearby bunker. Necks strained to confirm his findings. He rolled the small golf bag over with his toecap; five clubs, old as the hills, an umbrella and in the sand no longer hidden. The Armalite! He heard the sobs deep and animal, felt his soul crying.

— o —

The report lay on the desk. The words flowed easily, pages and pages of cynicism, full of confusion and innuendo. Exhausted, Colin had fallen asleep at his desk. He stretched. Tired but calm. His pen flowed, scratching and altering. He felt elated—at last he could tell the truth. Satisfied, he asked the duty clerk to make three copies. He marked them, 'Officer Commanding', 'Brigadier' and 'General Officer Commanding'. The original he put in his inside pocket. He stood over the impassive clerk, waiting, determined. He watched him place them in the post bag.

— o —

The staff orderly ushered him into the general's presence immediately on arrival. The spacious office was in darkness except for a solitary lamp casting its directed light onto immediate problems. The lamp's green shade shielded the man's eyes, its eerie shadows accentuating the high cheek bones. A soldier's soldier, they said. Rumour had it he wasn't flavour of the month with cabinet ministers. Diplomatic in judgment, he was too honest in delivery.

"There was no permanent military solution whilst the Catholic population lent active and passive support to the gunmen. Internment was not an alternative; it would not work on its own." Open-mouthed, they challenged his judgment, asking for an alternative. He gave it immediately. "Give me the authority to go out and shoot the gunmen. They call themselves soldiers; and soldiers get shot in war," he explained matter-of-factly.

"Major Monro," the voice was tired, "please be seated," naturally courteous. "I do apologize for not receiving you personally but this wretched pen is stuck to my hand." Each vowel was polished and rounded before release. Manicured fingers pushed aside the remaining papers and adjusted the lamp. The eyes were dark and filled with fatigue. The other hand reached into the dark, returning a coloured folder. "I have read your report on the incident in the North with deep regret," he said, raising one finger to prevent early comment.

Colin swallowed his words.

"I also have here," he continued, sifting in the shadows, "somewhere…?" The hand found it. "A detailed forensic report on the weapon used by the assassin," he declared, savouring the last word. He flicked the file's information tabs. "The experts tell me that the weapon used matches the bullets used to murder one of our own troopers. Quite recently," he stressed. "That, Major, is a fact! It is the only fact, besides a very messy body and the resulting situation that I have." He looked up, removing his reading glasses and looked directly into Colin's eyes. "I'm sure you appreciate my position." The report returned to the shadows. "Your report," he added, replacing his glasses, exposing the file pages, "although excellent in its presentation and emotional detail, contains not one fact on which to hang anything; never mind a man." The eyes continued to scan page after page. He looked up. "No court or jury would be able to convict on your evidence," he paused, allowing Colin an opening.

Colin said nothing. What was the use?

The General waited. He couldn't show mercy. He went for the kill. "For example, you say that you recognized the assassin fleeing on the motor-cycle. May I ask why you failed to recognize him when he was close, in the bunker?" he asked, "And not moving," he added. The eyebrows demanded an answer.

"With due respect Sir," Colin began, taking a deep breath, "you know as well as I do, one does not perceive a golfer as a threat to life. It is only when you're looking down the barrel of an Armalite, even as you say, at a distance; one remembers the eyes, never mind the face. A face we both know!"

The eyes lowered, taking the brow with them. "Granted Major, but do tell me how many jurymen and women have looked down a rifle barrel? My carefully considered advice to you, Major Monro, is to walk away from this one." The tone of voice was caring, confidential. He wanted to help this young officer, but how? The man had been hurt. Dreadfully hurt. "Otherwise, you are fashioning a rod for your own back and will undoubtedly be misunderstood by a large section of your brother officers and men; men who see the loss of a terrorist leader as a bonus, no matter who pulls the trigger." Had he detected a flicker of understanding? "We are both realists Major; one has to be to survive in uniform in this country. I am willing and ready to destroy this report," he offered. The folder slid easily into the darkness. "To put the whole incident down to battle fatigue. I, like others in this headquarters, would be sorry to see such a promising career founder on the emotional rocks of Ulster, exposed and crushed in open court," he sighed heavily. He had run out of time. It was time to move on.

Colin stood, shoulders straight but stomach churning. "Thank you for your valuable time Sir," he said respectfully. He swallowed loudly. "I do appreciate the sound advice and thoughtful offer which I accept in the spirit offered and would ask that you accept my resignation in a similar light." He could hear his voice breaking. His right leg began to shake. Jesus, he had to get out of here and fast.

"Major," the voice was low, sympathetic, "there are numerous types of casualty in war, some more obvious than others… Believe me, I am truly sorry," he stated, simply. "I envy you your freedom of conscience and respect your honesty. It is therefore with obvious regret but complete understanding that I accept your resignation." He paused. "Should you however," he searched for the correct phrase, "with time, wish to continue your chosen profession, in any theatre, I would be pleased to personally recommend your expertise and loyalty. To friends in the Oman for example," he suggested.

Colin felt the firm handshake lead him to the door. There was no going back. The door opened. "May I wish you every success, Major. Perhaps it would be best for all concerned if you would remain in barracks until things are confirmed. I'm sure that your colonel could do with an extra hand in

Operations now that Motorman is upon us. Should be quite a show, twenty-seven battalions," he couldn't help but boast.

The door closed.

The show went on and on and on...

— o —

There was no shortage of players but they were all on the one side—their own. Colin listened into the HQ network. It was a signaller's nightmare. Twenty seven battalions charging around the countryside with twenty-seven colonels chasing their OBEs—Other Buggers' Efforts! His coffee was too hot to drink. He blew gently, making waves. But people were making bigger waves out there. And it was becoming very obvious that nobody but nobody had any idea what was going down... A tank... A bloody whole tank had to be abandoned, its blade stuck in a Derry barricade... Battalions lost... LOST, for God's sake! Commanders, cursing their drivers, up a creek without a map... Dead-end streets with only reverse as a choice... Jesus Christ... What a cock-up!

Belfast was just as bad. The Protestant Shankill stood around watching troops push and prod at their barricades until, fed up with watching, they'd given a helping hand. The whole thing had been a bloody farce. Motorman driven by Mickey Mouse!

— o —

The television screen flickered its trite propaganda of speeding Land Rovers and scurrying troops with faces operationally blackened. The TV reception wasn't what you'd call great in Donegal but you didn't pay a license fee and the pint was perfect. Tom pushed his chair back from the crowded table. All eyes turned as one and voices died, some arrested in mid-flow. Hadn't he led them out of Derry and Belfast, safely into Donegal?

"Lads," he called them to order, raising his glass. "A toast," he proposed, "To the Black and White Minstrel Show. May they disappear up their own arses," he joked to public acclaim. "Wouldn't Danny have loved today," he said.

"God bless, Rest in Peace," the older men mouthed in remembrance, making the sign of the Cross. "Danny," they chorused. "Oh Danny Boy…" The tenor's notes rose above the hubbub covering them with an emotional blanket.

Tom waited, standing until the last note… "We'll be back, just you wait and see," he promised them. "Better armed, better informed and very soon." The cheers rang in his ears. The fight was on!

On until the last English bastard had left or died.

— o —

# CHAPTER SEVENTEEN

## MEN OF HONOUR – CYPRUS 1976

THE WORN TYRES followed the rutted lines of dust baked earth. They reminded Colin of the cold, wet tram tracks, set in the cobbled stones of his Belfast youth. He fought the reluctant steering forcing the battered Land Rover around the unconcerned donkey and its panniers, heading downhill for the morning market. The old man waved his staff in greeting, scratching at his buried crotch somewhere in the deep folds of his pantaloons. The donkey continued on its way on autopilot, ignoring his mumbled curses and efforts of chastisement.

The sun was bright and hurtful to the eye. Small beads of sweat sparkled on the hairs of his tanned arms. He swiped them away, wiping the dampness onto the seat towel between his legs. One more bend. It never failed to excite him and there it was bouncing into view—Kyrenia, in all its majesty, shimmering in the new day's sun.

He looked down on her medieval castle, casting its twisted and bent reflection between the flotilla of small boats, their double image stuck upon the blue mirror of the Med. His right foot pumped at the brake pedal bringing his own donkey to rest. He stepped down, stretching his body, feeling the exhausted sea breeze tumble at his feet. This spot had become his healing field, the irony not lost and so obvious; to find a personal peace on this divided island. The people so like his own. He retrieved the binoculars from the passenger seat, wiped the lens on a dry spot of his shirt. He focused on the horizon, sweeping inwards to shore, following a dying trail of white exposing the progress of the mainland ferry ploughing her morning furrow.

Tracking ahead he entered the harbour. His neck tingled. There she lay, at anchor, his schooner, his life. Her deep blue hull massaged by the gentle ripple of morning movement. His dream had come true, his reason for living; living those lonely years of retreat in the desert.

The last thing he had intended was to join another bloody army. But needs must. His gratuity wouldn't buy a rowing boat, never mind a charter yacht. He had no choice. The general had kept his word. He'd become a very well paid mercenary. A four-year stint, two tours should do it. Hard and tasking years but handsomely rewarded by his Omani paymasters.

The concept, his yacht had become a passion; comforting the hurt and filling the cold star-laden nights; a mixture of fantasy and reality. Arabian nights.

Jesus, he was so lucky. About to put pen to a new contract and Turkey invaded Northern Cyprus. Boats for sale, for cash, no papers..., well, Turkish papers, no questions. He'd found the boat he wanted. He'd paid the deposit. Now he needed a rich friend, a sub, a loan. Nobody would risk Northern Cyprus. He was buggered!

Wasn't life peculiar? It had taken him by surprise. Barbara, yes, why not, her husband was a city banker, a fat cat. Business is business. God bless them both.

A business loan at good rates, spread over five years. The wedding present had been well worth it. This would be his first season. Barbara and her party were pencilled in for September.

He had better get going, stop this day dreaming or there would be no supper. The morning's catch was already ashore.

— o —

The quay was crowded with spectators. Turkish voices were raised in anticipation at seeing family, hearing news, talking politics. Their applause was spontaneous and loud as they welcomed the final nudge to the harbour wall. Her skipper stroked his moustache, pleased with himself, whilst his crew tethered the gangplank in a chorus of harmonious discord. Colin followed the crowd, no hurry now, his supper in his bag. He paused... A glimpse, a sense, a mask, impervious to simple pleasures. His mind shuddered. Then it was gone, a face in a crowd, an image in the mind, gone and quickly forgotten.

— o —

The harbour lights rippled in floated reflection. Tightening rope creaked in the calm air. Distant voices drifted their amusement. One last twist of the rope and he'd be on his way.

"Major Monro." It wasn't a question. Adrenaline pumped its fear, moving his heart into overdrive. Muscles tensed and memories chased distant shadows. He'd become careless, fooled himself it was over, that nobody cared if he lived or died. He waited for the pain. They say there is no pain. Who says?

"Shit," he cursed aloud as he spun on his word of courage, dropping to one knee. Bloody stupid... conditioning. He wasn't armed. He smiled at his ridiculous position.

The outstretched hand waited, ghostly still in the harbour light, its body hidden in the castle's shadow.

Colin stood. "You," he hissed, drawing oxygen into his lungs. The impervious face from the morning ferry. "You," he repeated. "I can't believe it! You silly bloody bastard," he raged, relieved. "What in hell are you playing at? I could have shot you... If I'd a gun," he confessed. He pumped the empty hand. "Major bloody Philips," he confirmed. "It's true then, old soldiers never die. How long has it been?"

"Your passing out parade, I do believe," the visitor replied as if it had been only yesterday.

"What in Heaven's name," Colin started.

"Sorry about the introduction," the visitor apologized, cutting Colin's question short. "Not really my scene, cloak and dagger and all that stuff," he confessed. "Let me buy you a drink in recompense," he offered, taking Colin's elbow.

— o —

Jamal watched the two men touch glasses. Obviously old friends; military men. He could tell. Warriors; like his ancestors. He, Jamal, could tell them of real wars. Such tales. The younger man, his Mister Colin, his friend from the big boat was talking. He strained his ears.

"God, I needed that," Colin, gulped, releasing the ice cube back into the empty glass. He looked at his visitor, puzzled... wary... "Two questions," he asked quietly. "Why? And is it Colonel, Brigadier or General?"

"Neville will do, and as to the first, it can wait. We have a lot of catching up to do," he admonished the younger man. "Jamal!" he ordered.

Jamal poured himself some wine from the unmarked bottle. Blood red and full of history. His visitors had settled for his special brandy; fourteen stars. He could never fathom the English. When it's hot they sit outdoors, sometimes under an umbrella. When it's cool they sit indoors. He moved closer, ear wigging.

"Subtle as ever I see. Perhaps, we should begin by a toast to absent friends, wherever they may be," he suggested. "Absent friends." The glasses clinked.

Jamal wiped the table one more time. He could tell that they had nothing interesting to say. Only the names of dead friends, killed in that cold and wet island on the edge of the Atlantic. He shivered despite himself. Full of race horses and terrorists. Crazy Irish... Stupid English. Quiet tonight, he folded his arms on the counter and went to sleep.

"I see that our friend is finally at rest," Neville observed. "We can now turn to the question – Why? Turn to old friends again, but this time purely yours, not mine. Thomas Edward O'Neill to be exact," he paused, allowing time for recovery.

"Jesus!" Colin waited.

"Widow-maker extraordinaire," Colin heard Neville's voice continue from a distance, "who, not content with military and Irish targets, has now turned to mainland carnage; Guildford and Birmingham; twenty-four dead and two hundred and thirty-six injured. Some crippled for life; better dead in some cases but then you know better than most."

Colin stared into his glass, watching the amber whirlpool of thought rise to the surface. It would never go away; the wedding dress, limbs, legs, an arm, a human fucking jigsaw of death… Fuck them all… Fuck them all… Every last bastard mother-fucker. He was on his feet.

"Don't you understand?" he asked, "I don't want to know your bloody problems, I don't want to fucking care, I want you to fuck off. I want it all to… Just leave me alone," he pleaded. Jamal, woke with a start. Mister Colin's chair was overturned.

"Sit down Major," the older man ordered. Jamal rubbed his eyes. No longer friends, he thought. "O'Neill is stretching us, laying false trails. We know he is preparing for the big one and believe it will be military, possibly a parade or similar event."

Neville decided to play his trump card. "Involving Royalty," he whispered.

Colin's mind knee jerked refusal… Bloody Royalty… So what? Why should they be different? They wore uniforms. Drew Government salaries… Tax free… What did they expect? Get out of jail cards?

"Now you appreciate why we so desperately need your help," Neville continued, taking Colin's silence for alarm. "Only one man knows the target, the place and the exact timings. Yes, your friend O'Neill; and he never leaves the protection of Dublin. Except…," he paused, "he visits Donegal once a year and we know the time and the place. A virtual fortress," he finished, obviously pleased with himself.

"That's okay then," Colin said, leaning forward. "You don't need me. You can blow him away yourselves; just like you did Danny. I know a man, who knows a man," he offered cynically.

"An unfortunate incident, but totally warranted in the circumstances and on information available at the time," he replied without any hesitation or evasion. "Water under the bridge. But of course the Irish only bury the body, never the memory," he defended, in his own logical manner. "Things have changed, moved on. We understand O'Neill has undergone plastic surgery and you will enjoy this…," he said, smiling for the first time, "Nobody knows what he looks like. You couldn't make it up… Unbelievable," he commented, shaking his head.

Colin poured himself another brandy. He could feel the laughter building in his head; the awful bloody laughter of madness.

"Why me?" he asked, despite himself. "Why me for God's sake? After all this time. Why are you telling me these things? I'm out of it… Long gone. I haven't discussed the troubles or spoken with anyone since my last day in Lisburn."

"Exactly the point," Neville agreed, "We need your dependable silence and proven loyalty, but most of all we need your knowledge. We believe you are the only person available who can identify O'Neill in the limited timescale available and qualified to undertake the operation. Six months planning. Down to the last detail… And you are the last piece of the jigsaw. We are going to kidnap the bastard, yes, kidnap him right from under their noses without them even knowing," he declared, smugly. "The team is hand-picked, HALO specialists, every man. They have a limited window to get in and out. Our friend is very protective of his privacy," he smiled knowingly. "Yes, we have a contact in the area." He stretched his legs. "There you have our problem, time, always time. We haven't the time to argue whether or not we have the right bloody man in the bag. You see, we can't do it without you," he finished, convinced of his case.

Jamal put his cloth away. He didn't need to earwig. Mister Colin was shouting at the visitor; and very angry. Perhaps his brandy had too many stars.

"You're mad... You're all fucking mad, grown up Boy Scouts with guns. Go home and leave me be, play your bloody charades somewhere else and without my help. Idiots!" He was suddenly cold despite the warm night. He shivered. "You shouldn't be allowed out on your own," he shouted.

"You want something else, Mister Colin?" asked Jamal, cleaning the table top, replacing the chair.

"Thank you, no," the visitor replied, tossing a handful of notes onto the table. "You may lock up... Goodnight," he stressed.

Jamal swept the notes into his apron pocket ignoring the rudeness. He glared at the older man, staring into the cold dark eyes. Like the Greek fish in his fridge. "You okay Mister Colin?"

"Yes, that's fine, Jamal, we won't be long now," Colin confirmed.

Both men watched the broad backside waggle indoors. Jamal turned the finger-stained sign to Closed. The lock clicked shut.

Colonel Neville Gerald Anthony Pemberton-Phillips, late of the Brigade of Guards, White's and the Carlton Club, officially retired but still a servant of the Crown, waited until the Turk's face had disappeared from the glass frame. He had never liked the people of the Med; much too independent for service and too lazy for anything but self-employment.

The cicadas, hushed by the shouting, broke the waiting silence, their cacophony of sound restored to the velvet night.

"I apologise for my rudeness," Colin said, tired; embarrassed by his undisciplined display of raw emotion. "Please go," he requested. "Tell your masters they must find another sucker. I have nothing left to fight for, I am sufficient alone and content with myself."

"Quite, dear boy, and apologies accepted. You made an honourable decision at that time and we fully approved.

However, time as they say waits for no man. We move on to new things and new rules of engagement," he explained as if to a child. He eased his chair round to face the harbour. "Take your beautiful schooner and it's equally beautiful name… Sheila and Colum!" he stabbed.

Colin bristled, felt the anger and fear bubble their insecurity. He must control his emotions. He heard his voice low and controlled, "Are you threatening me through Sheila and her son?"

"Not really, dear boy, but one never knows what the future may bring. No, I'm simply pointing out the difficulties one can experience in getting various permits for such an enterprise as yours, and there is always the cost of insurance to cover unforeseen accidents. Accidents do happen to both people and property."

Colin back heeled his chair into the darkness, reaching for the bottle as he stretched across the table. "To men of honour," he smiled thinly pouring the remaining contents into his antagonist's lap. Credit due, the old bugger didn't even blink.

The Colonel watched Colin disappear into the night. Like the chair he knew that he would eventually return. He just needed time to let his frustration rage.

Colin sat on the bollard staring across the water at the sleek hull, its beauty reflected in the moonlight water. The name glinting his dilemma, Sheila, mocking his ability to fight back. Everything he'd worked for was drifting away beyond his control. They had him by the balls. Bastards! He'd make them pay, they needed him, screw them. He'd take them to the cleaners.

He returned to the table, composed, resolute.

He noted that Neville had removed his linen jacket, spreading it across his lap, avoiding any embarrassment to either party. A silver drinking flask stood next to the brandy glass. Its coat of arms twinkled under the coloured fairy lights.

There were no preliminaries.

"I will have complete operational control," his voice steady and unemotional. "McCready is to be my number two and it will be my last mission... and talking of Sheila. You would know that she has reverted to her maiden name and her address and details... I want the appropriate contract rate with double indemnity, all monies and my pension to go to her and I want the boy to board at a public school, of her choice, paid for out of one of your numerous funds; oh yes, it is to include a substantial cost of living allowance, index linked, like your own, all in writing and in my hand before we assemble. Finally, I want the loan on the boat cleared and all permits and the necessary paperwork paid for and cleared through our Embassies in Greece and Turkey for the next ten years. No excuses, no delays, stamped, sealed and delivered—or no deal."

"You have my word," he offered his hand. "Oh, and by the way, we have Rourke safely tucked away."

"That's useful," Colin acknowledged, ignoring the proffered hand.

"To men of honour," the Colonel raised his glass to Colin's disappearing back, his face retaining a fixed smile of triumph.

— o —

# CHAPTER EIGHTEEN
## THE MISSION – DONEGAL 1976

**T**OM AWOKE WITH A START. His head rested on the desk amidst scattered papers, the overflow strewn on the floor. Bleary-eyed he measured the remains of the accusing whiskey bottle. His level of guilt he called it, shaded by the morning light. Sleep was a luxury. Another dawn filtered through the gaps in the heavy velvet curtains covering Georgian windows from a colonial past. He knew he was drinking too much. His side ached. Probably the way he'd slept. More probably his liver, his mother would have said. He tried to remember the dancing words amongst the night's amber thoughts. He rubbed his eyeballs hearing them swim in a pool of liquid pain. Three years of pain.

Time didn't mean anything anymore; hopeless years of trying to co-ordinate and control an ethnic passion. Trying to guide the turbulent and confused emotions of young hotheads, always keen to get in on the act wanting to take over the business. But it wasn't an act anymore, it was a way of life and more often death.

He shuffled his cold feet back into crumpled slippers, pushing his body upright. Everything was a bloody effort these days. The thin leather soles slipped easily across the carpeted room, his guiding fingers touching the comfortable furnishings on passing. Old pieces his mother would approve of. He held on to the comforting texture of the curtain sash cord, silky soft and real. He heard himself sigh as he unfolded a new day.

Dublin Bay lay before him casting its misty shroud over Dun Laoghaire harbour. He counted eleven masthead pennants, their splashes of colour poking through the mist the only evidence of the silent and invisible sea dodgems below. Wouldn't the grave be warmer? If only he had the courage. He lit the first fag of the day, feeling his body tense, coughing the smoker's cough. He felt better. The death wish had become stronger lately.

The past was his purgatory. Danny's death had been his excuse, Bloody Friday the result. He alone had given the order. Twenty-two bombs had exploded in Belfast in one day of madness, opening the floodgates of hate creating the death squads and the tit for tat killings. That had been Danny's memorial and his own answer to death and betrayal. Feeding the martyrdom of Irish history with fresh blood and personal sacrifice. And so it had gone on and on; years of senseless bombings and killings on both sides; creating the black statistics, mirroring the body counts of the Vietnam War. Lists of the dead and injured recording the Irish disease and its evil tide of hate, watching it sweep backwards and forwards dropping its flotsam of death and jetsam of maimed across the divide.

He let the bathwater run for a while, watching the brown tinted water swirl into guilt pools of dark blood. He allowed his eyes to creep up on the mirrored image. Right enough, sometimes he didn't recognise himself. Hans Christian Anderson, the King's new clothes, he heard himself hum the Danny Kaye tune; that's me, he thought; a fantasy, a phoney, a chancer. A writer doing research at the colleges in the city; reading, typing and travelling. His periods of absence accepted by the locals and the Garda alike. Didn't he always inform them when he'd be away for any length of time? And didn't they look after his property for him? And weren't they always grateful for the bottle of Powers at Christmas? It was always best to hide in the open. He soaked for a while, still restless. The towel was a bit wet. He wiped at his body, rubbing his face and neck. Finished, he shouldered into the thick dressing gown. Tightening the cord, he returned to his desk. The hidden drawer opened to his touch. His fingers touched the worn cover of Colin's secret thoughts. Colin's expertise sifted and interpreted from his letters; his confessional tomes from the Middle East. He'd never replied. But they just kept coming to Dorothy. He hadn't intended to even read them but curiosity had won.

Colin's thoughts created that strange mixture of ideas; evolving in his mind and growing into a political and military strategy of five simple principles. Didn't he know them by heart?

One… You can't bomb the English into submission in Ireland.

Two… People are expendable

Three… The establishment write their own rules.

Four… Hurt the city and you hurt the economy which in turn hurts the government.

Five… Feed the media.

Now at long last he was ready for the opening move. His players were in place. He was ready to show the world that the rules had changed, nothing and nobody were excluded. He had laid the trail with care. Every move checked and double checked. He'd watched Westminster's hounds sniff the scent and rush to tell their masters.

His pencil stroked off yesterday's date. Easter had come and gone without any serious blunder. He had even decided to delay his holiday to Donegal, determined to put the fear of God into Liam. He needed to keep him quiet, allow him to be a part of the action, but only on a need to know as Colin would have said, the place and target but not the how? He couldn't take any chances. He couldn't afford to lose.

The sun touched his head, warming his thoughts. The mist had cleared and things looked good outside. He stretched, allowing himself a smile at his thoughts of Donegal. He needed to recharge his batteries for the final push.

— o —

Colin had forgotten the painstaking hours necessary to plan a successful operation; the teams of specialists so keen to justify their existence; departments determined to hold onto budgets, run by civil servants forced to carry their hearts in briefcases. One department, possibly the Foreign Office, had even asked why Donegal wasn't in Northern Ireland. Nothing had changed. Donegal, that beautiful county of rugged coastline isolated by the stroke of an English pen, stretching from the south-westerly cliffs of Slieve League to beyond Malin Head the most northerly tip of mainland Ireland. Donegal, Fortress of the Foreigners, unchanged in centuries, its people unconquerable. Tom had obviously retained his sense of history and an appreciation of the bizarre in selecting his bolt hole. Right on the tip of Malin Head where one lonely God forsaken road led in and out of the village. Quiet and lonely the village rested content behind the lace curtains of privacy touched by bony fingers capable of blessing the owner of a sneeze by name. Nothing could enter those last few miles between the village and Tom's cottage unnoticed or unannounced.

The photo recce Hunters had done their work well recording every nook and cranny of Tom's fortress. Black cliffs rose straight from the sea their rugged slopes covered in thousands of nesting birds; a multitude of raucous guards. The photo interpreter's china graph pencil marked the thin line of electrical fencing running east to west on either side of the farm gate; separating the unconcerned sheep from the minefield beyond. A professional job; not your farmer's string post effort. The Operational review confirmed that there was only one way in. Through that bloody gate, constructed of concrete and steel it pivoted smoothly on a delicate balance operated from a guard hut manned twenty-four hours. The only contact permitted beyond the hut was the nightly collection and delivery of Tom's mail by his personal bodyguard. His only link to the outside world. The mailman, as he was known, checked in at eleven o'clock every night. Tom came out to meet him, exchanges completed, he was on his way by eleven thirty. Returning to his digs in the village by midnight. Everybody agreed that it was bloody stupid but it was Tom's life and Tom's decision.

Colin had thanked the interpreters for their efforts and conclusion. Mission impossible! They had smiled knowingly and presented him with a masterpiece of topographical modelling from which he was able to identify every pothole and windswept bush. There was no hiding place. Even the sheep were numbered. Bloody marvellous but could they use it? Was it feasible?

The men in suits said yes. They would, wouldn't they!

— o —

The winds had rattled the window frames of the briefing hut for five days. Parachuting was out for the foreseeable future. Even the sheep lay hidden behind stone walls. Ground rehearsal followed rehearsal in the silent choreography of the covert until they were ready to go.

— o —

Time had run out.

The Hercules rolled down the windswept runway into the ebb of the late April showers. Only the colonies of rabbits sat upright, their ears flapping to take notice, watching it climb steeply towards the North-west.

Ears folded, they returned to their late supper in peace.

Colin fidgeted with the strap of his heavy helmet, his head rattled within as the skipper pushed the engine thrust to maximum in order to achieve height quickly. This was no rehearsal. They were on their way. He felt his lips move in silent prayer, pure habit; he'd never thought about religion, it had always been there just like breakfast. He closed his eyes, allowing his mind to wander. The face was clear, Tom's face, and always that never-ending scream. He pushed the image away. The plan returned. It would never work. The spooks had lost their marbles. A masterpiece of deception. Tom was to defect, come over the water and in from the rain. He was to impersonate Tom, leave by the front door as Tom whilst the real Tom would leave by the back door. Simple... He'd laughed in their faces. He still couldn't believe that Paddy had backed them, agreed to the scheme, agreed with the spooks and agreed to be his back-up.

"Think about it, Colin," he'd said. "Can't you just see the bastards in Belfast and Dublin turning and twisting like terrified turkeys on Christmas week not knowing who to trust. They couldn't trust their own shadows."

It was a nightmare scenario and it was about to begin.

His eyes followed the trail of dust and dirt sucked out into the vortex of the night as the aircraft's rear doors locked open. Reality flapped at every loose inch of clothing. The six men stared out into the night sky at a corridor of studded stars framed in velvet blackness stretching to eternity. Not even a wisp of cloud smudged God's backdrop. The heavy equipment container rested at the end of the roller conveyor, its automatic release chute checked and checked again. Where it went the men followed.

FIVE MINUTES.
The gloved hand pointed.

STAND UP.
Colin cleared the coil of black cable over his shoulder, tested the radio connection, listening to the aircrew make their final adjustments, recording their shopping list of wind speed, direction and time to run.

THREE MINUTES.
The team unclipped their breathing tubes from the mother console, transferring to their personal oxygen bottles. The loadmaster cleared the chocks holding the container in position, holding them aloft. Paddy took hold of the container handle, adjusting his balance, calf muscles tense, ready for the exit push. Colin disconnected the communication cable to his helmet.

ACTION STATIONS.
Men and equipment rolled forward on rubbery legs to the platform edge reluctant to touch or hold, their gloved fingers making final adjustments. Each man an island of private thoughts.

RED – ON.
Jesus Christ, this was a go... First time... Colin looked out and down into the canyon of darkness. They had crossed the coastline; he could see Inishtrahull Sound far below bathed in a dark green hue.

GREEN – ON.
Gone... they had gone headlong into the night, free of man's restrictions and free to decide for themselves.

Colin pushed gently, feeling for the air with his hands bending his legs at the knees, watching the team jockeying for position around the container. The sky was aglow with light, starlight, what a sight. God was at his work. Slowly he allowed his body to turn, following the coastline into the orange glow of Derry. The scene was magic, a child's cut-out model painted in garish hues. What had the bastards done to her? So small, so beautiful and yet so troubled. Londonderry, Derry whatever? Everybody's kicking post of hate; there she lay, bruised and bleeding from the mouth of the River Foyle.

The body of men had reached terminal velocity, falling in a frozen tableau of sinister blackness. Only the occasional rocking movement as the heavy rucksacks settled on muscular thighs betrayed their alien presence in the night sky. The container spun slowly under the stabilising chute, surrounded by a posse of sheep dogs, watching it's every move. Paddy gave a thumb's up.

Colin turned away, Derry forgotten. His eyes dropped to the twin altimeters glowing their information... Fifteen thousand and falling... Concentrate... Relax... Follow the coastline... Too far... Come back... There... Just before the headland... There it was... Their opening point. He completed a three-sixty degree turn and signalled a thumbs-up. Five thousand. Beautiful, the waves broke below huge white monsters... Handle... Left hand above head... Sit up... Wait for it... Wait for it... Three thousand... Check handle...

The first report rifle-like and to his right confirmed the container opening height. The canopy blossomed, then a second followed below and to his left. He listened for his own deployment. A mushroom of nylon flashed at the corner of his eye dragging a swinging body upwards and out of his vision. He looked over his shoulder watching the rigging lines snake upwards following his canopy. The opening shock shook him like a rag doll and captured air crackled above his head; conditioned reflexes hooked frozen fingers into the parachute steering toggles, turning his body in a sweeping arc below the canopy. Ghostly shapes flitted across his vision, stacking one above the other in landing formation following the container. The huge parachutes breathed silently above each man's head. Colin released the toggles, fumbling with the restraining straps of his oxygen mask. Grateful lungs sucked in the distinctive taste of natural air. He watched Paddy's misshapen bulk lead the parade of chutes as they descended on the unsuspecting target below. His ears popped as a crescendo of sound flowed into his drums, the sound of pounding Atlantic breakers crashing their final energy on the rocks below. It was truly majestic.

Five hundred yards to run... they were going to make it. Release personal container, wait for tug on the lanyard... Jesus... nearly took his side with it. He watched the Bergen rucksack swinging its pendulum sequence above the landing area... the air spilled from the canopies below as they applied their air brakes... Paddy had selected the landing area well short of the killing fields... The heavy equipment touched down releasing the chute on contact. It was working like clockwork. Where had the winds gone to?

The first man touched down followed immediately by the second. Colin rolled onto the soft wet earth of Donegal. He cut the automatic release hooks of the canopy and rested on his knees, pulling in his Bergen... checked his weapon... then his watch. Twenty-five minutes before Tom's personal protector arrived for the night shift.

The men paced themselves, gathering the discarded chutes, missing nothing. Everything pushed into the now empty container. The two men responsible for recovery shouldered their escape pulleys and ropes and melted into the darkness heading for the cliffs and the Special Boat Party positioned offshore.

"Jesus," Colin breathed his nervousness at Paddy's touch, signalling his readiness. He caught a fleeting glimpse of the rear guard cutting into the night towards the guard hut. The man with the body bag adjusted his load as they raced with measured strides towards the cottage. The three men crouched at the door listening, fighting to control their breathing. Colin nodded. Paddy grasped the door handle. Not a sound. Only the distant thunder of the waves competed with their heartbeats. Sweat trickled from armpits as he eased the door open. Colin glided past his accomplices into the darkened interior.

The room was empty.

A neglected fire smouldered in the small grate. Its aroma of turf filled the room. Colin touched Paddy's arm, pointing to the strip of light escaping from under the bedroom door. He knew the exact number of paces to the door. They entered the room in tandem, eyes darting and fingers poised. A figure was slumped in an armchair. Only the top of the head crowned with stereo earphones was visible. The chair spun at Paddy's touch, spilling the unsuspecting occupant onto the floor... Mozart filled the room as bodies collided. Colin scrambled for the socket, yanking the plug. He turned, hunkered and peered into the bearded man's eyes.

"Colin," the name came on a sigh, a statement of fact.

"Tom," Colin suppressed a chuckle.

The only surgery was nature's beard and passing years; just a simple beard. Tom's eyes danced, suddenly frightened, caught unawares as Paddy plunged the needle of the syringe into exposed flesh at the open neck. Tom's strong fingers clawed at the restricting hand, seeking his assailant. Too late he grinned feebly as his eyelids fluttered and closed. The room was still once again.

The bag man crossed the room, sweeping the assailants aside—he had a job to do. He dropped on one knee to check his prize, running his index finger around the inside of the slack mouth, feeling for the tongue and teeth. No dentures. Satisfied, he clamped the neck brace into position buckled the restraining straps and slid the plastic cover along the body like a well-worn glove.

Still no one spoke. Only the bag man moved; with practised ease he hoisted the inert load onto his shoulder and left the room.

The outer door clunked shut.

Colin bent low peering into the blackness beneath the bed. His fingers touched, then gripped a soft leather holdall covered in neglected fluff. The leather smelt expensive. He stripped quickly, tossing his outer clothing into the bag, pulled open the heavy mirrored door to the wardrobe and rummaged Tom's rail of clothing, selecting navy slacks and a cashmere sweater. Expensive stuff. The belt buckled into the grooved hole—they were still the same size. He gathered an armful of garments, stuffing them into the main bag whilst Paddy filled the outer pockets with a selection of papers from the desk. He waved the passport and revolver in triumph. Colin felt the panic rise. He looked around the room, his eyes searching desperately.

"Where's his bloody raincoat?" he asked. "Everyone in Ireland has a bloody raincoat."

They both stood still, their eyes checking all the obvious places. There was no sign; not a sausage. Colin could feel his breathing quicken. Think about it. He concentrated... raincoat, wet, hanging up, door, back of door... back door. He rushed through to the living room and into the kitchen and sure enough there it hung, the Irishman's dressing gown, its folds mocking his ignorance. His eye caught the label: Burberry of London. Good old Tom, no cheapskate, he. He slipped his arms into the sleeves. He spun, pivoting on his right foot, caught unarmed; the figure had emerged from the woodwork of the door, his weapon pointed directly at Colin's stomach.

"Suits you, boss," the voice mocking, eyes glinting excitement. "Any room for a weapon?" the lips smirked.

"Smart arse." Colin retreated into the bedroom, the rear guard following. "Any sign of the mailman's car?"

"It's on its way, boss."

"Are we connected to the beach yet?" Colin asked.

"No problem. Ready when you are. Those bastards don't like hanging about, they're always anxious to get back to mother in the bay. Our boys did well, piece of piss," he concluded.

"Okay, you'd better get going," Colin said.

The gust of cold air confirmed the rear-guard's departure.

Paddy checked the front door. They were on their own but not for long. Advancing headlights caught the cottage window bouncing the reflected image off the oval mirror above the fireplace, catching the imposter bare faced at the bedroom door. Colin's hands shot to his face—the beard, he'd forgotten about the beard! He hunched his shoulders, pulling the collar of the Burberry upwards covering his cheekbones. Paddy doused the bedroom light.

"Come on man, stop admiring yourself," he encouraged him forward. "Here comes our lift. I've got the holdall. That's a nice coat right enough," he admired.

Colin moved to the window keeping low. Paddy signalled for him to go first. Colin crouched lower as he crossed to the door ready to slip into the night. The blow from the snub barrel was sharp and precise, shooting his body upright.

"Stand up you idiot." The message held no hint of humour. "It's O'Neill, he's expecting not some bloody chimpanzee."

The driver killed the headlights, keeping his foot on the brake pedal. He was puzzled. Tom usually put the outside light on before giving him the mailbag. He watched Tom walk around the back of the car, a holdall in his hand—there was no mailbag that he could see. Wasn't the night as black as his mother's coal hole despite all those stars up there? He couldn't see Tom's face, his high collar turned up against the cold night air. They hadn't told him about any trip. He adjusted his silk tie into his button down collar. The car door opened letting in the cold night air. He turned his head for instructions. Cold hands covered his mouth and left ear. He was aware of the pressure applied to his skull, the accelerated neck movement suddenly arrested and reversed; he heard a crack like a dry twig breaking, not realising it was his own spinal cord.

Paddy released the floppy head, allowing the lifeless body to rest against the door. "Are you going to stand there all night?" he asked. "Or can I expect some help?" He slid forward into the front passenger seat, removing the lifeless foot from the pedal. "Come on man, move yourself," he demanded. "Get his jacket off and dump him in the boot and keep to the cottage side," he reminded.

Colin struggled with the warm corpse. He could hear Paddy cursing his luck.

"The shoulders are all padding," he struggled. "How the hell, am I supposed to wear this?" he asked. The sound of tearing was the distinct answer.

The headlights stabbed into the night fingering the now deserted headland as the car's suspension bottomed, its front wheels locked into the rutted track bouncing its occupants towards the guard hut. Paddy switched to sidelights as the car nestled before the gate, engine running. Colin wound the back window down a few inches, watching the harassed figure hug the hastily donned jacket to his body, caught off guard. The man was mumbling to himself. Damn it, he couldn't get his arm into the sleeve and wasn't it the man himself in the back. Well, what he could see of him. Posh raincoat and all muffled up and with his hand over his mouth. He heard the words *toothache* and *Buncrana*. Sure he must be bad if he's going to that old goat in Buncrana. Wouldn't he drill your ear for your mouth? He fished deep into his jacket pocket.

Paddy eased the weapon's safety catch with his thumb.

The man leaned forward, touching the rear window. Colin couldn't see what was in his hand; his toes gripped his socks as he stared into the vacant gums following the pointed finger to the stained dentures in the palm of the open hand. He waved his appreciation of the toothless joke as Paddy engaged first gear, flickering the headlights impatiently.

"Just you be holding your horses young fellow me lad," the older man rebuked, ignoring the driver, fitting his teeth in case of an argument; he swung the gate open revealing the downhill road to the village. "There you go," he declared, patting the rear boot as he would one of his cows.

Colin traced the map in his head: Ballygorman first after the village followed by Malin, then a right at Culdaff, through Gleneely and on into Moville where the boat was waiting and across Lough Foyle to Magilligan.

"Paddy?" The big man lifted his eyes to the rear-view mirror.

"I know," he grinned, "I'm bursting myself," he grimaced, "but you'll just have to wait until we're through the village."

The young Marine stood in the cold water, a rubber appendage to the moulded retrieval craft. His eyes moved constantly, traversing the coast road from Moville. Nothing, not a sodding thing. He peed into his rubber suit once again, feeling the warmth trickle comfort to his toes.

The Coxswain watched the youngster fidget; they had no patience these days. His fingers fondled the control rudder, feeling the mood of his idling engine burbling gently in the dark waters. His experienced eyes spotted the distant sidelights of the approaching car taking the fork to the golf club. He leant forward, tapping the craft's side to attract his keen apprentice.

"Make ready lad, our guests have arrived." The words rumbled majestically from pipes matured through years of issue rum and cheap tobacco.

The car turned sharply off the main road, its rear cargo shifting audibly. The signpost read Greencastle Golf Club. Colin stared into the passing blackness, remembering another golf club not too far away. The eyes appeared first, then the nose followed by the mouth, but there was no skull. He wiped desperately but the image remained reflected in the window of the passing night. Danny and Tom, the past and the present.

The wheels crunched their arrival dispelling the ghosts. Paddy turned in his seat punching Colin's leg.

"We did it!" he shouted. "We bloody did it, against all the odds." He opened the car door, ripping the restricting jacket from his shoulders. "You go on ahead. I'll tidy up and for God's sake cheer up." He tossed the holdall to the ground. "Oh, I nearly forgot, leave me the belt of your raincoat," he motioned.

Colin didn't ask why. He heard the car boot lid open and close. The cold waters of Lough Foyle lapped at his hesitant feet. Colin signalled for the Michelin man to come closer. The young Marine eased the bow in shore.

"We was told not to hang about," he bitched, the Brummie accent respectful but slightly pissed off and besides, his feet were cold again and that old bastard had spotted them first. Eyes like a hawk, a shite-hawk more like. "In and out, that was our brief," he continued. "Now you're here, can we all get in so we can all get bloody out of here?" he challenged, pulling the craft closer to the shore, muttering all the while. "Here's your mate at last—leaving a note was he?" He heaved men and holdall over the side with effortless ease.

Paddy lay on the floor of the small craft, feeling it ripple beneath his body, soothing his mind and body. He had done it, he had brought this one home intact.

The voice was pure Laughton straight out of the Bounty. "Welcome aboard gentlemen; blankets for the outside and rum for the inside. Now keep your heads down," he warned. The blunt rubber bow swung in a gentle arc towards the open water as experienced fingers tickled the controls, coaxing the engine to maximum revs. The bow lifted creating a cold spray.

"Hold tight to whatever you've got," he roared. They felt the surge of power as the craft raced for the home shore and the waiting Wessex hidden in the moon shadows of the round fort.

— o —

# CHAPTER NINETEEN

## THE INTERROGATION – HEREFORD 1976

**THE COTTAGE CLUNG** to the steep slopes hanging threateningly above the small village tucked below. From the bay window, Colin could see the windswept sands curving from Llandudno in the West to Rhyl's harvest of caravans in the East. He looked down on the narrow main street which provided all the inhabitants' needs in one long line—the greengrocer, the butcher, the pub and chapel; all drip-feeding the civil but dour inhabitants from cradle to grave. How he envied them their honest mistrust of all things foreign, retaining their tradition, their language and their pride behind the red mist of the Dragon's breath.

He had been proud to be Irish once, a long time ago. Proud of the Green warriors of Lansdowne Road and to wave his schoolboy pride. Then with age came confusion, a different ball, a different game, different names: Linfield and Distillery, Rangers and Celtic; supporters in tribal colours. Colours inherited at birth; colours of prejudice. Why had nobody said anything? Why had nobody explained? State and church, whatever, whoever, all of them part of the system. A dual system creating the religious lepers of the Shankill and the Falls. Protestant Shankill and Catholic Falls, side by side but worlds apart. All in the name of Jesus and the English Crown. Most of them honest people forever betrayed, slow marching their dead to tribal cemeteries, rubbing away the touch of a mad dog. What had they done to his people? All those needless deaths. Stroked in their grief by political hands wiped clean on hidden handkerchiefs. Why can't the Queen dance with the Pope?

Colin pushed the pen and paper aside, muddled and confused by his own past ignorance. Terrified for the future. What could he do? What could anyone do? The faceless ones had kept him away from Tom. He was surplus to requirement. Donegal was history, their history, three weeks old. One cryptic telephone call in the first week, then nothing. Not even a name, just the code word.

"Major Monro, we would be grateful if you could help us with some background information regarding our mutual friend. Childhood history, that sort of thing."

"I'll try," Colin offered. Anything to break the boredom but he must be aware of any traps.

"Thank you," the voice continued.

Colin had a desperate urge to ask him if he ever had a dog called Horatio. "Have you ever had a dog called Horatio?" he heard himself on the line.

"Sorry?" the voice puzzled.

"Never mind," Colin said, feeling foolish, "What do you want to know?"

"Can you confirm where you first met and the date?"

"Cookstown, 1949," he replied immediately. The questions continued, all pretty mundane.

"Nearly finished Major," the voice hesitated, "difficult to phrase the next question without sounding silly. Best to be direct. Had our friend any childhood fears, phobias? You know what I mean, like your own fear of snakes."

"How…?" Colin gripped the phone tightly.

"Your personal file Major, your jungle survival report," the voice replied without hesitation. "Thank you for your co-operation Major Monro, we will be in touch."

The line went dead in his hand. Colin listened for any telltale click, nothing, you can't hear a satellite sitting overhead with some clever monkey guiding it from Cheltenham.

So here he remained, coming up to the fourth week in what was known as a safe house, awaiting the men in suits. The men who needed credit like Sinatra needed applause. When would they ever learn? Tom would never talk. A high beam of light reflected off the picture rail disturbing his train of thought. He checked his watch; nobody moved between eight and ten—they were all in the pub. He crossed to the window. The large Range Rover's lights dimmed then went out, returning the street to darkness. The spooks had come for him.

— o —

The silence was disturbing. The room was of standard, middle ranking, civil service entitlement. Table, three chairs, a large mirror, light bulb; sixty watts with plastic shade, two pictures, both animal scenes and both crooked. Colin fiddled with the non-issue tape recorder, checking the mirror. The knock was loud, demanding, not requesting. He turned towards the door, his palms itched.

The prisoner moved slowly, head down, using the shuffling hospital gait of the weak. Tom homed in on the familiar chair with dogged resignation. He stopped before the seat, waiting.

"Sit," the escort ordered.

Tom's body folded onto the chair in a slouch of positive insolence. Colin leaned forward, clicking the switch, hearing the live hiss of recording tape. Tom ignored the movement. The beard had gone exposing thinner cheeks; untidy curls covered the back of his neck. Colin couldn't see the eyes but he knew they were still stubborn.

"Thomas Edward O'Neill," Colin read aloud, "Interviewee," he waited. Nothing "Interviewer, Colin James Monro," he declared for the tape. Tom's forehead jerked upwards catching age by surprise, spilling the worry lines beyond the hair line.

"I knew you'd come," he said in a tired voice, eyes alert. "You see I fed them your letters, told them of your philosophy. Only titbits mind you," he warned. "They're not too quick on the uptake that lot," he nodded towards the mirror. "Won't even admit we're in England." Tom laughed aloud at Colin's giveaway expression. "You don't think I would believe for one minute that any of those supercilious bastards would risk crossing the Irish Sea?" he said in a raised voice, giving Colin a big wink.

Colin tried to ignore the familiarity. He'd already decided that there was no point in playing bloody stupid games. "Yes, you're in England, somewhere between Guildford and Birmingham; names familiar to you no doubt."

"So's Hereford," Tom shot his arrow straight.

The watchers sat up.

"You make me sick," Colin continued, "how can you face yourself, never mind your God after that lot. You don't even remember what you're fighting for anymore. It's become a way of life. Women and children mean sod all to you; just another way to twist the knife in the soft English belly." He knew he was shouting. Tom hadn't moved a muscle.

Colin sat down.

The watchers were restless.

"We all do things we're ashamed of personally or through association," Tom replied. "You of all people should know that," he said softly. "Sometimes the cross of life picks us unasked," he paused. "I've learnt to live with mine. Have you?"

"Yes, I have," Colin replied immediately. "Danny's death was not my fault," he declared. God, it was a relief to speak those words.

Tom smiled patronisingly. "You can't really believe that a few letters, even from the soul, can absolve you and your masters of their sins," he challenged. "Jesus preserve us, wouldn't you think it was a Catholic I was talking to. No, you can't run to God on this one... I know that much," he confessed. "You showed no mercy to Danny... Lisburn knew that he had the agreement in his head until you blew it away. They were scared of him, weren't they? They couldn't face the possibility of having to cancel Motorman. Loss of bloody face but even more important loss of careers and they thought they had us. Just thick Paddys. We learnt quickly after that; you have to in war," he bragged.

The senior ranking of the watchers searched the file on his knee. Operation Motorman, July 1972. He recognized Colin's voice.

"Absolve!" Colin stressed. "Your lot don't believe in that game anymore. Oh no, you've joined the Shankill there. Fuck the Pope is common ground. The chapel is purely for funerals and grief; grief caused by your own bloody cause. And as to war, who said anything about war?" he heard his voice rise.

Tom waited.

Colin checked his tongue. He needed to slow down, avoid the emotional traps. "War," he continued, "Don't ever kid yourself that you and your gang of thugs are taking on the British Army... No Siree. You're taking on Westminster politicians, fighting for their political lives and miserable careers, hamstrung by democracy, but you don't need democracy. Let me tell you the facts of life. One, just one good Para battalion and a few specialists to close the border and you bastards would have to extend Milltown cemetery..."

The watcher put down the file, rising to his feet. This was much more interesting. He was aware that the prisoner was fully in control of his physical and mental response. The bastard was tough; you had to admit that but this line of attack... Might, just might... Monro's tone was ruthless.

"War, men fight wars," Colin twisted the knife. "Soldiers wear uniforms with rank and believe in principles. You do remember what those are? Principles, which don't include mothers and their babies in prams as couriers of death. Assassins in black masks and running shoes... your national warrior... too scared to show his cowardly face!"

Tom slapped the table. "You'll see..." He looked flustered. "I said that I wasn't proud of a lot of things done in our name. Principles, assassins, masks, uniforms, all words without meaning, spooks, slee... spies," he hesitated, changing his mind, picking his word. "...the dirty war, we are all involved," he defended, leaning on the desk, in control again, his eyes alert, "but you had better believe me when I tell you that we are more than proud of the men and women who have known nothing but fear, living and hiding in the ghettos of your making. Hunted like animals for years on end; years in which you allowed those smug Protestant bastards on the Shankill to fill their arsenals whilst beating their tribal drums of No Surrender. Years of digging trenches, erecting barricades and drawing what is laughingly called a Peace Line between two ghettos. The Shankill and the Falls."

The watchers advanced to their goldfish window, drawn to the drama... O'Neill was on his feet.

"What's another Paddy, green or orange? One less... that's all it means to your lot... one less to worry about. You tell me, Mister smart arse Major, whose side should you be taking? Forget about Catholic and Protestant, think Irish or English, you dumb bastard. What would you sacrifice, Queen or country? Or is it too late for you to think for yourself? Just tell me, you stupid mixed up anglophile quisling," he demanded, kicking his chair backwards.

Now they were both on their feet. It was always touch and go with these cursed people.

"Why should I waste my breath?" Colin returned. "The whole world has told you, over and over again. Every civilised society has told you. I've told you in my letters, you can't bomb and shoot a majority into submission. You have to talk, you have all to sit down and talk before it's too late," Colin pleaded.

The buzzer was harsh and final.

Tom swayed on his feet, obviously exhausted. He smiled at Colin's confusion. "Tea time at the zoo," he joked through a Pavlovian smile. "Your masters have heard enough for one day; time to put the animal back in its cage."

The door opened.

Tom turned, paused to select his lead foot and followed the escort without a backward glance. He would have to be more careful. He'd slipped that once... He hadn't expected Colin's attack to be so powerful. The reward was so close.

"Thank you Major, that was most enlightening, you have placed him exactly where we wanted." The same plummy voice but no Horatio at his heel, only two files under his arm. Colin smiled to himself. Tom and he were really together again.

"You are welcome to spend the night before returning to Wales," he offered.

"You mean that's it?" Colin asked, stunned. "I had him on the run," he stressed. "Hadn't I?" he queried.

"Quite," the man confirmed coldly. "However, our phase is over for the present, it is all down to the shrinks now," he explained, raising his eyebrows knowingly.

"I see," Colin acknowledged; his body shuddered involuntarily. "May I have a copy of this morning's session to take with me?" he requested.

"Certainly Major, we are all signed up to the same act, are we not?

"Thank you," Colin replied.

— o —

Tom opened his eyes, startled. He had lost track of time. Hours, days, weeks, everything had long gone. He was never alone, never without light. And the noise: white noise they called it, always in his head. There was no hiding place. He had set himself a daily task both mentally and physically. Sit ups, push ups followed by a paragraph, then a chapter a day: reading recall, *Wind in the Willows* had become his favourite. He had played every golf course in his head: sometimes in sunshine. Why hadn't he learnt to play chess? He heard the key in the door. It couldn't be more than two hours, he hadn't had any food. That bastard Colin; determined to keep going, to try his luck. Bastards.

This room was different. A second room led off to the right. He could see the immediate darkness with the presence of a strong light beyond. Tom allowed his eyes to adjust to the dimmed lighting. Three chairs and a coffee table; an informal session.

Two men entered the room, followed by two guards. Not a good sign. The escort he recognized, the other two were new; sports coats with leather patches, unpolished shoes and untidy hair, neither military nor career civil service. Academics, he surmised. Bet they could play chess. He wondered what their real game was.

They sat facing him. One had an envelope in his hands, the other an enamel bucket; he held it low enough to see inside: it contained a wooden spoon and a pair of gloves, large gloves like old motor cycle or gardening gloves. This was going to be some game. The envelope man spoke first.

"I would like you to look at some pictures," he said in a flat voice, without any change of expression on his face.

Tom watched his hands search the large envelope, extract some photographs and sort them, revealing nothing. "We might as well start with these," he suggested, placing the black and white photographs face up and turned towards the prisoner. "Bangor, Pickie Pool and Portnoo, Donegal, both quite beautiful," he commented in his superior English accent. "Worthy of picture postcards."

Tom sat on his hands.

"God's country some say, but unfortunately still two countries, according to some."

Tom had been watching the man's hands spread the photographs on the table top. He hadn't seen the second man reach for the envelope. He jumped, startled as the second man slapped a pile of coloured photographs on top of the first; bigger pictures, coloured pictures. Tom stared down at the mosaic of death in all its gory detail.

"You would know most of these, first hand," he accused in a tight Glaswegian accent. "The Abercorn, Belfast on Bloody Friday, Claudy and here," his fingers searched, "London," he stressed. "The Price sisters' handiwork and them so recently in the news. Homesick, they said they wanted to go home to their nice Irish prison. Leave us to get on with the sweeping up. Jesus, we have to be mad to let you away with this," he spat the words, his fingers wiping the spittle off the glossy print. "Then there was Guildford and Birmingham," he continued. "Look at them, you bastard," he hissed, reaching out to grab the prisoner's hair. "Look at your handiwork, O'Neill; legs, arms, hands, heads, all different parts, parts of different people, all bloody useless. All bloody useless."

Tom watched the man try to settle, still restless on the edge of his seat. Now for the good guy, he thought. Same old routine. They could blow hot and cold until the cows came home. He was saying bugger all.

"We," the good guy opened, "know you're plotting a big one, possibly against a member of the Royal family," he paused to extract two more pictures from the envelope. Tom could see that one was black and white and the other coloured. Surely the silly bugger had another routine, one of his own? "This one, I know you will recognize," he said, with an open smile. Tom stared down at the sepia photograph of his grandfather's old Cookstown. "This one you may not recognize," the good guy continued, placing a large coloured print on the table. "Dublin, the 17th of May 1974 to be precise, quite recent, you must remember. Twenty-two killed. No, I tell a lie, twenty-five. Three died later from their injuries, lucky people I'm told. Lucky to die for Christ's sake," he thumped the table scattering the pictures onto the floor. Tom watched the bad guy pick the photos off the floor and place them back on the table. All change, he thought, and he was right.

"Interesting photograph that last one," he said quietly, pushing its terrible details into full view. "Do you know why it's so interesting, Tom?" he continued in a friendly voice. "No...? Well, I'll help you there. You see, nobody has ever claimed responsibility; most people accept that it was the Ulster Volunteer Force; the UVF," he said, emphasizing each letter. "But, silly me," he hesitated, "Of course you would know, wouldn't you? Because it wasn't them, it had to be you, and even you wouldn't blow up your own. Or would you?" he challenged gently. The man smiled, directly into Tom's face, whilst his hands arranged the photographs in order, together on the table top. "There," he said, satisfied. "Look here, if that's what they can do to Dublin, what could they do to Cookstown?"

"You fucking bastard!" Tom yelled, launching his body across the table.

The man was ready. Tom landed half on and half off an empty chair.

"Hold the cunt still, cuff him if necessary, get the other chair," the man ordered. He removed the tight fitting perspex lid from the bucket at his feet, emptying the contents onto the floor. He sighed quietly, picking up the large wooden spoon with his right hand and holding the bucket in his left.

Tom felt the pain of the professional arm lock forcing him onto the chair. "Hold his arms and shoulders," he continued. "Now then," the voice had changed again, low but positive. "Your time's up, Tom. I can call you that, can't I? You see, I feel that I know you and your secrets." The man tapped the enamel bucket with the spoon. "Interesting piece of kit," he observed, hitting the bucket's side, using more force with every blow. "You can beat the shit out of it and leave the victim unmarked," he gloated. Tom felt the cold edges of the bucket scrape his ears; it smelled of bleach and he felt his body tense, his mind panic at the sudden restriction of oxygen; then his head exploded... The pain was excruciating, he couldn't hear his own scream.

Then it was clear again, he sucked in air, watching his tormentor through unfocussed eyes.

The man clapped his hands. "With us again?" he mouthed.

Tom struggled violently: he couldn't hear, he couldn't think.

"Good, plenty of fight left," he observed. He took a step closer and tapped the bucket in front of Tom's face. "No Tom, this one's not for you, that was only a sample. You're an educated Mick. You've done a lot of reading. You've read Orwell's *Nineteen Eighty-Four*... this one is specially for you and you alone... Take him next door," he ordered the escort, picking up the gloves and the lid. "And take these with you."

Tom felt the strong hands control his wrists and elbows, guiding him through the doorway into the darkness and beyond. His head was a hollow confusion of sound and fear, Orwell and *Nineteen Eighty-Four*, boyhood nightmares, lurking in his mind.

The chair stood in the middle of the room flooded by light. He was transfixed. Horror flooded his being, his very soul. He sensed rather than knew what was about to happen to him. He felt the waist belt tighten around his middle, pulling his back upright, then the leather straps on his wrists and ankles. The light made him sweat.

There was no seat to the chair, only a circle of wood making a hole, like a commode; an electric chair commode but without the electric cap.

"Bastards... Bastards!" he heard his curses as they pulled his head back, tightening the last strap around his forehead, forcing him to look directly at his torturers. He tried to spit but there was no spittle. There was only one man, the good guy, seated at a table, its top half hidden in the shadows.

The man's face and hands flitted from shade to light. "Time to go to work," he spoke to the darkness.

Tom sensed the presence of the Scottish git still in the room. Watching... His eyes followed the sound of the escort to the side of the table, where he placed two plastic boxes carefully on the table top, directly in Tom's line of sight. He felt his skin crawl as the animals' pink feet clawed at the clear plastic; he could hear their nails scrape at their invisible prison walls.

"Rattus Norvegicus; the brown rat, also known as the common, Norwegian, or sewer rat," the tormentor confirmed. "Dreadful things, vermin of course and deadly, vicious when hungry." He poked at the first box with his pencil point. The rat attacked immediately, no question of backing away. The man hesitated, before continuing. "Starving by the look of them," he quizzed the escort. "Three days without food," the escort confirmed. "That's why they're in separate boxes, bloody cannibals, would eat each other. Let our friend see for himself," he suggested.

Tom watched the escort reach under the table, producing another smaller plastic box. "A lunch box for one," he said as he placed it beside the nearest rat. "Who's the lucky boy then?" he asked the excited animals. "Bill or Ben? Ben," he decided, opening the box and removing a piece of flesh. "Pork, Ben's favourite," he confided, taking great care as he slid the lid back on the double compartment box, dropping the pork onto the box floor. He closed the lid. "And for Bill, only a small pill," he offered, repeating the routine.

The rat charged the divider, trying to grip the smooth walls, tearing at its prison, its juices of anticipation leaking from its mouth and onto its paws. The escort lifted the divider slowly, teasing the animal even more, working it into frenzy before setting it free to gorge its needs.

"Thank you," the torturer praised the man's efforts. "We might as well proceed; no point in keeping Mister O'Neill waiting," he declared. "Interesting observation, how their teeth can tear the pig skin apart in a jiffy whilst you and I have experienced the difficulty of preparing crackling, have we not?"

Tom hurled a stream of useless expletives at his tormentor's head, feeling the terror taking over his mind, then his body. He watched the escort produce the enamel bucket once again, placing it between the rats. The man pulled on the leather gauntlets as he picked up Bill's box.

"It won't be long until your turn," he whispered to the dozy rat. "You know the pill only lasts for five minutes and two are already over," he stated pointedly to the torturer. "Okay, take his trousers off, down to his knees," he ordered the second escort.

Tom knew he couldn't stop the nightmare but his body fought to survive the indignity. It was useless. "Push the bastard's prick down, between his thighs, that's better," he declared, satisfied with his minion's handiwork. "Now Tom, listen carefully, we have only two minutes left. I need to know your target, the place and how you mean to accomplish your hit. That's all, three simple questions and three simple answers. And if I don't have those three answers in one minute from now I will instruct our friend here to place that creature in that bucket and stick the bucket directly under your arse."

The escort picked up the bucket and crossed to the other side of the table. He opened the animal's compartment, transferred the twitching body and carried the contents to the back of Tom's commode. Tom couldn't follow him; he could only stare directly at his tormentor. He knew he had run out of time.

"One minute, Tom.

"Three answers; the target, the place and how, Tom?

"Thirty seconds Tom... Get ready," he ordered. "Oh yes, I nearly forgot, the quickest has been one minute, the slowest three minutes for the animal to reach the top of the bucket.

"Fifteen seconds,

"Yes or no, Tom?

"Do it," he ordered.

Tom felt the back of the chair lifting and the bucket scrape the floor beneath his body; then silence; a hushed waiting.

"We need three answers, Tom."

It was unmistakable... the sound of tiny paws, scratching their way to life; to food.... faster and faster...

"You spineless shit, you lousy cunt of an Irish asshole!" his tormentor shouted, pushing over the table, spilling the other rat box. "He's fainted," he declared to the startled room, already searching for the missing box. "Got it," declared a relieved voice. "Shit," the same voice continued but in panic. "The box is empty... the bastard's loose!" he shouted in a pronounced Glaswegian accent.

The escort checked his bucket; his rat was still there, the perspex lid in place. He could hear his colleagues scrabble around on the far side of the prisoner's chair, hunting in the darkness beyond the upturned table. "Silly bastards," he muttered, climbing onto the back of the commode.

The scream wasn't really a scream; it was a raw declaration of pure terror and pain ending in a gargle of words, trailing into a rattle of Scottish despair. The moaning was continuous.

"Somebody put the fucking lights on!" the escort shouted from his vantage point on the commode, his eyes glued to the black spot of trauma, his ears stretched to identify any new clues as to what had happened. He heard the light switch click on...

"Jesus," he whispered aloud, crossing himself as he stepped down. "How the Hell?" he questioned the harsh reality of the tableau exposed beyond the upturned table.

The man lay on his back, his legs spreadeagled. The front of his trousers; flares for God's sake, were ripped away from the waist band. The victim's eyes stared down at the bloody sporran gripped between fingers and thumb of both hands. The rat's head and his genitals were indistinguishable. He knew it was dead, every last breath squeezed from its body, its skull crushed between his fingers. He continued to squeeze, feeling his own body in its mouth. He didn't want to die. "Somebody, stop the bleeding," he howled.

— o —

# CHAPTER TWENTY

## THE RECKONING – BELFAST 1976

**COLIN PRESSED THE MASTER TAPE** once again. He knew every phrase word for word. Sick of his own voice, never mind Tom's. He knew that Tom was playing with him, using his roller-coaster mind. Playing for time. Time, that's what it was all about, everything, came down to that. They had wasted a month already and now it was June. The machine stopped at his touch. He checked the numerals and pressed the replay. "Play it again, Sam." It was his own voice. Live. Jesus, he was talking to himself. Talking to the machine. He was going loopy. He could feel his lips mouth Tom's words on the replay… "What would you sacrifice, Queen or country? Or is it too late for you to think for yourself?" Colin rewound the tape… "What would you sacrifice…" Colin thought he had it, he knew there was something he had missed. His finger touched the Play key: "Queen or country?"…"Queen or country?" He knew the target. All the pieces were there, he knew it, but only Tom could complete the picture.

The coffee splashed across his forgotten notes as he grabbed for the telephone. "Yes... yes, I want a number," his voice was high, his accent strong like Tom's. Colin hesitated, his heart racing, doubt flowing backwards, the receiver in his hand. "I know you're waiting and I'm trying to think how best to put it..." Jesus, there was no other way. "Yes... I know who I want," he confirmed. She sounded a superior little cow.

"Thank you," his voice sharp, knowing all the time it wasn't her fault. Sod her.

"Yes..."

"Buck House... get me Buck House!" he demanded. That made her hesitate. You could hear the silence. "Yes, I do mean Buckingham Palace... No, Downing Street won't do," he chastised, missing her point... "Yes, I'm Major Monro and yes, I'm deadly serious." He held the phone before his face listening to the loud dialling tone. She'd cut him off.

— o —

Colin braced the soles of his boots against the reinforced steel floor of his airborne taxi. Tom's body lay across the open door. The cold wind howled its private protest, beating on Paddy's goggles as the machine banked away from Holywood towards Carrickfergus. They were on their way.

"Okay Paddy, bring him in, he's got the message by now." Colin made his throat mike more comfortable. "Put Rourke over beside him where they can both see the door. Watch your back," he warned, "I want to have a look for myself." He moved forward, stepping over the third body on the floor. "Check my harness Flight," he ordered. "Flight... Are you okay?" he asked sharply.

The man hadn't moved. He looked ill. Even Tom's face was a better colour. Colin sank onto hands and knees and eased his own head out into the slipstream. The lights of Whitehead covered the mouth of the lough. Left at the lighthouse and there it lay, tucked away, nestling up against Island Magee, Portmuck Bay. Home to ducks, migrant geese and spooks.

Nobody would let him speak to Buck House direct. All requests had to be in writing he was told. Nobody would want what he had to say in writing. Colin's fingers toyed with the crinkled copy of the flash signal he'd sent. He knew it by heart, every word, every syllable...if only he could have seen his mentor's face on opening the signal.

> BUCKINGHAM PALACE.
> FOR COMPTROLLER EYES ONLY.
> TO MAJ-GEN PIGGOTT-SMYTH.
> TARGET IDENTIFIED AS HEAD OF FIRM.
> TIME AND PLACE TO BE CONFIRMED.
> GOD SAVE THE QUEEN.
> ROMULUS

The General had pulled out all of the stops. It was impressive by any standards. Even for the Comptroller of the Queen's household. Colin's shopping list had been approved without pen touching paper. A Jetstream, from Northolt to RAF Aldergrove. A Wessex from Aldergrove to Palace Barracks, Holywood with a Special Forces crew and Paddy, plus one in full kit. The Special Branch were to deliver Rourke stirred but not too shaken.

Colin, touched the paper copy once again, his comfort blanket. He was beginning to understand the temptation of power. Real power. Life or death was his to decide. Not in the heat of the battle but on the scales of justice and political necessity. The ultimate balancing act. Was he really capable? Did he believe that much? What if it went wrong?

Nobody would ever know. The spooks would see to that. But could he live with himself?

Yes... He had already. He was programmed just like the rest of them. Programmed to protect, to defend and to sacrifice. It was impossible to change.

The Wessex banked left, picking its spot. The pilot's voice echoed in Colin's earphones. It was all about to happen. He was in control. This was his world. This was reality.

"Overhead in five minutes," the pilot's voice was insistent. "Mostly overcast with a few holes visible to the East. Seven thousand. Stand by..." he finished in a clear and precise tone. Colin signalled to Paddy to prepare for action. Both men stood back-to-back in the confined space of the cabin. They didn't need to communicate. The briefing had covered all eventualities.

"Cargo ready for despatch."

Colin spun in surprise. The flight sergeant was back in the action.

"Thanks Flight," the pilot acknowledged. "It's your show from here on. Good luck..."

"Request three minute check," the flight sergeant responded.

"Copied," the pilot replied.

The men went through their routine, propping Rourke's body against the bulkhead, securing him with a safety harness. Satisfied, they turned to the third figure for the first time. All three bodies where now inches from the slipstream. There was no visible response and no safety harness for the third man. The flight sergeant supported the man's head on his knee trying to protect it from the constant vibrations. Whatever he'd done he couldn't deserve this. Maybe it was best if he didn't wake up. Poor bastard.

"Three minutes," the skipper's voice brought him back to work.

"Copied." The flight sergeant felt the sweat settle between his gloved fingers. He held up a three fingered warning. He watched the two men move to their positions. The big man, Paddy, had removed one glove. He couldn't see what was in his hand. Paddy sank the needle into the exposed neck flesh at the base of the skull, squeezing the clear liquid into the bloodstream. Close to the brain. The reaction was instantaneous. Rourke's vacant eyes fluttered as the sagging lips twisted into life. Eyelids wide, the startled eyes revealed the mind's incomprehensible terror.

Liam felt the soft clammy fingers of chamois leather clamp his bruised lips together, forcing his fear back into his mouth. He felt sick. It wasn't real. Nothing was real. He couldn't take anymore. Not again. They had promised never again. Bastards... He knew that they weren't allowed to do this, not anymore. The Government had promised. It wasn't real. He felt the wetness spread in his crotch. He squirmed... It was real. The voice was forcing words of spittle into his ear.

"Listen carefully," it said.

He knew the voice. But from where? The noise and the smell... Smell? The smell... the begonia man. Ballymurphy. Sheila's man. Liam's mind stumbled. He struggled to get free.

"Are you listening?" it continued its message. One of the hands grasped his hair, pulling his head back, rattling the words into his head.

"Listen good, big boy, because your own life and your friend O'Neill's depend on your answers."

It paused. The fingers tightened their grip, pulling his head around, forcing his lips to protrude. He could see his own lower lip. His eyes swivelled, seeking Tom... He tried to move his head.

"Yes," the voice confirmed, "Tom's here with us, right next to you but possibly not for long."

The obscene litany washed his ear. He jerked his head violently twisting away from his tormentor, leaving his defiant words lying in the gloved hand.

"Get stuffed, cunt!" Liam shouted, not scared any more. It was Sheila's begonia man. The hand returned squeezing harder, injecting new words into his ear. It left no doubts as to its capabilities. Liam held his breath.

"Listen up bog-man," the voice hissed. "We're all dispensable in this chopper. You, me, everyone... But there are some more so than others and believe me you're not high on the list. And this game's for keeps." The grip relaxed but the words continued. "You see, we didn't write the rules. O'Neill did that all on his own. But he got carried away. Got ideas above his station in life. Bog-men don't attend Royal occasions. They only serve at Her Majesty's pleasure."

The words screwed into his thoughts. He knew that he was losing control. He could feel spittle bubble from the corners of his mouth and trickle down the stretched skin of his lower jaw.

Colin watched Liam's eyes roll in his head unable to hide the mind's terror. He knew that the man was close to breaking point. Maybe even beyond, but he had no choice... He had to go for it.

"Right again," he answered the eyes. "We know who. We know when. What we want is how?... How you silly bastard?... How?..."

Colin reached low into Liam's crotch and squeezed hard. He ignored the open mouthed scream, wiping the spittle from his shoulder with the damp glove. He waited for the scream to subside. "And you call yourself Commander," he mocked, holding Liam's head upright. He knew that this wreck of humanity was their last hope. He could show no mercy. "O'Neill won't tell us but you will... Won't you?" he screamed into Liam's ear. Grabbing the pasted hair from the wet forehead, he looked directly into the terrified eyes. "You see you need him more than he needs you." Liam shrank away from the eyes. He wanted to die. He sucked air through his bruised lips. His body fighting to live. His mind raced in circles. They knew... How could they? The bastards knew.

Tom struggled to see what was happening to Liam, but Colin was in the way. He needed time to think. What were the bastards up to? He refused to believe what was happening. It couldn't happen... But there was no escaping the obvious. It kept returning... They were going to be killed. They were going to die. Thrown out into space. Falling, falling into the cold sea. He remembered the cold waters of Donegal and their teenage dares, the fear and the pain of high dives gone wrong. The concrete water. He lunged feebly catching Colin unawares with his foot.

Liam felt the sudden movement. He turned peering into the dark beyond his tormentor.

The prisoner's face stared back, a blank mask, the body hunched against the bulkhead. Quasimodo, the hunchback of Notre Dame.

Colin recovered his balance immediately... Now... It had to be now...

The flight sergeant watched the mimed nightmare unfold before his eyes. He had no means of contact with the two men.

He had stacked their unplugged radio leads. They were in their private world of need to know.

Paddy moved directly behind the still prone third figure closest to the open door. He sank to the floor. Seated and bent-legged, he rested his feet on the man's back. Colin nodded... The legs flexed once, thrusting the body out into the night. It was all over in a second... The rag doll bundle erupted into the jaws of the slipstream and was immediately whipped away on a chorus of silent screams. Liam felt his neck muscles lock into a hideous choral reflex of animal pain. There was nothing he could do. Nothing. He sobbed great gulps of despair as he watched them drag Tom to the door. Words wouldn't come.

"Bastards," he mouthed. "Tell them, tell them Tom... for God's sake tell them!" he yelled. "Before it's too late." It wasn't his voice, it was the voice of a hysterical child, broken and abused. "Tom... Tom, tell me... Help me... Please... What can I do? I don't know how... I don't know how... Only you..."

Tom shut his eyes against the tongues of pain whipping his cheekbones. Strong hands forced his head and shoulders into the buffeting slipstream. He knew what to expect this time... He hung in the blackness of purgatory.

Colin leant closer to Liam mentally recording every word.

"Tom... Tom... They know... They know it's her birthday... Tom... Please... God... They know... You can't do it now... They know... They know... Tell them... Tell them... It doesn't matter anymore... For God's sake, tell them," he continued to plead.

Liam's words followed Tom into the night. Tom felt the hands release him to eternity, his body falling, falling, forever falling...

Colin clung to the open door unable to avoid the stench of Liam's final indignity. He felt no pity for Tom's wretched disciple crumbled before his eyes. He smelt the Abercorn in his mind. There was no victory. There had never been any winners. They had all become the hollow men of Irish history. Void of friendship and trust.

He felt Paddy's arms enfold his body, lifting him in triumph. "Her birthday!" he shouted. "The Queen's birthday. The Trooping of the Colour!" he yelled. Colin nodded… "Horse Guards Parade. All those people. All those troops. They've got to be mad. Stark raving mad."

"In front of the whole world," Colin agreed. "Move him to the front, blindfold him and put his ear protectors on. Flight, ask the skipper to do a low run over the drop zone as briefed."

The chopper banked left, descending rapidly in a tight arc. The two men clung to the door struts, their monkey harnesses secured to their waist and bulkhead, eyes straining through the night-time goggles.

"There!" Paddy pointed. "Two o'clock."

Colin picked out the black dot on the surface growing ever larger.

The bosun kept his revs high enough to cope with the current.

"Now," he ordered.

The marine pressed the button issuing a clear green strobe of two-second duration.

"Let's go home Flight," Colin ordered.

— o —

# CHAPTER TWENTY-ONE

## THE PARADE – LONDON 1976

LIGHT CUMULUS CLOUDS, tinged with the hesitant promise of a fine June day tumbled across the Mall, skirting Horse Guards Parade. Waves of troops swept back and forth, sifting and examining every piece of gravel until every loose stone was logged or lodged. Dogs sniffed other dogs. Marksmen adjusted their sights. Radios crackled with incessant checks. The General was everywhere. This was to be his finest hour. He had planned to retire next year, take his peerage and sit on the red seats. He just couldn't believe his luck. But luck had nothing to do with it now. He was taking no chances. The word was out, O'Neill had been bought and Rourke had talked.

There was no hiding place. Lisburn had been swept with a verbal broom leaving no chance of any misunderstanding. The Falls had stuttered and gone to ground. Street corner whispers filled empty ears. Letterbox news rattled children from their sleep. The Shankill kept its head down.

The scene was pure history; a Canaletto. Colin looked down on Horse Guards, the most revered parade ground in the world; steeped in pageant and tradition. Very little impressed him these days but this was something else.

"Paddy, Colin here," he fumbled to retain the stupid earpiece in position. "Everyone in position... Thirty minutes," he read his watch. "Her front door closes in ten," he reminded. "Confirm all monitors working," he ordered. "Jesus," he exhaled aloud, his heart missing a beat. There had been no sound, no warning, only the hand reaching over his shoulder to flick the switch on the master monitor to close up... Opening the general channel.

"McCready, that's no way to treat an expensive sight," the general admonished.

Colin pushed his chair back, barking the man's shin.

"God damn it man, relax," he ordered. "We have everything covered except McCready's sight..." he explained, smiling despite having to massage his shin. The man didn't smile often. He put his foot on the chair pulling up the trouser leg, prodding the broken flesh back into place. "First class, team. First class. McCready knows more about scopes than the manual. Keeps the others on their toes," he confided.

The General crossed to the window. There below was everything he stood for, everything that gave meaning to his life.

"Good luck Monro," the hand was cold. Very cold but firm, making no attempt to withdraw. Embarrassing... Colin, felt his eyes drawn to the older man's.

"I had to do it," the General confessed, a slight tremble of his thumb on the back of Colin's hand. "I had no choice. Strangely, I believe that Danny would have understood," his voice positive. Their hands parted... "Thank you for today," he said abruptly, turning on his right heel and he was gone from the room.

"Colin, Paddy here. Is the old man wired?" he asked.

"Yes," the man replied for himself.

"Just checking, Sir. The front door has closed." Fifteen all, he thought.

Colin switched on the full bank of cameras; each one angled to cover a precise area; each area overlapping the next. He zoomed in on the VIP enclosure. Jesus, and they'd the cheek to mock the Peacock throne. The General's seat remained empty. A leather case containing powerful binoculars confirmed the man's intention to remain in visual contact. The master monitor picked up the BBC relay. The commentator droning on and on in that hushed reverence reserved by the English, for God and Royalty. The harsh eye of the unforgiving camera threw the still portrait of Her Majesty's dutiful mask onto the world stage. He adjusted the colour. The mask didn't change. He marvelled at her self-control. Not a flicker of doubt. Her decision made, fully aware of all the facts. Her eyes steady. One small gloved hand graciously receiving and acknowledging her subjects' homage; the other resting low on the animal's neck, giving comfort and assurance.

Suddenly the raised hand darted to join the other. Horrified spectators saw the animal's eyes roll and nostrils flare as the rider's hands fought to control the prancing hoofs. Small heels ordered the animal to behave; the lower leg comforted its unease. The mare lowered her ears, the shadows gone, reassured by the rider's touch. The mounted escort and family drew closer, swallowing their heartbeats; their personal feelings hidden within the sickly mask of duty.

The entourage swung right off the Mall allowing for the wide arc needed to complete their entrance onto the parade ground. Colin cleared his throat before going to open mike. "Okay everyone; she has just become our property." He was aware of the tremble in his voice. The General, now seated, raised the powerful binoculars sweeping the roof-top positions. Perfect, not even a fly could enter his air space. He knew every movement of Her Majesty's foot guards. Every step his father had taken before him and now at last he was the real protector of the sovereign. Her Majesty knew and his peers knew. Stature forgotten, status retained. The general concentrated on the young ensign, the escort to the colour. Good, very good, hands high, fingers grasping the folds of unfurled colour.

Colin adjusted the sound. The commentator was still audible: "This Royal phalanx."

He rubbed his eyes. "Rehearsing every movement until… in their sleep." His hand froze on the knob. Words; bloody words; Tom's words, tumbling like dice in his head. His eyes continued to follow the rows of now stationary guardsmen. Some looked too young to be soldiers. Boys really… 'Soldier boys are we'… boys marching to a drumbeat of command. Concentrate… Concentrate… He nearly had it. The chair toppled backwards for the second time today.

"Jesus," the word, filled the empty room. "The clever, cunning bastard!" he shouted aloud. "Tom's boys..." 'Soldier boys are we'—the Nationalists' anthem—sent to England... to grow... to sleep... *Sleepers*... of course, not spies, Tom's sleepers... Army sleepers... Irish Guards sleepers... Out there... Christ... How many? Where? Why me, Lord? Why me? Shit. The bastard... The cunning bastard... "Fuck him," he cursed loudly. He had to think... Control the moment... Think for fuck sake. Think!

The General's eyes checked his neighbour for any sign of embarrassment. She smiled sweetly; completely unaware. That word. With that accent... So loud... So clear..., ringing in his ears, in his head. Monro had cracked. He pointed the glasses at Colin's window. Nothing... Only reflected sunlight... Bloody Irish, all emotion and no logic. The man had taken leave of his senses.

The General rubbed at the sudden ache in his chest. He couldn't believe what he was hearing.

"Paddy, listen, they're out there," Monro's voice... Calm now.

"Who's out there?" McCready's.

"Tom's boys... His sleepers... Our soldiers."

"Talk sense man, this is no time for bloody riddles." McCready.

"Exactly McCready... exactly," the General muttered. Neighbours turned to stare at him, bemused, then concerned. The man was talking to himself.

"They are on the parade, damn it," Monro's voice, angry, insistent. "Listen carefully... Everyone listen out... This is an order," he heard himself swallow, "No questions... Any man, and I repeat, any man who breaks ranks or makes a sudden move towards the Royal party is to be shot immediately.

"I repeat... Immediately."

"Does that include yer man on the horse?" McCready's voice.

"Paddy!"

"Sorry boss."

Colin listened to the mixed accents of loyal men.

"Copied."

"Copied."

He wasn't alone.

The General's right eye twitched; a long forgotten boyhood habit. The audacity of the man. His glasses started their journey again. "Sit down Sir. I say, do sit down there." He felt the sharp pain surge through his veins, upwards into his eyes. The glasses were heavy, swaying; droplets of perspiration stung his left eye. He closed it. The other eye focused. There... The inner end corporal, number one guard... He was facing the wrong way... He was facing the Royal party... Against the escort to the Colour.

"Monro... Monro..." The General's shrill demand sliced into stretched eardrums. "He's in number one guard. The corporal, inner end, a mere boy..." he observed. The General felt the tug at his jacket, pulling him away from his duty. He couldn't hold the binoculars any longer; the pain was intense, escaping through his left nipple. He swung the heavy glasses backwards in an arc of panic. The tugging stopped.

"Oh, my God, he's killed her... Oh my God." He heard someone scream... More hands; clutching hands, pawing at his arms. He felt his body stumble. He felt himself go, backwards out of control. The face was vacant, its eyes closed, mouth open, her gums covered in gore. Her false teeth lay on her lap, to the right of his head. He could feel the binoculars still swinging at his elbow. He tried to apologize but the pain twisted his lips, draining his head, pounding his chest. He knew that his heart had stopped. The pain had gone. Only a piercing scream followed him into the darkness. His head toppled sideways, his hand twitched, its fingers covering the lady's embarrassment in her lap.

Paddy moved the scope slowly and precisely. Following the chest line of campaign medals, the colours of the Northern Ireland campaign on every chest, to the inner end of guard one... He didn't hurry... He inhaled deeply forcing his heartbeat lower... arresting his body rhythm... He would have only one chance... Stop... The image filled the scope... The corporal had dropped to one knee, as if in trouble... Scarlet red cloth stretched smooth taut across broad shoulders.

She was as large as life, filling the sight.

Both men released their firing mechanism at the same moment in time... Paddy exhaled waiting for time to catch up.

He was too late. He had seen the trigger finger move... there was no catch-up.

The assassin felt the precision of death enter his body.

There was no pain.

No cry.

Just his brain frozen forever on the unmistakable click of emptiness... blank... it was blank.

He didn't understand.

Some dreadful fuck up... he had unsealed Tom's package himself... The magazine had never been out of his keeping.

Colin stared at the pictures on the monitors. A huddle of concern surrounded the VIP seating. Every camera was trained on the excitable crowd. Bloodstained attendants rushed here and there. Husbands comforted distressed wives. The commentator had lost his hush and the director had found his story. He zoomed his camera in on the VIP stand. The General, the woman, both down...what a picture.

The parade, forgotten, moved on. A wall of polished boots in box formation surrounded the fallen body.

And the bands played on.

"Stand still," the order was explicit. The box formation of men remained fixed, eyes front, motionless, their ears straining to identify the medics' despairing efforts.

Recognizing the finality.

The zip of the black plastic body bag; the clink of a medal on metal; the rustle of final interment.

The enigma that is Ireland.

**THE END**

Lightning Source UK Ltd.
Milton Keynes UK
UKOW051826121211

183641UK00001B/29/P

9 781908 128263